HANK RATTLER
And The
SECRET OF THE CAVE OF KINGS

HANK RATTLER
And The
SECRET OF THE CAVE OF KINGS

ARDYTH BROTT

Library of Congress Control Number: 2024930966

ISBN (paperback): 978-1-963271-01-0
(eBook): 978-1-963271-02-7

Thousand Acres is an imprint of Armin Lear Press, Inc.
Armin Lear Press, Inc.
215 W Riverside Drive, #4362
Estes Park, CO 80517

To my darling husband Boris for his extraordinary mind and his never ending support and love.

And our children Alexandra, David and Benjamin who continue to bring me a part of his brilliance and gentle nature.

1

The Arctic wolf cocked his massive head and listened to the boy running along the side of the deserted country road. As he had for many nights before, he picked up the boy's scent long before he saw or heard him on the road. Now the wolf ran closer to the boy. He could hear the crunching snow and bits of ice beneath the boy's feet. The wolf had watched the boy for days and, looking up at the bright moon, decided tonight was the night he would show himself. This tall boy was a good, strong runner, which pleased the wolf. *You will need all your wits and strength to go where you're going*, he thought, peering through the dark trees, and catching a glimpse of the boy. It was time. He would finally allow himself to be seen against the blanket of snow under the bright moonlight.

Just as he had thought, it took barely a few moments. They locked eyes. The wolf saw the boy's fixed stare and heard

his sharp intake of breath. *Good.* But mostly, he listened to the boy's heart pounding.

You are clever, boy. You know better than to run faster. You will never out-run me.

The wolf could smell the boy's panic, and he wondered if he would lose his footing or run into a tree. But the boy didn't panic. The boy kept his head as the wolf closed the gap between them, so they were running side by side. The wolf's huge paws—at least six inches across—long legs and easy strides were built for running in the winter's thick snow. The boy was tiring and sweating profusely. The wolf expected this, and he edged a little farther away.

He watched as the boy ran the last stretch of road to the oldest woman's house. He growled softly to himself. He knew the oldest woman would begin with a small bit of the valley's secret. *Don't worry, young Hank.* He wondered if the boy could hear his thoughts; he hoped so. *I will not harm you. I am your protector. You need me.*

A moment later, the wolf watched the boy barge through the oldest woman's back door and heard it slam behind him.

The light of the moon illuminated the bright white coat and black tipped ears of the wolf as he sat in the yard. His large amber eyes trained directly on the windows of the house, as his small round ears pointed right and left as he listened inside its walls.

He could hear the boy's heart pounding, then *bang bang* as his boots were kicked off against the door. The oldest woman peered at the boy over her spectacles. The wolf knew she was drawing her pictures and could hear her scratching the charcoal against the paper. He had watched her drawing for years.

The smells and sounds of hot bubbling meat reminded the wolf he needed to hunt. *A fresh kill, perhaps a coyote or a deer or even a couple of foxes would start to fill up my aching belly.*

He turned his ears back to listen inside the house. He knew his hearing was much stronger than any humans. An icy breeze picked up sections of his fur as he leaned his head towards the house.

The oldest woman's voice cracked. "You certainly seem in a hurry." She cleared her throat. *Perhaps the oldest woman is sick. That would not be good. This boy was needed. You must teach him. Time is running out.*

Then out of the corner of his eye, the wolf spotted a good-sized hare darting through the snow. The wolf jumped over the back fence, raced after it, lunged, grabbed, bit, shook it hard, and heard its neck snap. It wasn't much, barely a snack, but at least he wouldn't starve. As he feasted on this small catch, he turned back to listen to the boy and the oldest woman.

He wondered if the boy could hear his thoughts; he hoped so. *Don't worry, young friend. I will not harm you. I am your protector. You need me. Eat. Be strong and brave. Listen to the oldest woman. We have much to do.*

Hank watched Mrs. Plunket reach for two large bowls and made his decision. He needed to tell a grown-up.

"Something was running after me."

Mrs. Plunkett turned, glaring hard over her rimless glasses. "What was it?" Her voice was a whisper.

"A wolf. Just like the one we saw in the backfield last winter."

Mrs. Plunkett had pointed out the massive animal. "Way bigger than any dog." Hank had seen it first, running through the fields behind their houses. The two of them had watched the powerful arctic animal bounding over the untouched snow.

"I see that wolf here a lot," Mrs. Plunkett had pointed as it effortlessly jumped through the deep snowdrifts. "He doesn't want to hurt us."

Hank had raised his eyebrows, knowing how dangerous this 6-foot wolf could be.

"It's not that he's tame," she explained, "it's just that he's used to seeing us. He has lots of game back here and doesn't need to eat us."

From the safety of the house's interior, Hank thought he saw the shadow of a smile cross her old face.

She stared unblinkingly. "It didn't growl or snap at you?"

"No. It ran right beside me." Hank thought it seemed more like a statement than a question.

"This wolf will protect you."

Hank watched as Mrs. Plunkett opened the kitchen door and trudged through the snow. The wolf made a low bass growl and reached up and leaned his massive head against her face. His head came up to her chest as she placed her hand on his snout.

"This wolf is the leader of a mighty pack," she called back to Hank, rubbing her hand over the short fur behind the wolf's ear. "He's been watching over our two houses for a long time now."

2

MRS. PLUNKETT SAYS GOODBYE

There was a furious snowstorm during the night. The windowpanes rattled and the house's old wooden frame fought with the strong wind.

At 5:45 a.m., Hank opened his eyes. He thought of the evening before. Old Mrs. Plunkett walking outside to pat an Arctic wolf as if it were a family pet—and this was his protector?

Hank pulled his thin blankets up to his chin and tried to push away the confusing thoughts. He thought about how much snow he would have to shovel. Kicking off his covers, he went to look out the window. At first, the swirling patterns of frost on the windows blocked his view. He blinked a couple of times and rubbed at the glass with the sleeve of his pajamas. His shoulders slumped. There was a lot of snow—maybe three-and-a-half feet, and even more where it had drifted.

Better get started. Hank pulled on his socks and long underwear, along with a heavy sweater, jeans, and a thick pair of mittens that used to be his father's. He barely glanced into his kitchen as he made his way past. He ate all his meals with Mrs. Plunkett now.

He tried to be quiet as he opened his back door, but the old rusty hinges creaked, and an instant later, Mrs. Plunkett's bedroom light snapped on across the yard. His gaze swept back and forth across the snow, looking for the wolf. There was no sign of him.

The shovel was under a deep drift of snow, with only the handle showing. Hank kicked at it to snap the storm's icy grip. Although it was still dark, there was plenty of light from the bright winter moon. The shovel's metal blade scraped along the back steps leading to the sidewalk between the two houses. The sound echoed softly around the still, windless night. He knew he'd have to hurry to shovel Mrs. Plunkett's walk before he left for school.

Hank cocked his head to one side and stopped to listen to a low-pitched *whooo-ooo*. He wondered if it was the same great gray owl he sometimes saw around the back of their houses. He thought it lived in the thick woods behind the shed.

A few days ago, Hank had been leaning against the back fence, looking at the different trails of footprints and wondering what animals had made them. He had watched a great

Gray owl tilt its flattened plate-like face to the right and the left as its tiny ears zeroed in on its prey. It had taken flight and, ghost-like, glided noiselessly over something moving under the snow. The massive bird—had twisted in mid-flight, re-adjusted its aim, and dived soundlessly into the snow. It wrenched his head up, clutching a squirming field mouse in its claws.

Hank gazed at the outline of the shed, wanting to go and look for the owl, but he turned back to the task at hand. *Maybe later.*

His arms were strong, and he soon settled into a rhythm: slide the shovel, lift the snow, throw the load over his left shoulder. *Slide–lift–throw. Slide–lift–throw.* He was warmer now, and the steam billowed out of his mouth with each shovelful.

By 7:45, when Mrs. Plunkett opened her kitchen door, he was just finishing her walkway.

"Hank Rattler, get in here. Porridge is ready."

There was nothing on earth better than Mrs. Plunkett's porridge—except perhaps her hot cheese biscuits. Once inside her warm kitchen, he pulled the sweater over his head, dropped his soggy mittens beside his boots, sprinkled brown sugar over the hot porridge, and dug in. The sweet steam swirled up to his nostrils as he watched the sugar melt into small rivers.

From the other side of the table, Mrs. Plunkett peered at him over her spectacles.

"Listen, boy; you come right home after school today. I'll have a good hot dinner for you. I'm leaving for the clinic in Birchton for a few days. I need to get some tests done."

He nodded through his last few mouthfuls. Mrs. Plunkett had been to the clinic before, but only overnight. 'A few days' sounded like a long time to be alone.

"Don't you worry, boy," she said, reading his mind. "I'll look after things for you. I won't let your mother down."

The mention of his mother made the porridge stick in Hank's throat. He glanced at the calendar on Mrs. Plunkett's wall, where a neat row of X's marked the time that had passed since his mother left. She'd been gone for 168 days.

"Do you think she's ever coming home?" he whispered as his finger traced the red and white checks on the plastic tablecloth.

"I think so, boy. I just don't know when. Time will tell. Time will tell."

"Will the wolf stay with me?" Hank wasn't sure why he asked the question. In some ways, the wolf seemed like a strange dream. But he liked the idea of having someone—or something—looking out for him while Mrs. Plunkett was gone.

"Yes. I told you, the wolf is your protector. You'll be safe with him."

Safe from what? Hank wondered.

He scraped his spoon around his bowl, gathering the last bits of porridge. "Why do I need a protector?"

"Everyone needs to be protected from something," Mrs. Plunkett replied, nodding her head. "Especially children. You have this wolf. He *is* old, but he's still powerful, and he's smart."

The corners of Mrs. Plunkett's mouth turned down. "Your wolf is a great fighter. I have seen him watching us for a few years." For a moment, the old woman looked off into the distance then snapped her attention back to him. Hank wondered what she was thinking. He was about to ask when she turned back to him. "You okay, boy?"

"Yup." He wasn't entirely sure that was true, but he knew it was the correct answer. Mrs. Plunkett needed to go to the clinic.

"Good. See you at dinner. And thanks for the shoveling."

That night after dinner, just as she had done in the past when she had to leave for the clinic, Mrs. Plunkett gave Hank a list of instructions.

"Leave the porch light on until you go to bed. Lock the doors. Don't answer the phone. Don't be late for school. Open the curtains every morning and draw them closed every evening. Take in the mail. Shovel the snow. Do your homework. Don't get sick, and don't get hurt."

Her voice softened a bit as she saw Hank's eyes widen and his gaze fall to the floor. "I'll only be gone for a day or two, three at the most. I've left enough food for you in the fridge—but nothing hot because I don't want you to make a fire in the stove." She gave him one of her rare smiles. "Maybe one day I'll get an electric stove, but for now, this is just fine."

Hank looked around the kitchen and then into the living room. Mrs. Plunkett's house was strange, and everything was old. The kitchen didn't have an actual refrigerator, but an old icebox with ice on the bottom and the food on top. He wondered how often she had to get a new piece of ice and who brought it to her, but like so much about Mrs. Plunkett, it was a mystery.

The stove was a blackened, wood-fired, cast-iron monster that took up one whole side of her small kitchen, with a wide pipe that rose through the ceiling to heat the second floor. There was a cracked porcelain sink with a copper faucet that only brought in cold water. Mrs. Plunkett hauled in her wood from the pile out back and refused his help any time he offered. He thought she was strong for someone her age but had no idea how old she was.

There were sketches thumb-tacked onto walls and pairs

of dirty shoes by the back door that looked too big for her feet. Pieces of rock lay on top of piles of books that took up almost every surface. Cobwebs hung in the windows, and when Mrs. Plunkett opened the curtains every morning, the dust danced in the light. Hank couldn't imagine anything anyone would want to steal, but he noticed how she always locked her doors and windows and left lights on.

The living room, too, was strange—or at least different from his living room or from his friend Sam Benedetto's house. The furniture was worn and colorless and looked as if it were a hundred years old. There were no photos or pictures. What there was, were books—hundreds, maybe even thousands of them. Almost every wall was lined with sagging shelves, all labeled with Mrs. Plunkett's distinct, black-inked printing. Sometimes, Hank would walk around, reading the titles on their spines and wondering how anyone could read so many books.

Mrs. Plunkett had plenty of time to read and never had any visitors, and he'd never heard her phone ring. It was as if she were alone in the world. More than once, Hank thought about asking her where her friends and relatives were. But he always decided against it. She didn't seem lonely, and she took care of him.

Hank did wonder about her eyesight. She squinted through her old rimless glasses, and her face was almost always in a book. The general mess didn't seem to bother Mrs. Plunkett, and Hank didn't care either. She was the only person who knew his mother had gone away and the only one who cared about him.

He wondered why she was going to the clinic. He'd asked her once, but she'd brushed off the question with a joke about being old. It worried him. *Was she sick? What would he do without her?*

He remembered a piece of advice from his mother.
Don't borrow trouble.

But he did worry about the upcoming science test; twenty-five questions on the bird unit they'd just completed— and he needed to get at least sixteen correct, or he'd have to write an essay. Mrs. Plunkett sat down on the wooden chair.

"What's the difference between a nestling and a fledgling?"

"The nestling doesn't have many feathers and can't hop or walk or grip onto your finger. A fledgling can hop and has feathers and a stub of a tail."

"Good. Give me two reasons why nests are unsafe for nestlings?"

"Umm . . . they're easy places for other birds or animals to find because baby birds are loud, and also the nests usually have parasites."

"What other birds besides Canada Geese recognize their parents?"

"Cranes, crows, and jays."

"How do hummingbirds sleep, and how much do they have to eat every day?"

Question after question. Whenever Hank hesitated, Mrs. Plunkett barked, "Concentrate, boy, you know this! Think! It's there in your brain."

Hank sighed. Mrs. Plunkett was strict about tests.

After all the studying and Hank's eyelids were getting heavy, Mrs. Plunkett threw a shawl around her shoulders, and Hank grabbed his coat. As she pushed open her kitchen door, they both stopped. Mrs. Plunkett looked up at the moon. "It's a full worm moon," she said as her breath huffed clouds into the night air. "It's when the ground begins to become soft, and the earthworms become more active. That is when the robins and other migrating birds come back. There are worms to eat."

An owl hooted nearby. Mrs. Plunkett stopped, cocked her head to one side, and smiled. "You have another protector, boy." Hank stared up at her. "It's a great gray owl who also guards our properties."

Hank stood in the snow and looked up at her eyes shining in the moonlight.

"How long has the owl been a protector?"

"Since the day you were born, just like the wolf."

"But why?" he asked, confused. "Why do I need to be protected by a wolf and an owl?"

"The wolf protects you from the ground, the owl from the air," Mrs. Plunkett replied. "They are a team—a good team."

Mrs. Plunkett walked out into the night and headed toward his back door. She stood on his back porch, and they listened as the owl hooted. The moon was bright, and Hank saw the glistening eyes of the wolf, he sat quietly in front of the shed.

"Time for bed, boy," Mrs. Plunkett said as she opened his back door. The conversation about his mysterious protectors was over.

When he woke the next morning, Mrs. Plunkett was gone.

3
THE YELLOW CAR

Mrs. Plunkett always told Hank to follow his gut. His gut told him not to take his usual route to school the next morning. Trudging through the snow at the back of their two houses, he hopped over the old wire fence and headed in the direction of his school.

Mrs. Plunkett owned the land, although she didn't farm it or keep any livestock. She used to say, "I don't care for neighbors much; they always want to know your business. I own just shy of a thousand acres back there, so I can do what I want and have some privacy."

Turning around, Hank wasn't surprised to see the wolf following him, its white fur camouflaged into the fresh, unmarked snow. The wolf stopped at the same instant Hank did and his amber eyes stared at him the way he had the night before. As if he knew him. Hank squinted once again at his black-tipped left ear.

Okay, wolf. What do you want with me?

That afternoon, just as he expected, the wolf followed him home. Hank watched as the wolf sat tall and still, in the same spot as the previous night.

After another one of Mrs. Plunkett's cold sandwiches, Hank threw on his father's old coat and opened his back door. Sitting on the top step of his porch and shivered. The light from the snow bounced off the clouds and had turned the sky almost into daylight. The wolf sniffed up at the sky, and Hank wondered if it would snow again that night.

Then the owl hooted off somewhere behind the shed. The wolf's ears were instantly low and out to the side.

Hank thought he heard its low growl, and his heart began to beat faster. At the same time, the wolf looked over at the road between the two houses as he lowered his head and stretched out his chin. His upper lip curled, and his growl was low and steady. Hank listened as the sound became deeper and more threatening.

Hank crept along the back of the house and peered around the corner toward the street. Nothing. He took a deep breath and hurried over to the woodpile stacked up against the side of the house – an excellent place to hide. There were no streetlights this far into the countryside, but the wolf's eyes remained fixed on the road.

Then Hank saw a car. Its lights were off, and it was

driving slowly, almost silently, along the snow-covered road. The moonlight reflected off the hood of the yellow car. Hank held his breath, and his throat tightened.

Where are you, Mrs. Plunkett?

The car stopped on the side of the road, between the two houses. The driver turned off the engine as two people sat in the front seat, looking at the two houses. The wolf stood motionless at the back of Hank's house; his teeth bared as he growled quietly.

The light went on inside the car as the passenger's door opened. A man stepped out smoking a cigarette and pointed it towards Mrs. Plunkett's house. Hank watched the cigarette's amber glow as the man trudged into the snow. The passenger's window was open, and the second man leaned out, talking in a low tone. Then the two men laughed softly.

Hank's throat tightened. The man with the cigarette pulled a massive knife out from his coat. As he twisted the blade around, it caught the bright flashing glow of the moon.

Then Hank heard the owl. The sound pierced the cold night air from somewhere behind the house. He wanted nothing more than to run – as fast and as far as he could – but his legs were heavy and frozen to the woodpile, and his heart thumped so hard he thought it might burst out of his chest.

Whooo whooo-ooo. This time the owl sounded louder and more urgent.

The man with the knife chuckled and looked back at the man in the car. He continued to walk towards Mrs. Plunkett's front door. Then everything exploded. The wolf was a blur of white, streaking toward the man with the knife. The owl flew a few feet above, his wingtips almost touching the wolf's back. They both headed straight for the man with the knife. Alerted by the owl's cry, the man turned in their direction, but was too late. The owl dove straight toward his head; the wolf growled and barrelled into him, knocking him flat on his back in the snow.

The man shrieked and tried to stand up, his knife flashing again in the moonlight. He looked directly at the wolf as it lunged and sunk its teeth into the hand holding the knife. The wolf pulled and shook it, like a shark killing its prey. The man yelled as the frenzied shaking continued. His screaming filled the night air and echoed across the empty land. It sounded angry and then quickly weaker and weaker.

The wolf's low rasping growl continued. Hank leaned out from behind the woodpile. He was close enough to see the disbelief on the man's face. For a moment, the man looked straight at him, their eyes locked, and the man's mouth twisted into a painful grin.

"They know where you are, kid. They'll come for you. Even this wolf can't protect you." The man laughed and then coughed and choked up blood. His eyes widened, and he yelled as the wolf's jaws closed around his neck. The wolf shook it hard once. Hank heard a bone snapping, then nothing.

A moment later, the owl landed on the car's open window, as the man in the car punched and screamed, knocking the owl out of the window onto the road.

"No! No! Get Out!"

The man rolled up the window as the owl lunged at his head.

"Stop! No! No!"

Hank heard the man screaming as he watched the owl fight to get into the car. He turned his eyes away, but he could still hear the fight.

Several seconds later, the wolf stood over the dead man lying in the snow right next to Mrs. Plunkett's front door.

Hank took a couple of slow steps toward the wolf. Its ears moved, and it backed up further as if he were showing off his kill. Then Hank turned and realized the yelling from the car had stopped. There were no other cars and no other sounds. Had the owl killed him too?

In the moonlight, Hank could see the man wasn't moving. His eyes were wide open and unblinking. His eyes were fixed straight up at the stars. The knife lay on the ground beside his bleeding hand, and the snow around his head was quickly turning red. A small river of blood was pouring out of his neck. Hank had never seen a dead person before, but he knew this man was dead.

Then he heard it—a painful moan coming from the car.

Hank looked away from the dead man and the wolf. He could see the owl standing on the yellow roof, staring back at him. He took a step toward the car, and the wolf growled menacingly. Hank lifted his foot as if to take another step, and the wolf's barad his massive teeth.

Hank could just see something moving inside the car. *The other man was alive! He must have managed to roll up the window.*

The wolf stepped between Hank and the car. He continued to growl, his amber eyes staring and his upper lip quivering. Hank ran back to his house, pushed the back door open, and, taking the stairs two at a time, ran into his parents' bedroom.

Outside he heard the car's engine start. Pulling the curtains aside, he saw the owl still on the car's roof. Then the wolf jumped onto the front hood, stamping his front paws against the windscreen, and biting at the window. The owl pecked at the roof and shrieked as it flapped its wings.

Inside the car, the man's high-pitched screaming started again.

"No! No! No! Get away!"

The car sped up as the owl and the wolf kept up their attack. The wolf's snarling and the owl's unearthly screeching reverberated through the frozen countryside. Hank watched the car swerve dangerously from one side of the road to the other until the night finally swallowed it up.

Hank looked down from the window at the lifeless man lying in the red snow.

What am I going to do with a dead man?

It started to snow. There were big fat flacks of it and within a short time, the snow almost covered the dead man. Even the red snow was disappearing.

Hank heard the owl's *whooo*, as it swooped into sight, flashing its magnificent wings as it flew around the yard. It landed on the edge of Mrs. Plunkett's roof as the wolf appeared running down the road. He stopped beside the dead man and lapped up some of the blood still trickling from his neck.

Then the wolf grabbed the man's coat collar and began to pull. He stopped several times to get a better grip and then dragged him toward the shed. Hank ran outside again and started to follow the trail of blood staining the snow. The wolf dropped his grip on the man and growled at Hank. The moon was so bright; Hank could see its vast white face and torso were bright red.

The owl perched on a nearby branch. It was so close

that Hank could see the yellow irises of its eyes and its large, yellow-green beak. The wolf growled softly at Hank.

The snow fell harder, and the flakes were bigger and thicker now. Hank went inside. What else could he do? There was no one to tell, and the danger seemed to have passed. In his dark, silent house, he thought about the dead man and wondered if the wolf or the owl had ever killed anyone before. *Probably.*

Peering out of his bedroom window, he saw nothing. No man, no blood, no indentation in the new snow. The falling snow had covered up everything. It was as if nothing had happened.

He slid into his cold bed. He slept with his clothes on and dreamt of nothing. Layers of wool blankets seemed to hold onto him.

Sometime during the night, he awoke to hear the wolf's long bass howl. Hank knew it would be heard for miles around on this windless still night.

4
WINGED MYSTERIES

The next morning, Hank jumped out of bed and went to the window. There was nothing to see: no dead man, no blood, no knife, no yellow car. He looked over to the shed and saw the wolf looking up at him and the owl perched on the edge of Mrs. Plunkett's roof.

He knew there was nothing to do but get to school. Forgetting breakfast, he got dressed and headed off. He had almost forgotten about the science test.

Miss Clutterbuck's bird unit test was hard. He chewed on his pencil and thought about Mrs. Plunkett. Where does she find these difficult questions?

The answers are in your brain, boy. You know this. Just pull them out!

The classroom became quiet, and streams of slanted sunlight shone through the windows. *Twenty-five questions.*

Thirty-five minutes. Find those answers. Hank stopped chewing his pencil. Half an hour later, he got to the last question.

"What's the difference between a nestling and a fledgling?"

Thanks for the help, Mrs. Plunkett. The right corner of his mouth jerked up in a crooked smile.

After school, Hank and his two science project partners, Ruby Basher and Sam Bennedetto walked to Sam's house. As soon as they got to the Bennedetto's driveway, Sam yelled. "Yes!" he yelled. "She's making my favorite—lasagna!"

"How do you know?" Ruby green eyes flashed as she raised her eyebrows.

"I can smell it," Sam grinned.

Hank sniffed the air. "I can't smell a thing."

"Me neither," laughed Ruby.

"I've always been able to smell things from far away," Sam smiled.

A second later, Mrs. Bennedetto waved them into the kitchen for a snack. The radio was on, and she was singing an Elvis Presley song. Not knowing when he would get home, Hank ate four cookies and drank a large glass of chocolate milk. Then they went to the garage and stared at their project. It was a life-sized pterodactyl.

There were lengths of thin wire wrapped around the bird's wings. Each piece had been cut off and anchored on the underside of the wing to look like feathers.

Ruby ran her hand up the side of one of the wings. "These look good. We'll thread strips of cloth through the wire, and they'll look almost real." She squinted as she examined the model. Hank and Sam exchanged a glance. It was an expression they knew well; it meant Ruby was thinking—hard. "Remember," she continued, "the question we're asking is 'Could the pterodactyl fly?' We need to make sure our model isn't too heavy looking, or the judges will never believe the bird could get off the ground. And the shape of the wings must be thicker at the front but then long and narrow. I've been reading about birds and how the shape of the wings creates lift. Paleontologists know that pterodactyl bones were thin and hollow, just like the bones of birds today. And these guys *needed* to fly to get away from predators, have mates, and find food."

Sam peered in the pterodactyl's mouth. "We need some nasty-looking teeth."

Hank watched as Ruby ran her fingertips along the inside of the pterodactyl's open mouth. "You're good at making small pieces," Sam praised her as he remembered a school art project. "Can you make the teeth?"

Ruby grinned. "Yup. Paper-Mache and toothpicks." She turned to Sam. "And I need two identical marbles for her eyes. Big ones."

Sam nodded. "No problem. My brother has a whole tin of marbles."

Hank tilted his head as he studied the bird. "We need a better rib cage and a good, solid spine. Then we hook on the wings. They're big. They have to be balanced perfectly. Their small legs should be no problem, but the claws must look scary. The head will be hard because the beak and crest are so big, they might snap off," Hank said, tilting his head and studying it.

"We'll reinforce it with this thicker wire" Sam picked up a coil of wire on his dad's workbench.

Ruby nodded. "We need to make the crown on the top of its head a bright color."

"What color?" Hank asked.

Ruby shrugged. "No one knows. Red? Orange?"

"We might have some red paint around here." Sam stood back and squinted at the bird and nodded his head slowly. "I think we have a chance of winning."

"Yes." Hank grinned. "And that means we'll all get to go to camp."

A few hours later, Hank stood on Mrs. Plunkett's front step, feeling around in his pocket for the thin brass key she'd given him. He pushed it slowly into the lock, turning it, and opened the door just enough to slide in and shut it behind him. He turned on the kitchen light, the porch light and saw the wolf sitting in the snow. The black tip of his nose and his amber eyes stood out against the camouflaging snow. Opening the kitchen door, a crack, he looked across the snow at the wolf and then slammed it shut just as the owl swooped down and landed on the shed's roof. As strange as it was to have a wolf and an owl, Hank was glad they were there.

He ate his sandwiches slowly. It was strange eating alone and even stranger to think about passing a whole evening with no one to talk to and nothing to do. After dinner he wandered into the living room, thinking he might find a good book. When he got into the room, though, the stairs and not the bookshelves caught his eye. He'd never been upstairs. As he started up to the second floor, he felt as if Mrs. Plunkett was nearby. He didn't think she would mind if he looked around. Perhaps she even expected it.

On both sides of each step were piles of books with almost no room for his feet. All the spines faced outward, so Mrs. Plunkett could see each title as she was climbing.

Walking up the stairs, he expected to find the same layout as his own house. Reaching the top of the stairs, Hank was startled to find one large bedroom and a small bathroom. A single bed stood in the room, with a radio perched next to it on a stack of books. Like the living room, the walls were lined with sagging bookshelves, all labeled with Mrs. Plunkett's distinct, black-inked printing.

Hank slowly passed the bookshelves, reading title after

title. His own house had a few shelves of his father's engineering books and his mother's art books, but nothing like this. Here, though, Hank noticed, most of the books were about science or mathematics, except one shelf of atlases.

Hanging over Mrs. Plunkett's bed was a piece of wood with the word *fandian* painted on it. "Another mystery, like almost everything in your house," he whispered.

Hank sat on the floor next to Mrs. Plunkett's bed. An old atlas lay nearby, open to a map of China's Gansu Province. He could see Mrs. Plunkett's distinctive black lettering in the margins, connected by arrows to points on the map: *Late Jurassic Period: Gasosaurus—small meat-eater; Shunosaurus—plant-eater; Yangchuanosaurus—meat eater.* Hank flipped through the atlas and found other pages marked the same way.

Until Hank had started work on his science fair project, Mrs. Plunkett had never even spoken to him about dinosaurs. But she sure seemed to know an awful lot about them. Hank wondered why she'd never mentioned it—not once during all their conversations about school and science and the natural world. He leaned back against the bed. *She sure is a strange old lady.*

After spending most of the evening poring over the atlas and Mrs. Plunkett's notes, Hank slipped out of the old woman's kitchen door and locked it behind him. He heard the now-familiar hoot of the owl and felt less alone.

Good. You're here.

The stars were bright and glistened above the fresh white snow; it was almost like daylight. A shadow glided along the snow leading out to the shed. Standing perfectly still and closing his eyes, Hank waited and listened. He tilted his head so his ears could get a better fix on the sound.

A moment later, he felt a strong *whoosh* of air against his face. He opened his eyes in time to see the great gray owl directly in front of him, flapping its gray-brown wings and staring right into his eyes. For a moment, it hovered, suspended in mid-air, and then flew off toward the dark woods.

As Hank slipped inside his back door, he reached for the light switch, but something stopped him. "Don't turn on the light. Not tonight." Hank closed the door and looked back through the window toward the shed. The owl was perched on the roof, and the wolf sat between the two houses. He stared at the wolf. "I could sketch you," he whispered. His eyes went over the wolf's massive head and thickly furred ears, his left one tipped in black. It was turning slightly, listening to every sound. His long, dense layers of fur shielded him from the winter's frigid night: his broad face and square muzzle housing its mighty jaw and deadly teeth. Its amber eyes were edged in black and seemed not to blink.

Hank guessed the wolf weighed about 200 pounds and

stood at least three feet tall at his shoulders. Where was his pack? Was he a lone wolf? Probably an alpha wolf.

Outside, the snow kept falling.

He slid into his cold bed sleeping in his clothes and dreamed of nothing.

5
THE PROTECTORS

Hank awoke early and wondered if it had all been a strange dream. He looked out of his bedroom window. The wolf was sitting in front of the shed, watching him.

This isn't a dream. I will call you Raif. In a science class, he'd learned the name meant wolf counselor.

Grabbing his sketchbook, he propped himself up and started with the wolf's head.

The owl sitting still as a stone, watched from a nearby branch. Hank drew for a long time, paying no attention to the clock. Then he slid the sketch under his bed, thinking of what Mrs. Plunkett would think of his drawing. Who else could he tell of his two protectors? Maybe Sam?

He was hungry. Last night's cold sandwich was a long time ago.

It had snowed even more during the night. He looked at

the new blanket of white as he trudged across to Mrs. Plunkett's kitchen. He stuffed one of her sandwiches into his book bag and headed off to school. He cut through the back of her property and, thirty minutes later, was running past the post office, two blocks from school. A man stood outside reading the newspaper. Hank slowed down and edged closer, trying to get a look— "Constellation Missing from Galaxy"—about how Orion's Belt was missing from the night sky. Another headline caught his eye. *Wolf Nears Closer to Town: Attacks on Livestock Increasing.* His stomach clenched. Could this be his wolf? Who would he attack? One thing for sure was that his wolf could be in danger.

As he continued to walk, he began to wonder who Mrs. Plunkett really was. He'd thought perhaps she was more than just a neighbor—she seemed to care about him more than a neighbor would. And then the thought just struck him: *Could she be my grandmother?*

On Monday after school, Ruby joined Hank and Sam in the garage. Her red hair glowed under the bare light bulb as she chattered away at them. "He looks like he has one wing longer than the other. He must be perfect. Get out the measuring tape."

She groaned. "Hank, what are you *doing?* I told you that wing is too long. And I don't think his mouth should be open so far."

"Ruby, stop it! I like it half-open. How do you know if pterodactyls flew with their mouths wide open? He's hunting for smaller dinosaurs or fish, and he's near the water, ready to grab one."

Hank watched Sam trying to ignore Ruby, who provided a running commentary of their work: "Good, I like that. That will fall off . . . fix it, and move the talons out further. They don't look dangerous like they're going to rip you apart. We need more wire to reinforce his head and his eyes. What are we going to do about his eyes?'

After about an hour of this, Hank had had enough. He'd been happy to hang out with Ruby and Sam, after a weekend spent with only a wolf and an owl, but Ruby's constant comments were getting on his nerves.

"Enough!" Hank said. He stood up and stretched. "I have to go study now."

Their end-of-term science test would be fifty multiple-choice questions. Hank needed to get thirty-five right. Hank rolled his eyes. Mrs. Clutterbuck sure knew how to motivate her students.

He headed for the front walk as Mrs. Bennedetto called, "Hank, dear, stay for dinner."

"Have to get home. Thanks anyway," he yelled and waved, taking the front steps two at a time.

The streetlights lit up patches of pavement as he started

his run. Out of the corner of his right eye, he glimpsed a white blur. *Hello, Raif.* The two of them took alleys and ran behind backyard fences. Once they'd passed the last house, Hank felt a sense of relief. It wasn't likely anyone would see "his" wolf away from town. Hank pushed himself to go just a little faster, and Raif easily matched his stride, his tongue hanging out of the side of his mouth.

They ran so fast that Hank almost felt as if he were flying. He was doing everything right; then, for a split second, he stopped concentrating and focused instead on the feeling of power he felt running with his wolf. And that was all it took. That was the moment he lost his footing and knew he would fall. He twisted his body to save himself, but it was too late. He landed hard on his side.

As he lay on the gravel on the side of the road, gasping. Mrs. Plunkett's words sounded in his ears: *Don't get sick, and don't get hurt.*

Raif's cold, wet nose sniffed around Hank, nudging him to get him up. Hank's breath came back in large gulps, and he shivered in the cold.

"Okay, okay," he said, pushing the wolf away as he stood. "I'm up, boy. Let's see how bad it is."

His left ankle was throbbing, and as he began to walk, the pain raced up his leg. The trip home from this spot on the road would be no more than a thirty-minute run. But running was out of the question. He hobbled along slowly, leaning against the wolf.

When he finally arrived home three hours later, he had sweated through his clothes and was dizzy with pain. His ankle was swollen and pushed out angrily against his boot. He wrapped it in a snow-packed towel, swallowed two aspirin from the medicine cabinet, and crawled into bed. He pulled out his sketch book to study and a minute later was asleep.

6
WHO ARE YOU, MRS. PLUNKETT?

Hank awoke at 4:35 a.m. to pain in his bulging ankle that took away the rest of his sleep. He swallowed the last two aspirin in the bottle and hobbled outside to get more snow for his ankle. The moon was bright, and the wind was still. Raif growled a soft, low greeting.

Back inside, Hank sat down on a kitchen chair and leaned his head back. He was hungry, dizzy, and in pain. He needed help—from Mrs. Plunkett, from his mother, from someone. Having a wolf and an owl for protectors was fine, but they couldn't feed him or drive him to school or go to the pharmacy for more aspirin. He closed his eyes and was asleep in seconds.

When he opened his eyes again, there was sunlight streaming through the window. He sighed, knowing he'd missed most of the morning at school. *One more day*, he

39

rubbed his eyes and hopped over to the sink for more water. *One more day, and Mrs. Plunkett will be home.*

Hank sat at the table and studied his bird notes, reading each sentence out loud and making notes in the margin. He wished Mrs. Plunkett were home to quiz him. He studied his notes and textbook for most of the day and drank a lot of water to fill his stomach. There was nothing left to eat.

When the sun began to set, he put on his coat and hobbled over to Mrs. Plunkett's house, hoping that he'd missed something in the back of the icebox. The house was damp and cold. The kitchen stove hadn't been lit since Mrs. Plunkett left.

"Nothing," he sighed as he looked inside the fridge.

"There must be food in here somewhere," he whispered, opening cabinets, and pulling out drawers. No luck. There was nothing for his aching stomach.

He hopped over to the cellar door and opened it. The air was stuffy as if the door hadn't been opened in a while. Hank peered down into the darkness. Maybe she kept canned goods down there? A jar of pickles, or some apples or potatoes? His left hand felt around for a light switch and snapped it on. Holding onto the rail with both hands, he hopped slowly down the basement stairs, careful not to knock his sore foot into anything. At the bottom, he stood on his right foot and looked around. The last sliver of the setting sun was streaming through the basement window. It cast an orange hue as it lit up the wall in front of him. He sighed. Gardening tools—tons of them—pots of every shape and size, and bags of dirt. But no food.

He leaned against the stair rail. He thought about Ruby and Sam, who were probably in Sam's garage working on the pterodactyl. If Mrs. Bennedetto had asked him to stay for dinner tonight, he would have said yes. But it was too late for that. He'd missed school and any chance of a good meal. Now, he'd have to wait until lunch tomorrow. He would pretend he'd forgotten his lunch; he knew Ruby and Sam would share.

Hank rubbed his eyes. There was no point standing around here in the dust. He needed to get back upstairs and head home. But as he turned to hop back up the stairs, an odd sound stopped him in his tracks.

He cocked his head to the right and then the left, every sense alerted.

There it was again . . . faint but noticeable. A crinkling noise, almost as if someone were breaking crackers—but far away. Was it behind the stairs? A mouse making? Hank squinted into the darkness behind the steps, waiting, listening. When the sound returned, he looked around. It wasn't coming from under the stairs, but the lower shelf where Mrs. Plunkett stacked her gardening tools.

Hank stared at the shelf. He hadn't noticed the straight crack in the wall above the top shelf. His eyes followed the straight-lined crack to the floor.

That was strange. Cellars around here often had cracks. Hank knew from his own house—but they were crooked and spindly, not straight as an arrow. He couldn't reach the gap at the top of the shelf, where it ran along the line of the ceiling, but if he angled his body just the right way, he could touch the one on the wall. His fingers traced the smooth edge down the wall to the floor. He crouched down and found it. In the dark space under the bottom shelf, he saw it: a thick metal ring hidden behind a basket of wooden pegs.

He cocked his head to the left and listened, but the sound had stopped. It didn't matter. Hank was sure it was coming from behind the wall. It had to be. He slowly turned the ring. He heard a faint click, and then the entire shelf sprang inward. A moment later, the whole wall opened slowly and silently.

Hank squinted as he reached into the dark. He slapped at the wall and found a light switch. When the bright overhead lights hummed to life, they illuminated a vast room—bigger than the rest of the house. He tried to picture the layout of the floor above him. If he was right, this room ran underneath Mrs. Plunkett's garden and then back to the fence, maybe even farther. Wooden shelves lined all four walls. They started halfway up the wall and continued almost to the ceiling, and each labeled with Mrs. Plunkett's distinct black print. Under the shelves, about every eight or ten feet, was a desk with a lamp.

Hank hobbled farther into the vast space, turning on a couple of the lamps as he went. The breaking-crackers sound started again. *Something is living in here.* He looked around the floor and up to the ceiling. *Is there something alive in here?* A label on the nearest shelf caught his attention. *Wing Finger. Triassic Toothed Jaw.*

What is that? Hank looked at the object on the shelf above the label. There was a skull about three feet long, with a long, pointed beak with about three-inch teeth. Hank peered at the wings. They looked twice as long as the beak, with small hands protruding halfway up the wing. In an instant Hank knew what it was. It was their science fair project, a pterodactyl.

He took a deep breath and whispered into the empty room. "What are you doing with pterodactyl fossils hidden in your basement, Mrs. Plunkett? And why didn't you show them to me when we started work on our science project?"

There was a ladder hooked onto a rail and running along the top of the shelves. Hank limped to the end wall and hauled himself up a few steps. The first label he saw read *Broken Jaw—Pterodactyl.* He felt along the shelf until his fingers touched something rough and thin. *Teeth.* He was so surprised he dropped it and almost fell.

Better watch it, Hank. No one will find you if you fall off this ladder.

He read the other labels he could see from his perch.

Distal Syncarpa. Proximal Syncarpal. Trailing Edge Tendon. Upper Arm, Forearm, Digit IV. All pterodactyl bones, all labeled in Mrs. Plunkett's bold script. He reached up to the next shelf and ran his fingertips along until he felt something. He pulled down a claw. It was about two inches long and smooth to the touch. He felt a chill run down his back as he inched the ladder along and kept reading.

Rhamphorynchus muensteri. Tibia 48 mm. Femur 36 mm. Radius and Ulna 67 mm each. Humerus 37 mm by 19 mm wide.

He removed a large fossil from the next shelf and held it in his hand, turning it over and over. He looked closely, trying to sort it out. Something didn't make sense.

Then his brain realized what his eyes already knew. What he was holding was smooth and light. *These aren't fossils! They're bones! Actual dinosaur bones? They don't weigh enough to be fossils, and they're not rough enough.*

Hank's ankle was throbbing, but he kept looking at shelf after shelf. Then he stopped and looked at all the shelves. They were filled with bones. Hundreds of them. How was this possible?

At the far end of the room was a long table covered in paper. Hank hobbled over, switched on the lamp, and sat on a well-worn chair with Mrs. Plunkett's orange sweater draped over the back. He blinked hard. There were pages and pages of dinosaur sketches. Mrs. Plunkett was often drawing, but she always closed the book whenever he came near. Why would she hide this from him? She was always encouraging him to draw. All right, he would draw. He picked up a blank sheet of paper and a piece of Mrs. Plunkett's charcoal and set to work. Each sketch was more detailed than the last. Drawing had always been Hank's talent; his fingers drew what his eyes saw; there were claws and teeth and spines and skulls. There were ribcages and wings, flippers, and several large vertebrae, plus stegosaurus plates. He filled sheet after sheet, consumed by the secret contents of this room.

The noise sounded again, drawing Hank's attention toward the wall on the other side of the table. And then another sound—Raif's distinctive howl, far away but still easily recognizable. Was the wolf trying to tell him something? Hank wanted to listen to his protector, but he couldn't leave the room. Not yet. He stood up, tucking his sketchpad and charcoal under his arm, and limped over to the wall. He probed along the same wall he'd done earlier, near the shelves in the cellar.

Several feet from the wall, he saw another handle. It

turned quickly, and the door opened into another room. It was warmer, and the light was much brighter. In the center of the space, a glass incubator sat on a metal table.

Hank inched closer for a better look. Inside, six large, light-blue eggs sat in a perfect circle. He stared at them for a long time. The largest egg moved in a back-and-forth rhythm. Then he heard the noise again, *breaking cracker?* As he leaned in toward the egg, he felt the heat of the lights. His fingers were almost touching it when the rocking stopped, then started again. He pulled back his hand.

"What are you guys?" he asked softly. "And what are you doing in Mrs. Plunkett's basement?"

The rocking picked up again, faster than before. Hank reached for his sketchpad and charcoal and began to draw. The pitted egg's shell looked rough but showed no cracks.

Whatever you are, you're not ready to hatch.

He drew and shaded each bump on the eggs, taking great care to find the correct line of each egg's shape. Soon his hands were covered in charcoal from the smudging and shading, and his fingers cramped and sore.

Much later, he hobbled back to the main room, closing the door behind him. He didn't know for sure, but he guessed the warmer air in that room was essential to the eggs. He made his way back to the cellar and closed the shelf of gardening tools behind him.

He sat on the bottom step looking through all his drawings, especially the egg sketches.

"Who are you, Mrs. Plunkett?" he whispered into the emptiness.

He limped up the stairs holding his sketches in one hand and gripping the railing with the other. When he reached the kitchen, he could see Raif's glistening eyes through the window.

Hank lay down on Mrs. Plunkett's old sofa. Still clutching his sketches, he pulled up a blanket and fell asleep. He had found something extraordinary, and he wanted to take it to sleep with him. Neither the pain in his ankle, nor his hunger, nor the cold in the house could keep him awake.

7
THE TEST

The following day, he limped out to Mrs. Plunkett's kitchen and looked at the clock over the stove: 6:45 a.m. He wanted to return to the secret room and see the eggs again, but that would have to wait. He had to get to school, and there was no way he could cut across the back fields today. The test was at nine o'clock. He needed to get moving.

He found a pair of long socks and wrapped one and then the other around his ankle, holding them in place with a safety pin. Then he looked through the boots by Mrs. Plunkett's back door and found something that fit. He wondered who's they were. They were a man's boots, though he'd never seen a man at Mrs. Plunkett's house.

He slipped his dinosaur sketches into his backpack with his science notebook, put on his winter coat, and tied a scarf around his neck. Once outside with Raif, he pulled on his mittens and took his first deep breath.

"Time to go."

Taking the wooden walking stick he'd sometimes seen Mrs. Plunkett use in the back fields, he started down the road. Raif stayed nearby, his white coat like a textured ripple against the stark white snow.

He stopped and rested every few minutes. As time wore on, his ankle swelled in his boot, and he had to rest more often. As the bell finished ringing, he shuffled into the school-yard. His ankle throbbed, and the boot was tight. When he entered the building, the lines on the hallway floor swayed and lurched in front of his eyes.

The tests were being handed out when he hobbled into his classroom. Miss Clutterbuck gave him an annoyed look, then saw him limping. She nodded and almost smiled.

Sam and Ruby looked at him, wide-eyed.

"I called you last night, but nobody answered," Sam hissed across the aisle.

"You may start your tests *now*!" Miss Clutterbuck sounded like a drill sergeant. "Keep your eyes on your papers."

Hank took several long, painful breaths as he scanned the exam. He let out a sigh of relief. His studying had paid off. The answer to each question was on the tip of his tongue. He could hardly believe it. Twenty minutes later, he finished.

The rest of the morning was full of questions about the science fair and a math class. Hank spent most of the time trying to ignore the hunger rumbling in his stomach and the throbbing in his ankle.

When the lunch bell rang, Hank looked over at Sam.

"I forgot my lunch, Sam. Any chance you have extras?"

"You kidding? We're Italian. My mom always packs enough for two."

Hank winced. "My foot's kind of sore too. I don't think I can walk to the cafeteria."

"That's okay. We can eat here today. What happened?"

"I just slipped on some ice and twisted it."

"How much does it hurt? You want me to get the school nurse?"

"No!" He almost yelled. "No, nurse. I'm okay."

"You sure? Looks kind of swollen in your boot."

Hank tried to smile and change the subject. "I'm starving."

As Sam unpacked his lunchbox on his desk, Hank tried not to stare. He could hardly believe what he saw: two ham sandwiches and a container of spaghetti and meatballs, slices of buttered bread, and pickled red peppers. Sam opened a selection of cookies wrapped in waxed paper.

"I'm not very hungry," he said, glancing over at Hank. "Why don't you have it?"

Hank tried to eat as if he weren't starving. He tried not to gulp, but he couldn't help himself. It took him only a few minutes to devour the entire meal.

"My mum's picking us up after school to work on the project," Sam said, smiling. "She thinks it's too cold to walk home." He narrowed his eyes and looked right at Hank; the smile gone from his face. "You walked here today, didn't you?"

Hank nodded slowly. "I walk every day."

Sam said nothing.

Mrs. Bennedetto was waiting in front of the school in her blue Ford. Hank lowered himself into her front seat and leaned his head back. The purr of the engine and the warmth of the car put him to sleep almost immediately. He awoke as the car engine stopped. "Lean on me," Mrs. Bennedetto took his arm. She helped him into their warm kitchen and handed him a piece of pastry. He wolfed it down as she eyed him carefully. "Thanks, Mrs. Bennedetto," he said, making his way to the garage. Mrs. Bennedetto called after them. "You're staying for dinner, and then I'll drive you home. No discussion."

He knew he couldn't argue with her—what reason could he have for refusing a ride? He had no idea how he was going to explain his dark, empty house. Mrs. Bennedetto would be suspicious, especially if Sam spilled the beans about him walking to school and having no lunch. For a moment, he imagined himself telling her the truth.

I live alone in two houses out in the country with a white Arctic wolf and a great gray owl as protectors. My mother left months ago, and I can't remember my father. Mrs. Plunkett is old and lives in the house next to me, by herself. She has no family and is the only person looking after me. I have no food and no money. Oh, and by the way, Mrs. Plunkett also has a collection of dinosaur bones, six large eggs in an incubator, and partial dinosaur skeletons in a secret room in her basement. I drew sketches of them yesterday. Would you like to see them? They're in my backpack."

Hank sighed. No, that wouldn't work.

As the family gathered for dinner, Mrs. Bennedetto ordered Hank to take a seat.

"We're putting a tensor bandage on that foot, Hank. Sam, get me some ointment. Hank, dear, who's at home now? Never mind. I'll speak to your mother when I drop you off." She finished what she was doing and spooned spaghetti into his bowl.

Later in the car, he closed his eyes and thought about how good it felt not to be hungry for the first time in days. Then he thought about going home to a dark, cold, empty house in the middle of the country. He still had no idea how he was going to explain things to Sam's mother.

For a moment, he considered having Mrs. Bennedetto drive him to a stranger's house, one with all its lights on. He could open the car door and run toward it while waving goodbye. But he knew that wouldn't work either.

The game would soon be up, and he had no way out. He opened his eyes to see how much longer he had.

"Just a little farther, Mrs. Bennedetto."

A moment later he spotted Raif running along, away from the road, keeping up with them. Hank smiled. He'd made it through one more day without being shot.

"I think I just saw a wolf!" Sam cried. "A big white one, running along the edge of the forest."

"They're not usually this close to town." Mrs. Bennedetto didn't sound concerned. "Probably just a big dog."

Hank closed his eyes. The food that had felt so good just a little while ago was starting to make his stomach ache. And his ankle felt tighter in his boot. The throbbing pain was back, and there was no more aspirin.

Soon all the questions would have to be answered.

As they approached the two houses, Hank took a deep breath, preparing to tell Mrs. Bennedetto everything. He glanced out the window and noticed the moon was playing tricks with the light. The snow seemed lighter near Mrs. Plunkett's house and his house. But wait. No. It wasn't the moon at all. Every light was on—in both houses.

Had his mother come home?

Had Mrs. Plunkett come home?

Had the half blind robber returned?

Had the Children's Aid Society come to take him away?

Just as Mrs. Bennedetto stopped the car, the front door of his house flew open, and Mrs. Plunkett marched out into the snow, wrapping her old coat over her old wool dress. She smiled and waved.

"There you are, Hank! I'm sorry I was late getting home from the doctors."

She eyed him closely through the window in the back seat.

"Hello, Mrs. Bennedetto. How kind of you to drive Hank home. Oh, don't look so worried, Hank. Your old grandmother is just fine."

She made her way around to the driver's window and leaned forward. It was minus 22 degrees Fahrenheit, and she huffed out clouds of frozen air that looked like smoke.

"Won't you and Sam come in for some hot chocolate, Mrs. Bennedetto?"

"Thank you, Grandma Rattler, but not this time. Sam has homework." Mrs. Bennedetto smiled and turned to Hank.

"Look after that ankle of yours, dear."

Hank nodded, unable, for a moment, to form any words. He felt as though the freight train coming at him full speed had suddenly stopped. He climbed out of the car and looked into the back seat at Sam. They held each other's gaze without blinking while secrets floated in the frigid night air like the beginning of a storm.

8
THE SCIENCE FAIR

Hank and Mrs. Plunkett walked slowly toward her house. Then she stopped exactly where the man had died.

"What happened here Hank?"

"The night before last night two men came in a yellow car."

Mrs. Plunkett stood still and slowly nodded her head.

"One man had a knife and was walking toward your front door."

"And what happened?" Her eyes didn't blink.

"Raif attacked him. Right here." Hank pointed to the spot in front of her house.

"There was blood all over the snow. Just before he died, the man saw me and said they know I am alive and where I live."

Mrs. Plunkett's eyes widened. "Then what happened?"

"Raif broke his neck. Right here. Solvor tried to kill the man driving the car. He got away in his car."

She nodded slowly, and her eyes didn't blink.

"There was blood all over the snow. Raif dragged the dead man to the back."

Hank took a deep breath. "Do you think Raif ate him?"

Her voice was clear and strong. "Yes. Every single bone. No one will ever find a piece of him."

As he went into her house, Hank blinked in disbelief. Mrs. Plunkett's counters and small kitchen table had food everywhere.

"Who's all this for?"

"It's for you, boy. In case I have to go away again."

He watched her move around the kitchen, picking up heavy roasting pans and casseroles. Fear returned, a hard lump in his stomach.

"Why would you have to go away again?" He tried not to let his voice tremble.

"Sometimes I have to go to the clinic. That's all."

"Are you sick?"

She didn't answer, but her look said, *Boy, that's none of your business.*

He wanted to ask her when she would go away again.

He swallowed hard. He took a deep breath and kept on talking. "I've named him Raif—it means wolf protector. And

I've decided to name the owl Solvor; it means strong and full of fury."

Mrs. Plunkett put down a casserole and looked at him over the top of her glasses. "Good names. Carry this for me, boy. It needs to cool down." She pointed to a platter of steaming meat and led him outside to the back steps.

"Aren't you afraid an animal will eat that?" he asked as Mrs. Plunkett gestured for him to put the platter down on the steps.

"No animals will steal this food. Not from this house. Not with Raif and Solvor watching." She looked at Hank square on in the brightness of the glaring snow, then back up at the sky.

"Look at that sky, boy. Remember your science lessons —the North Star? Look how it comes off the end of the Big Dipper. Remember your history? That's what guided the runaway slaves when they were running to freedom. Running to the northern states. Running to Canada."

Hank stared at her, trying to figure out why this mattered. He'd just told her that a wolf had killed someone—right in front of her house—and now she wanted to talk about history and stars? If Mrs. Plunkett noticed his confusion, she didn't let on. She just stood on the porch, looking from one side of the sky to the other and back again.

"The dippers are common. Everyone can find them.

Look there, boy, at Hercules and the winged horse. Perseus is hard to find. Now, find Orion's Belt."

"There." Hank pointed.

"Anything different about it? Different tonight than when you've seen it before? How many stars is it supposed to have?"

"Three."

"Correct. Three bright stars—Alnitak, Alnilam, and Mintaka. These stars are easy to find because they're evenly spaced and in a straight line, like notches in a hunter's belt. How many does it have now?"

"Maybe six," Hank said, squinting. "It's a bit blurry. Is it six?"

"Could be." She stared up at the sky for a long moment.

"Remember the constellations," she said finally, her voice soft and low. "Remember Orion's Belt."

She turned back to him and picked up one of his hands and then the other. She turned them over until they were palms up. Even in the moonlight, his fingernails were black and gray where he'd rubbed and shaded his sketches. "Show me your drawings, boy."

"They're mostly under my bed. Some are at the Benne-detto's—for the science fair."

Mrs. Plunkett left the door swinging open as she headed

over to his house. Hank noticed how she ran between their houses. She was much faster now.

He followed her up to his bedroom. She was kneeling on the floor, pulling out sheet after sheet of his drawings from under his bed.

She said nothing as she concentrated on each sketch, her hands careful not to touch the soft pencil work. She stopped when she came to the last drawing.

"It's difficult to draw bones. This pterodactyl bone is a powerful sketch because the edges are well defined. Unlike fossils."

She peered closer then stretched her arm out, holding the page up and away from her face.

"You've done well with the edges, but you need to work on the proportions and angles. This bone has a greater curvature than you've given it. Remember the basics of sketching, boy—shape, proportion, perspective."

Fifth finger joint. Mrs. Plunkett put down the drawing and focused on his sketch from the secret room. He'd been so excited he hadn't climbed down the ladder but had remained leaning into the top shelf turning the labeled bone so he could capture each angle. As he'd sketched, the dwindling light and rising shadows had made the digit look like it was in the shadows.

"This fifth finger is an extraordinary part of the bird," she said. "You've done well with this one Hank. Some of the others are quite good, but this is your best work yet."

He stood with his spine against the doorframe of his room as she turned to look at him. She'd never called him by his name before. The doorframe pressing into his back gave him the courage to speak his mind. His voice quivered with emotion.

"The rules of sketching? That's all you have to say? You're not even going to mention the bones I found in your basement?

"Don't be impertinent, boy."

"What about the eggs?"

Her chin rose, and her gaze became cold. "I said, that's all for now."

Hank stared back but said no more.

Hank was up early the morning of the science fair. At 8:00 a.m. sharp, he and Mrs. Plunkett opened the wide doors to the shed and climbed into Mrs. Plunkett's car. She rarely drove, and when she did, Hank noticed she went too fast around corners and merely slowed down for Stop signs.

They arrived at the Bennedettos just in time to help carry the display out to the Bennedettos' truck. They moved it carefully as Ruby winced and moaned. "Watch it, not too fast, watch the wingtip." Mrs. Plunkett gave her several sharp looks but remained silent.

After securing it in the back, tying it down, and double-checking every piece of the pterodactyl that could break, the procession to the Science Fair started. Mr. Bennedetto drove the truck with Sam in the front seat beside him. Then another big station wagon packed with more Bennedettos followed. Ruby and her parents followed carefully behind as if they were suspicious of pieces of the pterodactyl flying off. Hank and Mrs. Plunkett followed the Bashers.

The giant bird swayed around corners and bounced along the gravel roads. Hank couldn't take his eyes off it; he was sure that a wing would break off, or the jutting beak would smash into the roof of the truck. Ruby had measured it the night before. "Exactly eight feet across, wingtip to wingtip, and about three feet eight inches high." Hank remembered that it matched the measurements of a fossil found in the basement.

Both Hank and Mrs. Plunkett let out a sigh of relief as they stopped at the light just in front of the County Fair Hall. He could see the banner draped across the front of the building: WELCOME TO THE 1957 SOUTH FOOTHILLS COUNTY SCIENCE FAIR! He took a deep breath to calm the butterflies in his stomach.

"Now, all you have to worry about is Ernest Foster," Mrs. Plunkett said.

"Who?"

She snorted and shook her head in disgust. "He's one of the judges—the one who gives the prize money and pays for the winners to go to camp. Here's an important piece of advice for you, boy: If he comes over to ask questions or talk to you, don't look straight at him."

That was a strange piece of advice. Weren't you supposed to look at people when he spoke?

Mrs. Plunkett continued "he's easy to spot. He has three birthmarks under his left eye. If you see him coming in your direction, keep your eyes down. Just look at your feet. You understand me?"

He didn't—not at all—but he nodded anyway. There was no time to discuss it. They needed to get inside. The Fair started at 10:00 a.m. sharp, and their project had to be displayed perfectly.

The hall was filled with the buzz of eager voices as contestants carried in their projects. They found their assigned spot and got to work. They were fast and had the exhibit set up in a few minutes. The pterodactyl was the focal point of their exhibit, with its open beak, dangerous teeth and outstretched claws pointing directly at the audience as if it was ready to attack.

Hank, Ruby, and Sam made their way around the hall, looking at the other students' work. There was "Are Fingerprints or Their Patterns Inherited?" and "Do Different Kinds of Orange Juice Contain Different Levels of Vitamin C?" The participants for that one had small samples of orange juices as a giveaway. The three friends exchanged an uneasy look. Free orange juice and genetic fingerprints were much more exciting than a strange bird that had been dead for millions of years. *Maybe ours isn't so good after all*, Hank thought.

Finally, it was ten o'clock. The doors opened, and people swarmed in. The loudspeaker blared announcements over the sound of scraping shoes and babies crying. A steady stream of teachers, parents, and students visited their display, asking question after question. Ruby quickly became their spokesperson.

It was about 10:45 when the three judges turned down their aisle: two men and one woman. Hank peered at the two men. Which one was Mr. Foster? His eyes sought out Mrs. Plunkett. She was across the aisle, looking at a project of a series of different colored volcanos erupting. She turned and looked at him, almost as if she could feel his eyes on her back.

Then the judges were in front of them, blocking his view. He looked down at his shoes. From the corner of his eye, he tried to get a look at the first man's face. No birthmarks. As the second male judge asked Sam about the construction of the bird, Hank stole a quick peek. There, under his left eye, were three birthmarks. He clenched his fists, closed his eyes, and tried to focus on what the judge was saying.

"Whose work might this be?" Mr. Foster asked.

"Oh, not mine, sir," Ruby answered. "That's Hank's work. He draws all our pictures."

Hank opened his eyes but kept his gaze locked on his shoes.

"This is an interesting drawing of the fifth finger, young man. Did you copy it from a book or use a fossil as your model?"

"Fossil, sir." Hank tried to keep his eyes facing down.

"Hmm . . . very good. It looks almost real, doesn't it?" the man asked turning to the other judges. Together they slowly walked around the pterodactyl, reading Ruby's descriptions. They peered at each of his twelve drawings, then stopped and looked at the fifth-finger sketch again.

"This fifth-finger drawing has a real energy to it." Mr. Foster leaned over and peered at the sketch more closely. "You would almost think you've seen a real pterodactyl digit."

And then they were gone, moving on to the next exhibit.

Mrs. Plunkett appeared beside him. "You did just fine, boy, just fine."

"I didn't look at him, even when he asked me a question."

She nodded again.

"He sure looked at my pictures a lot," he said.

"Yes, he did." Her voice was soft and lower than usual. Hank couldn't remember ever hearing this tone before. "He did indeed." She put her arm around his shoulders and gave him a quick squeeze.

"What do you think?" Ruby asked.

"They liked us a lot." Sam smiled for the first time all morning.

"What's the matter, Hank?" Ruby said, her eyebrows knitting together. "You sick? You look like you've seen a ghost."

But Hank didn't answer. He was too busy watching the strange judge as he examined another project. When the man turned back to stare at Hank, Mrs. Plunkett nudged him. "Don't look back," she said gruffly.

Hank didn't know why he suddenly felt sick. His stomach churned, and his head felt woozy as if the room were tipping around him and making him lose his balance. The man's head inclined slightly in Hank's direction, smiled and walked around the corner, out of sight.

At one o'clock, the loudspeaker shrieked to life.

"Welcome once to the 1957 South Foothills County Science Fair. The judges have made their selections. Join us as we announce this year's winners."

It took a few minutes for everyone to gather around the small stage at the front of the room. Mrs. Plunkett stood behind Hank. He felt her hand on his shoulder.

Mr. Foster took the microphone.

"Good afternoon. Thank you for joining us on this important day—a day when we come together to see the hard work our science students have done over the last few months. We've had a chance to look at each project, and we congratulate all of you. However, this *is* a competition, and the judges have made their choices."

There was a rumble of voices before everyone fell silent again.

"Honourable mention goes to the team from Winston Churchill Elementary for their project entitled 'The Egg in the Bottle Experiment.' Congratulations to Marijana Wilson, Jennifer Stein, and Alex Laplante."

There was applause as the students made their way to the microphone to accept a small silver cup and shake the judges' hands.

"Second place goes to the project submitted by Mr. Mathews' class from Blue Grass Elementary— 'Musical Instruments: The Scientific Principles Behind Them.' Congratulations to Alex Trecartin, David Newton, and Ben Sherman."

Another round of applause rippled through the hall

as the second-place winners hurried to the microphone to accept their silver cup and three red ribbons.

A hush settled over the audience as they waited for the first prize. All eyes returned to the judges. Hank watched the man with three birthmarks as he scanned the faces of the crowd.

"And now, competitors, teachers, parents, and fellow science lovers, we're pleased to announce the winner of the first prize for the 1957 Science Fair—and remember, the prize is two weeks at Camp Brown Bear in the Rocky Mountains. The winner is 'The Pterodactyl: Could It Fly?'"

There was a burst of applause, and the chairman held up his hands for quiet.

"Congratulations Ruby Basher, Sam Bennedetto, and Hank Rattler, from River Rock Elementary!"

Louder applause rose from the crowd, and Hank turned to find Mrs. Plunkett smiling behind him.

Together, he and Sam and Ruby rushed up to the stage, and one of the judges handed them a large silver cup engraved with the previous winners' names. She also shook their hands and gave them blue ribbons with first-prize medals. They put the ribbons around their necks and then held the cup high over their heads. Hank found Mrs. Plunkett in the crowd, then Ruby's parents and the Bennedetto family. They basked in the sound of the wild cheering.

The three judges shook their hands as the crowd began to file out of the hall. Hank tried to keep his face to the floor, but the man with the three birthmarks extended his long bony fingers, and Hank had no choice but to meet his gaze.

"Congratulations, young man," he said, his voice low and intense. "Your drawings were a tremendous addition to your team's project. Your last name is Rattler?"

Hank nodded, trying to pull his hand away. But the man tightened his grip, and his gray eyes never left Hank.

"I'm Mr. Foster. I'll keep an eye out for you. I'm always looking for talent."

Hank slid his hand out from the man's clutches and almost ran off the stage.

9

A DANGEROUS SUMMER

The days flew by until the end of school. When Hank opened the heavy door to the playground when the last bell had finally rung, the sun shone, and the air smelled like freshly cut grass. It was summer—and almost time for their trip to Camp Brown Bear. Hank, Sam, and Ruby had just three days to prepare for two weeks in the mountain wilderness.

Hank gathered everything on Mrs. Plunkett's camping list: waterproof matches, a sleeping bag, a pocketknife that opened into a thick blade, file blade, a toothbrush, first-aid kit, a small shovel, fishing line with hooks, four short candles, a sewing kit for emergency tent repairs, a waterproof watch, and an old map of the other side of the mountain.

"He thinks he's a dog," Hank remarked as Raif followed him. Ever since the end of school, Raif had been nearby,

almost like a third member of their little family. This morning, Hank had opened the door to the kitchen, curious to see if the animal would enter. He had.

"He's an Arctic wolf, boy. And don't you forget that. He never will."

She surveyed the items lined up on his mother's bed. "What are you missing?"

He stared at all the equipment, ticking off items in his head.

"I guess I could take my sketchpad and some charcoal."

The corners of Mrs. Plunkett's mouth creased into the slightest smile.

"Now you're thinking, boy. Never forget where your talents lie." She reached into the pocket of a long sweater that she'd hung over the bedpost. "I've got something for you—to congratulate you on winning the science fair." She handed him a pocket-sized sketchbook. She'd never given him a gift before.

"Use it well, boy. You've got an artist's eye. You never know what you might want to draw."

"Thank you," he smiled and flipped the pages over and felt the paper. "I can't wait to use it."

Mrs. Plunkett nodded. "There's something else, too." From the pocket of her long skirt, she handed him a compass.

"It's waterproof, so you'll be able to use it no matter the weather."

Hank took it and turned it over in his hands. The back was silver and slightly tarnished.

"It was my husband's," Mrs. Plunkett said quietly.

Hank looked up, startled. She'd never mentioned a husband before.

"What was his name?"

"Max." She whispered the name so that only the tiny room could hear her voice. "He's been gone for a long time."

Late that night, long after all of Hank's gear had been stowed in his backpack and Mrs. Plunkett had gone home, Hank wandered through the quiet house. He'd tried to fall asleep but was too excited. The prospect of making new friends or wondering if Mrs. Plunkett would be safe worried him. And then, just before he fell asleep he thought about his mother.

Hank rummaged through his mother's dresser and looked for the hundredth time as to where she might have gone. Nothing. His father's dresser was almost empty and only had an old gray vest, a navy sweater with a black patch on one elbow, a few pairs of mismatched socks, and a pair of rumpled summer trousers with holes in the knees. Opening these drawers left him with an odd sensation. He had only faded memory of his father—small snapshots that seemed out of focus as if tucked behind a sheer curtain.

At the bottom of the last drawer, his father's watch was in a worn leather pouch. It was an ordinary old watch, and some of the stitching was loose. This time, though, as Hank looked at it more closely, and saw the word—*waterproof*—stamped on the back. Winding it and putting it to his ear, the ticking sounded perfect. Taking the watch to the workshop in the basement and using a small nail, he punched a hole in the strap and tried it on. It fit perfectly.

On the morning of their departure for camp, Hank awoke to the sound of Solvor hooting softly in the tree outside Mrs. Plunkett's house. A moment later, the owl glided onto Hank's window ledge. His wingspan blocked almost all the early morning light as his enormous claws gripped the wood, tearing off some of the paint. They peered at each other through the pane of glass.

"Are you coming with me, Solvor?" Hank asked softly, pressing his nose against the glass, and staring right into his eyes.

He and Mrs. Plunkett enjoyed a quick breakfast, then packed the car.

"Remember, boy," Mrs. Plunkett turned to look at him as she closed the trunk. "Use your talents—and your wits and your intuition."

He nodded as he climbed into the front seat. From his usual spot near the shed, Raif watched, ready to run along after the car. Hank smiled, knowing that his wolf and his owl would be traveling with him. He might not always know exactly where they were, but he knew they'd be nearby.

Hank, Ruby, Sam, and their families gathered at the station where the bus for camp waited. They were the last three to arrive, and the other campers stared as a counselor checked their names off a list after a round of goodbyes—Mrs. Bennedetto gave each of them 3 Italian cookies wrapped in tin foil and then they climbed onto the bus.

At last, the bus's engine sputtered to life, sending out a cloud of exhaust. Hank peered through the rear window as they pulled away from the station. The Bashers and the Bennedettos were waving and yelling. Mrs. Plunkett stood alone, off to the side with her head cocked to one side and her arms folded, watching them until they rounded a corner.

10
INTO THE MOUNTAINS

Camp Brown Bear was two camps, boys camp and girls. The trees were primarily huge pine with a few white birches. The main lodge was enormous, with long tables and crude, uncomfortable benches. The flags of all the Canadian provinces and the U.S. states hung from the rafters. The stone fireplace at one end, big enough for someone to stand in.

The cabins were old with weathered wood slates and small windows. Inside, the bunk beds were narrow, and the floor looked as if it had been walked on by thousands of feet. In the back corner was a tiny bathroom.

The boys camp was to the east of the rock-face cliff, and the girls camp was tucked under an outcropping of rocks further along the creek.

The camp director Mr. McGibbon was a tall, thin man who wore a small silver whistle at the end of a brown cord around his neck.

"I've been the director of Camp Brown Bear for years. I know all your tricks. The girls camp is *out of bounds*." He looked at each one of the 148 campers in turn as if daring anyone to disagree. "The *only* time the girls come to our camp is for special events. So don't be brave or stupid. *Off-limits* means just that."

"Each cabin is named after an animal in these mountains." Sam and Hank made their way to their cabin, called Grizzly, and met their counselor Frank a tall, skinny guy.

Hank and Sam spent the first two days learning the camp setup: the cabin's location with all the climbing gear neatly laid out on hooks; the nurse's cabin with five beds. There was a locked metal cabinet with jars of ointments and packages of bandages, tongue depressors, and thermometers. Hank looked at the metal beds and wondered if anyone ever got sick enough to stay overnight. Nurse Mary rattled off the rules about faking illnesses but warned them that if they were ill, to get over to her cabin pronto.

In the afternoon of the second day, Counselor Frank brought his group down to the boathouse. Hank saw the life jackets on hooks and canoes and rowboats in lines at the dock.

"A mountain stream feeds this lake, and so it's cold. Remember, no swimming on your own ever." Counselor Frank eyed them suspiciously.

Hank was an excellent strong swimmer thanks to his

mother and Mrs. Plunkett, and the pond on Mrs. Plunkett's property. But this was different. With a grimace, he wondered how deep the lake was. *The mountains are so high—are the lakes just as deep?* Maybe it was better if he didn't know.

The dock boards along the waterfront were weather-beaten and gray. Hank could almost hear the thumping of the summers of bare feet running across them. Even though the sun shone, and the outside temperature was over eighty degrees, Hank was cold and nervous. From the moment he'd arrived at camp, he'd looked around for both Raif and Solvor, but so far, they were not there. Last night, Hank thought he heard Solvor but was wrong. It was an owl, but not *his* owl.

On the third day at camp, the weather turned. Menacing dark-gray clouds hovered over the side of the mountain, stretching across the lake, and they could hear the distant thunder rumbling like falling boulders.

The campers and counselors spent the day in the dining cabin learning how to tie knots. Sam found knot making easy, and his fingers grabbed the ends of the ropes and tied knot after knot. Hank was all thumbs, and after countless failed attempts, he finally got the hang of the three knots, the Monkey's Fist, the Cow Hitch, and the Bowen.

He smiled as he looked over at Hank. "You'll get it. Try it again."

But Hank wasn't any good at it.

That night, the rain pounded on their cabin roof. The constant noise kept them awake, but eventually, the rhythm drowned out their chatter, and most of the boys settled into their sleeping bags and drifted off to sleep. Just as Hank felt his eyelids getting heavier, there was a faint thud on the roof. He stared at the ceiling and waited, but there was nothing to hear now except for the rain. No sound, no movement. The plywood ceiling had vibrated under its weight. A hawk, maybe, or a raven? He strained his ears and listened harder. After several minutes, he heard it. *Whoo-ooo. Whoo-ooo.*

"Hello, Solvor. Where's Raif?" Hank whispered into the night.

It rained for the next 5 days. Then the morning finally arrived with sunny skies and a light breeze.

"Perfect weather for our trip around the north side of the mountain," Counsellor Frank said. "One group at a time. Bring sleeping bags and toothbrushes, a sweater, and whatever else you think you'll need for three days. I'll need help carrying the tents and food."

Hank, Sam, and two other boys from their cabin—Oz Solomon and Zebi Littlecrow set out. The road was bumpy. They had to stop the truck several times to clear the rocks and branches in their way.

The narrow road wound around the foothills of the Rocky Mountains. They got their first glimpse of the high mountains after driving about twenty minutes through majestic pine forests dotted with small rockslides. Even though it was summer, a few of the mountains still had snow at the top. Hank had always seen the mountains from a distance, but now they jumped out at him. Counsellor Frank kept up a running commentary about the dangers of wandering off, but no one was listening; they all stared at the mountains.

When they arrived at their site, Frank set up his pup tent and then showed them how to set up the larger one. "Remember, stay together, no wandering off." He jerked his head down the steep slope and stared at them. "And stay away from that lake. It's stone-cold and drops off straight into deep water."

Hank squinted toward the sun, looking up high into the trees and the crags of rocks for Solvor. *Where are you, boy? Are you waiting for Raif?*

After a quick lunch, Counsellor Frank showed them around.

"See this plant?" He pointed to a pink, daisy-like flower. "It's called Arctic aster, and it grows like a weed around this mountain. And only *this* mountain, though nobody knows why." He moved a few steps to his left and touched the leaves of another plant. "Here's something else that grows only here. It's called Sideritis syriaca, commonly known as ironwort. People used it to heal wounds that soldiers got from iron weapons. It grows in Greece on the sides of mountains. We have no idea how it got here, but it's been around this camp for a long time." The boys leaned down for a closer look. "Our indigenous people use it to make tea. I'll make some later; it will take the chill off the mountain air."

Hank didn't want tea. The sun was high in the sky, and it was hot.

Later, while looking up at the craggy peaks, he stopped and stared. There was a flash of white across the rocks, then the familiar distant hoot of an owl. *Hello Solvor. Hello Raif.*

Hank spent the afternoon sketching: the Ironwort and Arctic Aster, as well as a pine tree, half dead with most of its branches gone.

When the sun started to dip in the sky, the boys helped Counsellor Frank with dinner: hot dogs, more apples, and lemonade. They ate around the fire pit and roasted marsh-mallows on sticks.

"I'll boil some water for the tea," said Frank. When the water was bubbling, he added several good-sized sprigs of ironwort, removed the pot from the fire." He poured each of the boys a cup. Hank took a sip and almost spit it out.

"Not to your liking?" Frank's laugh echoed across the rocks. "It takes time to get used to it." He looked at the sky, which was getting darker. "We've got a busy day tomorrow, so let's get to sleep early." He looked up again and frowned. "We may have some bad weather; the wind has shifted direction to the northeast, and that's usually where the storms come from."

He stood up and looked at the sky again. "Wash your dishes and put them in your backpacks. You never know when we'll have to move fast. And remember to put out the fire." He said goodnight over his shoulder and disappeared into his tent.

Zebi was the first to speak. "He may be right," he stood up and peered into the night sky. "I thought I heard some thunder . . . way off in the distance. I don't feel like turning in. Let's stay up for a while." He dragged his fingers through his shoulder-length black hair and sat down beside Sam.

Oz was the tallest, even taller than Counselor Frank, and his gangly legs stuck out almost to the firepit. He had blue eyes, wavy brown hair, and a knitted brow from a curious mind. He pulled a harmonica out of his pocket. "Let's try this one." "She'll Be Comin' Round the Mountain." Sam's clear voice rang out into the night, and an owl hooted in the woods. Hank pulled out his sketchbook and drew Oz's face as he played. Capturing the angle of his head was difficult, and the holes on the harmonica were smudged, but he knew the upper part of Oz's face was good.

After a few more songs, Zebi wandered down to the lake with the pail. Hank watched as he sat on his haunches and looked across the still water. There was the slightest feathering as the wind picked it up. Ripples spread outward like the shading in a picture. Zebi stood up and carried the pail back to the fire and looked up at the sky. Then he carefully poured it over the half-burnt logs and kicked the logs apart. "Let's sleep."

Hank awoke to the sound of the wind pulling and buffeting their tent. The doorway flaps were vibrating so hard he wondered if the zipper would hold. He looked over at Sam, Oz, and Zebi, their sleeping bags pulled up to their chins.

He listened for some sign that Raif and Solver were nearby. So far . . . nothing.

In the few minutes he'd been awake, he could hear a difference in the sound. It had started with loud, persistent static as if the radio station wasn't on the station. The cracking and splitting tree branches followed, like rifle shots echoing along the side of the mountain. The rain started, not lightly but in angry sheets, smacking and whipping at the tent.

A moment later the zipper was pulled open, and Frank hollered at them through the gathering storm.

"We need to get back to the truck! Now!"

In an instant, Zebi, Sam, and Oz were awake, jumping and banging into each other and the sides of the tent.

Hank was ready first. Oz couldn't find one of his shoes, and Sam's backpack was still outside next to the fire pit. Zebi moved more slowly and carefully than the others, and Hank wondered how he was so calm.

As the four of them half crawled out of the tent, the wind almost blew them over. The ground was alive, with small rivers racing toward the lake.

Frank ran ahead. "Hurry up!" he yelled over his shoulder. "Follow me!"

At first, they crept along together in a tight knot. But then Oz lost his footing and slid sideways into a rock. He yelled in pain, and in the next burst of lightning, Hank could see the side of his face glistened with streaks of bright red blood. He tried to wipe it off, but the blood poured out, and the rain didn't stop.

Frank ran back and knelt beside him. "Can you walk?" he yelled over the howling wind.

Oz nodded, blinking hard and gasping.

Frank peered at the cut without touching it. "You sure?"

Oz nodded again.

"Stay with me, and stay together," Frank yelled. He pointed ahead with his small flashlight, growing dimmer by the second. "I'll find the path."

But nothing was left of the path that had led from the parking area to their campsite. Frank stood, peering back and forth in the dark. Hank knew it was no use: the path was gone, wiped away by the pelting rain and the rivers of mud running down the hill.

The stars had disappeared behind clouds, and the sky was pitch black. Rain battered into their faces, propelled by wild gusts of wind. A thunderous crash shook the ground. Hank looked back at their campsite. A tree had fallen, slicing straight across their two tents.

The noise jolted Frank into action. "Come on," he yelled, stepping around a fast-moving creek. "There's another way to the truck, over here, south toward the camp." He led them along the side of the mountain, away from their campsite. "Keep going! Don't stop! Stay together."

They half-ran and half stumbled, blinking and wiping the water from their eyes.

Frank stopped abruptly, turning the flashlight around into the blur of the pounding rain, yelling, "I'm not sure this is the way to the truck."

"You're the camp counselor, and you've got us lost?" Zebi shouted angrily over the wind.

Frank held up his hand. "Stay here! Keep an eye on Oz, and don't move from this spot. I'm going to look for the truck," he said, pointing to a craggy hill covered in mud. "I think we can get to it that way, but I need to be sure before we all go."

They stood, soaked to the skin, and watched in disbelief

as he disappeared into a wall of water, his running shoes slipping and scrambling up the stony ridge.

They waited in the howling storm's blinding rain. Another tree crackled, and a huge branch slammed into the ground, not twenty feet from where they stood. The lightning lit up the sky every few seconds. Blood ran down Oz's face and into his ear, dripping off his chin. With the next flash of lightning, Hank looked closer at the large gash through his right eyebrow. Both sides of the cut looked raw, and in the center, he could see the white of the bone.

Hank shook his head and bellowed over the wind. "We can't stay here! Too many trees are falling!"

Zebi pointed up toward a cliff on the side of the mountain. He cupped his hands around his mouth. "That's where we have to go—against those rocks. There's supposed to be a secret cave, but no one's ever found it. We might find an overhang of rocks, or at least a ledge to protect us from this."

A moment later, as they stood rooted in the mud, a sound cut through the howling wind—a loud, huffing, low-pitched screaming growl.

"What is it?" Hank gasped and stared into the trees.

Zebi held up his hand, waiting for the next flash of lightning, then spoke at machine-gun speed. "A bear—a Kodiak or a grizzly. Maybe it's a female, and we're near her cubs? Or we're on her trail? It's huge! I think it's a male—too big to be female. Only males can make that sound. It could tear us to pieces. Let's go—we've got to get down the hill, then climb up that cliff!"

Zebi turned and ran, falling, picking himself up, sliding, and crashing and barely missing the trees. Sam followed, missed his footing, and lost his backpack as he fell, rolling in somersaults until he stopped at the bottom of the hill. Hank grabbed Oz's arm, and they followed the others down. Hank reached out to snatch Sam's backpack as they slid past rocks and mud. Up ahead, Zebi had started to climb the cliff. Hank and Oz slid into Sam, who had managed to keep his glasses on. Hank shoved Sam up with a quick "Go! Now!"

The bear roared again. Hank spun around to find him. There was so much lightning; he could see the dark brown bear standing in a clearing. It looked about twelve feet tall as it reared up on its hind legs and looked straight at him. The bear's jaws were wide open as it stomped on the ground, swinging its head from side to side. In another flash of lightning, Hank could see the hair on its neck and back was raised, and its ears were sloped backward.

How close was it—fifty feet? A hundred? What did it matter? Hank didn't know much about bears, but he knew they were fast.

The animal roared again and dropped onto all fours, his

long front claws furiously raking the mud. Hank saw the big hump between its shoulders. *It was a grizzly.* Its roar was rasping and powerful as if it dragged it up from deep inside its throat to echo and ricocheted off walls of rock. The bear was getting ready to charge. Hank saw the saliva oozing around its mouth and drooling down in strings. It thrust his chin into the air.

"Get going," Hank said, tugging Oz's arm.

Oz's teeth were chattering. "Bears can climb trees!"

"But maybe they can't climb cliffs. Come on—now! You go first. I'm right behind you!"

Feeling with their fingers, they found wet footholds and craggy bits of rock to grab. Step by step, they began to climb, creeping up the side. The water poured down the rocks and splattered into their eyes. Up above, on a narrow ledge, Sam and Zebi were perched, Sam shouted a warning: "Don't look down! Don't look down!"

Below them, the bear bellowed. Hank ignored Sam's advice and looked. The beast was at the base of the cliff now, just below Hank's feet. It turned its massive snout from one side to the other, trying to read their scents. Looking up, it roared again, enraged they might be out of reach. The sound seemed to go straight through their backbones. Then the bear started swatting at the rocks and began to climb.

Hank turned his face back toward the rock. "Keep going,

Oz. Concentrate and don't slip, or we'll end up in that bear's mouth." But Oz didn't slip, and he didn't look down. Inch by inch, he crawled up toward the ledge where Sam and Zebi were waiting. Then another sound cut through the howling storm. It was a human voice—two human voices, actually—and one of them sounded familiar. It was the same voice he'd listened to during months of work on the pterodactyl project.

Holding on to the rock, Hank looked down and over to the right. And there she was: through the rain and another flash of lightning, he spotted Ruby's red hair as she and another girl started their climb.

"Ruby!" he yelled. "Up here!"

The bear turned to the sound. It dropped back onto all fours, releasing a long note of fury while shaking its head. The storm was not moving away from them, and the lightning continued to light up the sky.

Hank looked past Oz, up at Zebi and Sam, and then back down at the girls. He thought the four of them were far enough up the cliff to be safe, but the bear could still reach the two girls.

Sam and Zebi reached down, and each grabbed one of Oz's arms. In one swift movement, they pulled him onto the ledge. Hank scrambled up behind Oz. The lightning still wasn't slowing down as they looked down at Oz's face. It was the color of chalk, and his left eye was swollen shut. Blood covered the side of his jacket. "He smells my blood. He's after me."

Hank leaned over the edge and found the girls again.

Ruby was only a few feet up the cliff, several feet over from where they had climbed, and the bear was heading straight toward her.

Hank wanted to close his eyes but didn't. Was he about to watch Ruby getting mauled to death? And where was the other girl? Maybe the bear wouldn't attack both of them.

Something caught his eye as a white blur streaked across his line of vision. *Raif.*

His wolf let out a terrible growl and leaped at the bear's face, bitting, and hanging on to its snout. The bear roared and swung its head, but Raif hung on, his teeth digging in as the bear tried again to shake him off. Its enormous claws ripped and bashed at Raif, but still the wolf didn't let go. With a tremendous roar, the bear swung its head even more violently. Raif flew through the air and landed on his back, sprawled out. He didn't move.

The bear looked at Ruby and then back at Raif. But before the animal moved in either direction, Raif jumped to his feet to face the standing bear, head down, jaws open wide, and teeth bared past his gums. The bear dropped to all fours and charged.

The attack was so fast and furious that for a few seconds,

it was hard to separate the bear from the wolf. Brown and white fur, mingled with blood, flew in every direction.

Raif's jaws clamped onto the bear's snout, and his white face had turned red with their blood. The two animals screamed and roared into each other's mouths before the bear once again batted Raif lose. This time when the wolf landed, he didn't get up.

Hank looked away, focusing instead on the horrified faces of Ruby and her friend as they continued to climb. Moments later, Ruby reached out her hand to him. The other girl was still far beneath them. A fierce growl echoed off the rock walls as the bear looked up and banged his paws onto the stone steps.

Hank grabbed Ruby's hand and pulled her onto the ledge beside Oz. The bear threw its head back again and roared at the other girl. She stopped, paralyzed by fear as it swatted at her. Its claws missed her trembling feet by inches and smashed against the rock, sending small fragments skittering down the cliff into its eyes.

"Juliana, one step at a time!" Ruby yelled from the ledge.

The bear started to climb, and Juliana began to scream. But the terrified girl just pressed herself against the side of the cliff; no amount of coaxing could get her to move. Hank closed his eyes.

WHOO-OOO WHOO-OOO . . .

Hank's eyes snapped open as his head spun in the direction of the sound. *Solvor!*

The owl swooped down, his vast wings skimming the side of the cliff as he flew straight toward the bear's head. It was like watching a torpedo hit its mark. Solvor drilled his beak straight into the bear's left eye. The bear roared as the pain sent it reeling away from the cliff.

"Juliana, you can do it. One more step." Ruby reached down. Ruby and Hank reached out pulled her up onto the ledge.

Twenty feet below, the bear ran in confused circles, bellowing in pain. Nearby, Raif lay on the ground bloodied and lifeless.

The small group pressed their backs to the rock and watched the bear. Hank pointed to the sleeping Oz.

"He needs his eyebrow stitched," Ruby said, leaning over and peering into Oz's gash.

"I've got a sewing kit!"

As Hank rummaged in his backpack, Zebi looked up. "Before you do that, we need to climb up to that bigger ledge and get out of this storm," he said, pointing at a wider outcrop about ten feet above them with a shelf above it.

One by one, they climbed to the higher ledge. Hank went last, pushing Oz up before him.

Once they were all safely on the ledge and out of the rain,

Hank handed Ruby his sewing kit. With the help of the continuous sheet lightning, she guided the black thread through the needle and then bent down close to Oz, her mouth next to his ear. "I'm Ruby, and I'm going to stitch you up. Be still, okay! No quick movements. This is just a small needle—not nearly as bad as that bear attack."

Oz closed his eyes and flinched as Ruby dug the needle into his flesh. Hank and the others watched as Ruby gingerly pulled out the thread of her first stitch. She made six well-placed stitches and re-attached Oz's split eyebrow. The bleeding stopped, then seconds later, Oz was asleep.

Ruby looked at her work and nodded. "He'll feel worse when he wakes up."

They huddled on the ledge. Everyone but Oz watched the unmoving Raif. Solvor perched on a nearby tree, his keen eyes following the injured grizzly's path through the trees.

If Raif is dead, why is Solvor still guarding him? Hank wondered. Then he thought he saw Raif's chest move. *Is he breathing?*

"Is that your wolf?" Zebi asked quietly.

"Yeah," Sam blurted out before Hank could answer.

How long has he known?

"I think he's still alive," Zebi said. "I saw his head move."

"I want to go and get him," Hank stood up. "He saved us, and I'm not leaving him there."

Juliana peered into the darkness below. The rain had slowed to a fine mist. "We'll have to be quiet. Grizzlies have incredible hearing."

"Sam and I are coming with you," Zebi glared at Ruby. "Ruby, stay with Oz; he can't be moved, and watch that he doesn't pull out his stitches or roll off the ledge. Juliana, you're our lookout. Listen and watch. If you see or hear that bear, start yelling. We'll be as fast as we can. Sam, bring your pack—we're going to make a sling from your rope."

Sam pulled a rope from his knapsack, slipping the end into knots and winding it into lengths about five feet long. His hands worked fast, and in a few moments, he'd made a sling.

It took them barely a minute to descend the cliff, and once at the bottom, they looked back up at Juliana. She gave a thumbs-up.

They rolled Raif over and wrapped the sling around him. Sam wove more rope in and out of the sling until he knotted Raif in a rope cocoon.

"I think he weighs about 150 pounds," Hank lifted his end.

"We can carry him" Zebi nodded.

After Juliana gave them another thumbs-up—the boys picked up the wolf. Hank scanned the treetops until he found his owl. *Watch that bear, Solvor.*

At the base of the cliff, Sam and Zebi took the top of the sling, with Hank grabbing the bottom. Raif's legs and bloody snout stuck out through the gaps. The rain had almost stopped, and the moon and the stars lit up the sky. Zebi was the strongest of them, and he heaved and grunted as he started to climb. Slowly and carefully, inch by inch, they carried Raif up the cliff.

As they huddled on the ledge, the storm started again an hour later. Oz woke up every few minutes and then slipped back to sleep while Raif opened his eyes but didn't move. Hank ran his hands along the wolf's legs and found one paw was badly cut. Blood oozed down over his snout, and as Hank pried open his jaw, he saw he'd lost two teeth.

"Best to let him sleep," Zebi muttered.

They waited.

Ruby was the first to break the silence. "We can't stay here forever. Maybe there's some shelter up here." She inched her way across the ledge, away from the group.

"Wait—I'm coming with you." Zebi crawled after her.

Hank, Sam, and Juliana watched them crawl farther and farther away until the ledge veered left, back toward the mountain, and they were out of sight.

"Where are they going?" Juliana sounded frightened.

"Don't yell," said Oz, his voice gravelly with sleep. "It could spook them—or attract the bear!"

They waited in silence until they heard Ruby's voice—a loud whisper coming from around the bend. "Over here! Follow the ledge."

"We've found it!" Zebi sounded excited. "The cave—it's here!"

Sam, Juliana, and Oz started to crawl. Raif struggled to a sitting position and then onto all fours, limping as he put weight on his wounded paw. Hank was last in line.

The rock on the ledge became wider and smoother as they crawled along.

"Don't look down. Don't look down." Hank could hear Sam repeating the words as his hands moved forward.

The ledge ended at an uneven staircase. At the top, Ruby and Zebi stood, grinning. Behind them was a small opening in the rock—*the secret cave.*

11
THE SECRET CAVE

The cave's entrance was no bigger than a bushel basket and hidden by an outcropping of rock.

"I'm going in," Zebi shimmied head-first through the hole. Ruby thrust her head in after him. "What do you see?"

"It's big," Zebi's voice sounded hollow and far away. "Big and dark and there are bats, but they're sleeping."

"Upside down?" Juliana asked nervously.

"Yeah, they're sleeping upside down." They could hear Zebi chuckling. He whistled from deeper in the cave. A perfect whistle, pure and clean, a kind of *holy-cow-look-at-that!* whistle.

One by one, they squeezed through the hole. Hank went last, pushing Raif from behind as Sam and Juliana pulled from the other side.

The storm was starting to push east, away from the mountains, and the full moon was at the perfect angle, shining

light into the cave. Hank looked around. The roof of the cave seemed to be about twenty feet above, and the "room," if you could call it that, was about the size of Mrs. Plunkett's secret dinosaur room.

Farther back, with the help of the moon, Hank saw stalagmites coming up from the floor, meeting the stalactites descending from the ceiling. They stretched across the entire wall, almost touching, like a prehistoric jaw full of colossal teeth. Beyond that, the walls of the cave continued back into darkness.

They were quiet— out of the storm and safe. Zebi was close to the cave opening, listening for anything from below. Oz had curled up on the floor and was half asleep, ignoring Ruby as she leaned over him, inspecting her stitches. Sam sat against the wall, cleaning his glasses. He looked at Hank, wide-eyed, and then farther up the wall to the bats. Julianna was asleep beside the opening to the cave as if she might have to make a quick escape.

Kneeling next to Raif, Hank felt around the wolf's body. He found no broken bones, and the bleeding from the cuts on his face was slowing down. Raif's amber eyes found Hank, and he made a soft, low growl. Hank motioned to Ruby, who crawled over to have a look.

"What do you think? A few stitches to close this?" he pointed to a large gash over Raif's left eye. Ruby nodded and held up her needle to the light to thread it. Raif didn't flinch as Ruby dug her needle into his bloody flesh. His right eye stayed open, watching her closely. After she finished, Raif limped around sniffing at bits of rock, then sat down and began to clean the blood off his fur.

Outside, the rain and the wind picked up, but the cave was mysteriously quiet, safely holding them in its walls halfway up the side of the mountain. There, on the steep, smooth rock wall, were a series of drawings. Hank's eyes widened as he lit a candle and held it up to the wall.

"Whoever drew these was very good," he said softly.

Moments later, Sam was at his side, staring at the mural. "What kind of animals are these?" he said, taking the candle from Hank. "You should sketch these!"

Hank nodded. Pulling his sketchbook and pencil out of his pocket, he began to draw. There were teeth in mammoth jaws dripping with what looked like blood. There were claws with pieces of flesh stuck to them and tails raised as if in battle. At the top of the wall, as if looking down on the rest of the drawings, was a pterodactyl. Directly over the pterodactyl, someone had painted the word *FANDIAN*.

"Hold the light up," he murmured, his hand searching for the outline, shading, and skeletal structure. He felt as he could lift pieces of these beasts off the walls and set them onto his page. He wondered if he was the first to capture the secrets of this mural.

Sam pointed to another section of the wall. "Over here. Look at this one. It's just a tail and it goes from here," he said, walking almost twenty feet, "to here."

Hank's pencil raced across the page as his drawings came to life.

As Hank sketched, Zebi peered out of the cave again. "It's still pouring out there," he said. "And I don't see Frank anywhere."

"It's getting late," Hank said, "and it's too dangerous to leave. We're going to sleep here. Ruby and Juliana, you can use my sleeping bag, and I'll sleep in my jacket. Who else has a sleeping bag?"

"We lost them all coming up the cliff," Sam said. "But it doesn't matter—at least we're safe for now."

As his exhausted friends lay quietly on the stone floor, Hank held up his candle and continued to draw. His hands blackened as he worked long into the night, sketching each detail of the cave drawings. Raif lay at his feet, occasionally opening one eye. Everyone else slept.

When the images became blurred, and he felt as though the sand was grinding into his eyeballs, he closed his sketchbook, crawled close to his wolf, and was soon asleep. Very early in the morning, Hank could hear Raif moving around. He listened as the wolf, no longer limping, sniffed, and scratched as he explored, going deeper into the cave. He returned several times, lightly touching Hank's cheek with the tip of his cold nose, and then he was off again.

Hank stood up, stretched, and followed Raif through the teeth of the giant jaw. The storm had cleared away the clouds, and the bright morning light pushed into the cave. The deeper they went, the narrower it got until they were in what looked like a tunnel. Raif's white coat shone, and Hank stayed close. When Raif stopped, Hank stopped too. He waited and then heard Raif's tongue lapping water, then hunched down and reached out his fingers: cool water. Cupping his hands, he took a drink after drink.

"Come, Raif," he whispered. "Let's see what else we can find."

After a few minutes, the tunnel widened. It was pitch dark here, but Hank noticed the air felt cleaner, less stuffy. Raif stopped again. Hank heard him sniff and then pick up something in his mouth. He brought it to Hank and pressed it into his hands. Hank felt the rough surface as he traced its contours with his fingers: it was a bone, about three feet in length. *A bear?* he wondered. *Did the animal die here, or was it carried into the cave?*

Carefully, they ambled through the small room to what

seemed to be another tunnel. The floor tilted upward, and the air was even fresher.

"Okay, Raif," Hank whispered. "Let's go back and get the others."

"Why are we going *this* way?" Sam looked suspiciously at the opening of the "jaw" and then hastily threaded his way through the stalactites and stalagmites. "Maybe we should go back. Maybe the storm's over. Maybe the bear's gone."

Hank smiled. Even without looking at his friend's face, he could hear Sam was nervous. "We're going to follow this tunnel and see where it goes," he said, following Raif.

"But I'm hungry," Sam muttered.

"Remember how hungry that bear was?" Juliana's frightened voice floated through the darkness.

Sam said nothing more.

"I only have a few more candles," Hank said. "Let's just feel our way in the dark. Okay?"

They crept along the tunnel, their fingers barely grazing the rough stone walls and their eyes staring into the pitch blackness, searching for any hint of light. Their ears were open and twitching for any sound.

Sam gasped. "I smell something. Yes. *Delicioso!*"

They all stopped, including Raif.

"You're just hungry and imagining things." Juliana's small voice piped up. "All I smell is stone and dust and . . ."

BOOM!

In an instant, the floor collapsed beneath them. They were falling, and their legs and arms flailed outward as they tried to grab hold of anything solid. Hands reached through the air, searching for other hands as they tumbled down. And then, just as suddenly as it had started, it was over. They landed in a heap, not on stone but soft earth.

Hank put out his hand to find Raif. "Everyone here?" he asked, looking around what appeared to be another cave. But this one wasn't dark—somehow, there was daylight here.

The others moaned and gulped to catch their breath.

"Ozzie, is your eye okay?" Ruby whispered.

"I think so . . ."

"What *was* that?" Ruby's voice was shaky.

"Where are we?" Oz barely managed to spit out the words before giving in to a coughing fit. They must be the stones that were on the floor of the cave above.

Before anyone could answer, something moved on the other side of the cave. A man, very tall and very old, stood watching them.

Hank's hand remained on Raif's head. Curiously, the wolf did not growl; he just showed his teeth as his eyes remained fixed on the bearded figure.

Then the man spoke.

12
MASCAN ARRIVES

"**W**ell now . . . you're here at last."

The man, well over six feet, stood very still, his piercing eyes taking in each one of them. Traces of rock dust still filtered through the air, but they barely noticed. They gathered into a tight group, shoulders pressed together, and waited.

Hank studied the old man. His heavily bearded, wrinkled face almost hid his mouth. His nose was long and hooked and drooped at the tip. His right eye was a bright blue, and the left forest green, with flecks of amber in a ring around the middle. They seemed not to blink and held each of their gaze. His eyebrows looked like thick white needles, poking out in every direction. The beard itself was long, white, thick and curly, and Hank noticed that his left ear poked through his hair, and he wore a small earring with a bright red stone.

The old man's gaze moved from one to another. His eyes widened as they settled on Hank.

Hank stared back at the extraordinary figure whose right hand was over his heart while the left gripped a tall, wooden staff.

"I expect you're all hungry. I've made some soup," the old man's voice quavered.

Ruby nudged Sam. He'd been right; he *had* smelled something.

"Who are you? And what do you want with us?" Hank tried not to let his voice shake.

"I will ask you three questions. Then you can decide what to do."

No one moved. Raif growled a low, soft warning.

"It's Raif, isn't it? That's what you've called him?"

Hank blinked but said nothing.

"Question one: Do you believe you just stumbled upon this cave, where no one has been for centuries?"

He held up his hand as Ruby opened her mouth to speak.

"Question two: You've just fallen through a stone floor in a secret tunnel and landed safely, without a scratch. Do you think it might be possible that something extraordinary is happening? And if so, do you want to miss it?"

"Question three: Are you hungry? As I said, I've made some delicious hot soup."

Juliana cleared her throat. When she spoke, it was in a voice none of them had heard before—loud and strong and angry. "That was *four* questions, not three, and before we answer them, we have questions of our own." She tapped her fingers as she counted them off.

"Question one: Who and what are you?

"Question two: Can we leave, and when?

"Question three: What's in the soup?"

The man shrugged and reached out his hand, palm up as he moved around the cave. "I am very old. Some call me a seer. I live here, in this cave and a few other caves nearby. My name is Mascan."

Hank noticed how the old man's hand brushed against the walls of the cave as he walked. He also noticed that when Mascan spoke to him, he didn't look directly into his eyes. *I think the old man is either blind or almost blind. How can he live here in this cave and be blind?*

Mascan gestured further along the cave. "There is a second cave that joins this one. That is where I cook and where I like to study." He smiled slightly through his beard as his eyes creased into slits. "These two caves are close to the Cave of Teeth, where you found shelter from the storm. But over the centuries, people have dug secret tunnels throughout this mountain. Some of the tunnels are still standing. I have one last underground tunnel that takes me to the Cave of a Thousand Bats. If I am in danger, I can escape to my bats."

He tugged on his beard and smiled. "As I said, I am a seer. I see the past and possibly the future. You can leave whenever you want. Now, if you like."

They exchanged glances, and then six pairs of eyes returned to Mascan.

"Go on," Juliana stared back.

"I can bring you something few humans will ever witness. Beyond this cave is another world—a world not on any map. You know this, don't you, Hank? It isn't supernatural. It's real and filled with adventure and danger."

Hank cringed as he felt five pairs of eyes staring at him.

"And Zebi—you knew about a secret cave, but how? Your tribal elders murmur about strange beasts and odd powers, don't they?"

Zebi's black eyes held the man's gaze. He nodded slowly.

"Juliana, in 1881, your great-grandfather arrived from China to help build the Canadian Pacific Railway. There was hardship and discrimination. He had to pay a tax to immigrate to Canada and was paid just a dollar a day for his dangerous work. The non-Chinese workers were paid double. Ah Hoo Wong told many stories about that time, but he also spoke of ancient beasts just over the mountaintops from another valley. Ah Hoo returned to the valley, but no one ever believed his stories."

Juliana remained still. Her shining eyes fixated.

Mascan's eyes went to Oz. "We need to look at that eye of yours." He reached into his robe and pulled out something that looked like a carved stone egg. "I have some ointment" he handed the egg to Ruby. "Just apply a little. It will heal." He half-smiled and continued, "I watched you climb that sheer cliff. You never lost your head, even though you could see with only one eye."

"And Sam . . . your father is a great engineer. Maybe one day you'll be as well. The pterodactyl you made for the science fair was well designed and very sturdy. And you have a good nose for food."

The man's eyes moved to Ruby. "Your stitches are excellent. You have a good eye and a steady hand. You acted quickly and with a clear head."

He looked once again at Hank. "Raif and Solvor have protected you, Hank. Mrs. Plunkett is pleased."

The only sound in the cave was Raif's low steady growl.

"And now, we move to the next cave?"

"Just a minute," Juliana snapped. "The third question: What's in the soup?"

The old man smiled. "Ah yes, the soup. It has mountain greens, root vegetables, and meat. I made it last night."

As they followed Mascan into another tunnel lit with fat candles, Hank could hear his stomach growling.

They followed Mascan to the next cave. It was circular, about twenty-five feet across, with walls that reached about 40 feet to a blackened hole in the roof. Along the left side of the cave were several small openings, about the size of a man's fist. Hank peered into one of them and could see the light. The fresh air felt good. *Were these strange tunnels a ventilation system?*

As his eyes adjusted to the dim light, Hank noticed something else about this cave.

The word *FANDIAN* was painted on the wall—just as it was over Mrs. Plunkett's bed and just as it was in the Cave of Teeth.

The cave's walls had a massive, brilliantly colored mural. The walls were in six parts, each the same size and joining at the dome. They all had drawings of rivers that joined at the ceiling.

Hank pulled out his sketchbook and gazed at each section. The first river started in a turquoise lake. Its waves carried it to the side of a mountain, where it disappeared under the rock. On the shore of the lake were small, glittering rocks decorated with symbols. He saw no animals or fish in the lake, only shining water. This part of the mural had been drawn in charcoal and looked to be the oldest of the six sections.

Parts were missing or so severely smudged they were nearly invisible.

The second river had vivid blue waves that were bigger and drawn in greater detail. The pale, stippled riverbed reminded Hank of sand. Trees grew on either side, and the artist drew the back of a large animal watching the river from its perch on the nearby bank. It had rough-looking skin, like an elephant, Hank thought.

The third river thrust straight out of the side of a mountain into a narrow waterfall that measured five or six feet across. The painter had dotted the waterfall's glittering stones so they appeared to leap out at the viewer as the water tumbled to the ground. On one side of the waterfall, two men walked along a stony pathway; one was tall, the other short, and both carried heavy burlap sacks over their shoulders. The short man wore no hat. The tall man's face was a mystery, hidden in the shadow created by a wide-brimmed, floppy hat. He looked angry and appeared to be shouting and shaking his fist at the other man.

Hank peered more closely at the small, angry man and sucked in his breath. There, above his right eye, were three small birthmarks. Hank's eyes traced the picture down to the bottom, which ended near the cave's floor. He got down on his hands and knees and stared at the image. The painter had continued to draw, showing where the men walked on a stone pathway leading to a tunnel. Hank squinted. Were those children in the tunnel? Hundreds of them bending over and picking up rocks in the long, dark space? Other than the glittering stones in the waterfall, someone drew this river in black charcoal.

The others followed Hank and Raif slowly through the cave, stopping and starting as Hank sketched.

The fourth river looked to be the smallest. Someone had painted from a bird's-eye view in muted colors that were faded and flaking off. It bubbled up from the ground in front of a sheer cliff of rock at the base of three mountain peaks. The water's surface was blurred, and the riverbed was invisible. Hank looked up.

"Zebi, can you lift me?"

A moment later he was perched five feet higher on Zebi's strong shoulders. He placed both hands on either side of the river image and looked closely, the tip of his nose inches from the wall. There was a small detail in faded gray, but it was there, in front of him, just like on the mural in the secret cave, and exactly like the one in Mrs. Plunkett's basement. *The fifth finger of a pterodactyl,* he whispered to himself.

The fifth river was tiny—more like a creek that spurted out of a deep-blue rock halfway up the side of a cliff where the tree line ended. There were polar bears and Arctic foxes on the river's banks, but it was the color of the water that caught Hank's eye: vivid green and purple, almost electric. *The Northern Lights?*

The sixth river was entirely underground. There were no clues other than the water flowed through what looked like an abandoned mineshaft. The wooden planks used for the mine's supports were faded and split, with rusty spikes sticking out. An old torch hung from a single nail and a mining cart was shoved against the side of a wall. There was a painted sign that said *The Devil's*

The remainder of the last word was lost beneath the water.

The old man cleared his throat, interrupting Hank's sketching. From the folds of his robe, he removed a large brass ladle and six spoons. He brought out a stack of bowls.

"And now, my six visitors, it's time to eat."

13

WHEN IS YOUR BIRTHDAY?

It didn't take long to devour the soup. Hank couldn't remember ever being so hungry—not even when Mrs. Plunkett had been away.

Mascan turned his hands upward. "You must have many questions?"

Juliana went first. "Who are you?"

"I've already told you." He gave a slight smile. "I am a seer. I came from another country long ago."

"Are there extraordinary beasts beyond this cave?" Sam peered unblinkingly through his glasses.

"Yes, Sam *extraordinary* beasts. You'll know what they are, though." He held up his hands as Zebi opened his mouth to speak. "You can ask me more questions soon enough. But now I think I will tell you *your* story. Did you know you are all born on the same day—June 21, 1946?"

Hank looked at Sam, who returned his gaze and then at the others. He and Sam had always known they shared the same birthday. But all of them? He looked back at Mascan. "What is much *more* interesting, is that your first heartbeat also happened at the very same instant—before you were even born. Six brand-new hearts beat for the first time at the same millisecond on October 24, 1945, at exactly midnight."

"How do you know this?" Juliana whispered. "How *can* you know this?"

"It's part of your story. How I came to know it isn't important. Not everything in life can be explained."

"How old are you?" Sam asked.

"I am four hundred and three, to be exact."

"Would that bear have killed us?" Oz asked, his face still pale and his injured eye still swollen shut.

"Hold on," Hank spoke up before Mascan could answer and before the others could ask more questions. "This is crazy! Supernatural beasts! Hearts that started beating at the same instant! A magical world! This man is telling us a fairy-tale. For some reason, he wants us to go into this valley. How can we go into a valley with strange, wild beasts by ourselves?"

Mascan looked at him calmly. "You are right, Hank. I do want you to go into the valley, but you cannot go as you are. Still, you are not as powerless as you think. You *can* go—if I show you the powers you have."

The cave was silent. Even Raif was still.

"You all have them," Mascan continued slowly. "Remarkable powers. Beyond your wildest imagination. Shall I continue?"

Six heads nodded in unison.

"When your hearts were forming—when *you* were forming—something happened that even I cannot explain. The six of you are joined in an extraordinary way. No matter what happens in your lives, you will always share this connection."

He stood with outspread arms and looked at the six rivers.

"I want you to follow the path of each river and see where they end?"

Six necks craned to look at the domed ceiling.

"It looks like nothing, but it isn't nothing. It is the secret of this valley. It is why we are all here."

"Our powers?" Hank asked, his hand moving quickly as he sketched Mascan's face.

The old man pointed toward the dome of the cave and the six swirling rivers that became one. "Each river is different and carries its secrets. When they meet—at the northern tip of this valley, where it reaches the Arctic Ocean—they converge and become one river. And it is this river that keeps this valley's creatures alive."

Mascan held up his right index finger. "However, the

convergence of the six rivers only happens on the twelfth crescent moon every year. For just one day. It is this extraordinary day when every living thing in this valley must drink from this convergence to have a chance to live for one more year."

He stroked his beard and folded his long, crooked, fingers.

"Each river brings something extraordinary to the convergence. If even one river does not reach the convergence on the day of the twelfth crescent moon, then everything in the valley will die."

Mascan pointed to the mural. "The first river is Calx. See those glittering, silvery-white rocks? That's the calcium, sodium, and magnesium in the water. These are important minerals for humans and animals."

Hank stopped sketching Mascan and flipped back to his sketch of the river mural. He jotted down the chemical symbols for calcium, sodium, and magnesium next to Calx.

"Ingemar is our second river. It's a piece of the ocean and reaches into the valley like a giant finger. It drags sparkling sand and ocean mammals into the valley with it.

"I have never seen Adamas, the third river. There are ancient stories of robbers and prisoners and diamonds. To our knowledge, no one who has gone looking for Adamas has ever returned."

"The fourth river, Ladon, is on the other side of the great valley. It is the home of the flying beasts that protect the valley from the evils of Adamas.

"The fifth river, Alme Tulah, means 'sky fires'. It is the farthest north and very important. We cannot keep the secret of the valley without its purple and green colors.

"The last river is unknown. Most of it is underground. Its ancient name is Colli Auf, meaning 'lost gold.' No one knows where Colli Auf surfaces because it's different every year. But occasionally, we see small glittering pieces of gold emerge from the ground after the snow melts."

He stopped and closed his eyes. "These powers, your powers, are extraordinary." His eyes blinked open. "How many senses do we have?"

"Five."

"Almost, Juliana. We have six: sight, hearing, taste, smell, touch, and the last one ... intuition."

"Six rivers, six senses, and there are six of us."

Mascan looked over their heads and zeroed in on Ruby. "Precisely."

"If you decide to go forward into the secret valley, each of you will have one of these senses, which will become a kind of power for you. And with these powers, you will be able to work together to defend yourselves."

"Why do we need to defend ourselves?" Oz asked, squinting up into Mascan's face.

"Because outside this cave, there are very dangerous beasts beyond anything you could imagine. But if you think and work together"—Mascan looked directly at each one of them, his voice becoming a whisper, "you will be *almost* invincible."

Mascan's words swirled in the air around them. Hank put down his pencil and closed his book. Oz opened his injured eye and stared intently at the old man. Sam studied the back of the beast in the second river. Juliana gazed up at the dome and traced the routes of the rivers. Zebi pressed his ear against the small tunnels. Ruby crouched down in front of the third river and looked at the small faces of the children.

"Why?" Juliana whispered from behind Sam. "Why would you give us these great powers and send us into a valley we don't know? What do you want us to do?"

Although Juliana had asked the question, Mascan looked directly at Hank as he answered. "This extraordinary valley is in danger. There are secrets here—some good, some bad. I need your help to put an end to one of the sinister secrets. But before you can help me, help this valley, you must pass a test."

"I have two questions," Hank said slowly. "How do these powers work? And what does the word FANDIAN mean?"

"Are you ready to move forward, Hank? Will you and

your friends leave this cave and see what is beyond it? I will show you your extraordinary powers." The old man held up a gnarled finger and pointed it at the word FANDIAN. "It's an old word, but a simple word. It means *test*. If you accept this mission, this challenge, you will have to prove that you will take the powers I give you and use them wisely. You must think quickly and *always* work together. You are a formidable team, but alone, you will be almost helpless."

Mascan waited as if he expected another question. When none came, he continued. "I believe there is something hideous going on across this valley. I hear snippets of information from the Queen of All Birds; you will meet her very soon. With your powers, you will see and hear the evil man responsible for what is going on. I believe he has a diamond mine possibly filled will children. I believe this mine is diverting one of the six rivers, and unless the rivers can flow into each other, this valley, and all the creatures in it, will die."

He gave them all a feeble smile. "Will you try?"

Hank looked at Mascan and then at the walls of the cave. He didn't know what to believe. Was this secret valley filled with extraordinary creatures? It did sound dangerous, and Hank had enough danger in the last few weeks. And the evil man Mascan had mentioned made his heart pump faster. But what if what Mascan said was true? What if they were the only ones who could save this secret valley? Could they say no? Could they pass Mascan's test, his Fandian?

He looked at each one of his friends and tried to figure out what they were thinking. Like him, they looked nervous, but he noticed Zebi nodding slightly and Ruby raising her right eyebrow the way she did when she found something interesting. Finally, Hank spoke. "We can try, but we're going to need those powers."

Mascan nodded and then motioned for them to follow him.

The next cave was brightly painted, with four phrases scrawled along the walls in an ornamental script:

The purple will touch the crescent moon before the six entwine.

The sky will rain with blood-tipped claws when danger follows close.

Beware of knowledge not completed before you drink from the valley's nectar.

Thundering rocks will charge from the ground and not from the air above.

There were also names written in turquoise ink along the tunnel's roofline: Geoffrey Blackwood; Mortimer Muir; Alice Longbow; Pip Wong; John Van Duzer; Max Granger, Jeremiah Levi. The list ribboned along the roof toward a shaft of light. At the end of the list, somebody wrote the word *FANDIAN* once more.

Mascan pushed on part of the stone wall, and it swung open to an outside ledge.

He took Hank's arm and held him back from the others. He smiled faintly, leaning against his wooden staff. "And lastly and most importantly, you may only stay in this valley while there are six bright stars in Orion's Belt. If one of the stars disappears or begins to fade, you must get out that night." He turned and grasped Hank's hands in his. "Do you understand?"

Hank nodded slowly. "How do we get out?"

"When the time comes, I will guide you."

Mascan and Hank followed the others outside.

Mascan stopped and held up his hand to the six of them. "Here, on the ledge, you are high up and away from most dangers. Wait and watch and feel. Listen, smell, and taste the air. Absorb all these things, and then you will know which power will be yours."

Hank looked down as he felt Raif's cold nose barely tap his fingertips. He wondered what place his wolf would have in this Fandian and if he'd be safe.

The stone ledge was about thirty feet long and fifteen feet wide. Above the ledge was a canopy of roped vines woven into a tight ceiling. The sun was bright, and there was no wind. They looked out over a beautiful valley, green and still.

Hank squinted into the light as he looked westward,

across the valley, to the ridge of mountains. Even with the heat of the summer, three of the peaks were snow-capped.

Mascan turned away from the valley and looked at everyone. "Does anyone see anything living in those mountains?"

Oz's voice was calm. "There's a moose down near the base and what looks like mountain goats farther up. And I see something over on the second mountain. It could be a grizzly bear. Not much else. There aren't any roads or trails or any sign of people; just rock and sheer cliffs."

Hank looked over the floor of the valley. It was a low, rolling plain of thick, long grass, with some scattered scrub pine trees nestled closer to the bottom of the mountains. A small, meandering stream seemed to cut the valley in two.

Oz whistled softly. "Can you see up the valley to the north, that mountain with the three tops? It goes for miles."

"How far?" Ruby asked, peering into the distance. "I can only see the three mountains."

"I can see farther. Much farther. Is that the second river? It's blue, with waves as big as ocean swells. And something is walking along the banks, and it's big and white. It's a polar bear. And there's blood on its face. Must be twenty miles away."

Mascan's eyes were closed, but he nodded. "You have chosen your power, Oz. *Sight!*"

"Listen!" Zebi leaned forward, cocking his head to one

side. "Do you hear that? There are birds in those trees on the other side of the valley. And something is moving *inside* the trees. Grubbs. I can hear them!"

Mascan nodded again. "And what else, Zebi?"

"Something far away. It sounds like thunder, but it doesn't look like we're having a storm.

It sounds like walking—large animals walking in this direction."

"I am happy you've chosen *to hear!*"

"I chose it?" Zebi looked questioningly at Mascan.

"It's something that comes instinctively to you. Something you will be good at."

Juliana spoke next. "I taste fire in the air. Smoke, but not from a campfire. And salt from your river, Oz. Calx, the first river, I think."

"Yes, Juliana. You will do well with *taste.*"

"What is *that*?" Sam asked. He was sniffing at the air and wrinkled his face in disgust. "Rotten meat? It stinks. I smell mud and poop. It reeks! Oz, do you see any poop around here?"

"Maybe . . . down the valley by the three mountains. What a pile! What kind of animal makes that much poop?"

Hank smiled as Mascan nodded again. *Of course, Sam would choose smell!*

Ruby fingered the roof over her head. "This is made of

feathers, not vines. They feel tough as nails. The spines are like ostrich feathers, but bigger."

"How clever of you to choose touch, Ruby. It will serve you well in the most unexpected circumstances." Mascan smiled through his beard.

Then Hank spoke quietly. "I feel as if something is going to happen. It's almost here. I can sense it like a mist sitting in the air. I can feel and smell and hear it."

Mascan opened his eyes and raised his arms. "And so, you have each chosen your gifts, your extraordinary powers. I am pleased with your choices. Sam, you have a remarkable sense of smell. You, Zebi, have the gift of acute hearing. Oz, spectacular sight is your power. Juliana, you can taste all that surrounds you. And your powerful sense of touch, Ruby, will serve you well."

He looked at Hank.

"You've always had intuition, Hank. Just wait and see how well it will serve you. Use these powers wisely and remember . . . *stay together.*

Mascan reached into the folds of his garment, and his right hand emerged, closed into a fist. "A small tool for unexpected mishaps," he said, opening his hand. In it lay a beautiful egg, perhaps the size of a chicken's egg. It glowed from within. They all leaned in for a closer look.

"It's carved amber. About a thousand years ago, someone

found it on the banks of Ingemar, the second river." He unscrewed the top, releasing a powerful smell into the air. "Calendula and rose, melaleuca and frankincense. It will help heal any type of injury to the skin." Screwing the top of the egg back on, he handed it to Ruby. "Keep it safe." She slid it into her pocket.

"Guard. It is a mighty tool in this valley of secrets. There will be dangers so remember your powers. They will serve you well. I will use my weakened, ancient powers to watch over you."

"How can you watch us? You're blind." Hank felt ashamed as soon as the words were out of his mouth. He turned to Mascan, ready to apologize, but he was gone, and so was the entrance to the cave.

"Oz, where's Mascan?" Juliana blinked.

He shook his head as he stared at the solid rock that had moments before been a doorway. "He's gone. And so has Raif."

They stood on the ledge, staring at the spot where Mascan had been standing.

Ruby ran her hand over the rock, feeling for the entrance to the cave. "I don't understand. How could he just disappear?"

A moment later Ruby gasped. "Do you feel that? It's shaking the ground. Is it an earthquake?"

They all listened. It started as a quiet hum—more a feeling than a shaking—then it changed.

"No. Not an earthquake. But something's coming."

"It's coming this way. From down there." Zebi pointed to the southern part of the valley. "And there's something else. Animal sounds."

Oz squinted in the direction Zebi was pointing. "*There! Look!* That cloud of dust over those trees."

"Ozzie, a dust cloud doesn't sound like that unless there's a storm coming," Ruby held on to the overhanging roof of feathers and then leaned out over the ledge to get a better look.

Hank pulled out his sketchbook. "They'll be on us any minute."

Small bits of stone crumbled away from the ledge and tumbled down the side of the mountain. The hum became a louder, low-pitched rumbling.

Oz moved closer to the edge. "Large animals . . . beasts."

"What kind of beasts?" Sam shouted over the noise.

Hank and Oz inched to the far end of the ledge and peered over.

"It's a . . . it's . . . a" Oz could hardly speak. *Stegosauruses?*

"Two stegosauruses are heading right for us!" Hank yelled.

"Come on," Ruby snapped. "You can't see them, and

Ozzie only has one eye working. Do you want me to believe there are dinosaurs heading our way? DINOSAURS?" Ruby snapped.

"It's my power, Ruby. I can *feel* things."

Sam stamped his feet on the ledge as the roaring grew closer. "Are we safe up here?"

"They're herbivores, Sam. Plant eaters," Ruby shouted. "They won't eat us."

The vibrations changed. Beyond the rumbling of several feet, they heard a slower, more deliberate sound: *thud, thud, thud.*

"They're being chased!" Hank tilted his head and stared. "By a . . . Tyrannosaurus rex? I think there's more than one!"

The roaring pushed into their eardrums as their eyes widened, transfixed, and terrified. Huddling together on the ledge, they were afraid to move. Hank looked back to where the entrance to the cave had been—it was still closed.

"We need to use our powers. What's coming now?"

"I can see them," Oz was gulping his breath. "You're right, Hank. Two T-rexes and maybe two, no three stegosauruses. They're heading straight for the opening in those trees in front of us.

"The stegosaurus leading the pack is huge, but the other two are smaller," he continued. "They're running fast. The T-rexes are about a hundred yards behind them."

"I smell blood and rotting flesh," Sam said, his nose in the air. "One of them is injured."

"Juliana, what do you taste?" Hank looked up from his sketchbook.

"I can taste the blood just like Sam can smell it. Nothing else is moving in the valley. The insects are gone, and no birds are flying. I taste none of their scents."

"Zebi, what else do you hear?"

"Nothing but this roar," he yelled. "I think Sam is right. One of them is injured. Probably a smaller stegosaurus. It's got a higher-pitched squeal."

Finally, the beasts burst into view charging and roaring and fighting. The biggest stegosaurus swung its tail and hit one of the T-rexes across its back. The two smaller stego-sauruses used the bigger one as their shield.

The dinosaurs stopped, breathing heavily. Blood poured from the neck of the smallest stegosaurus as it limped and wailed.

Hank looked away from the battle.

"Something else is here—very close to us. I can feel it." He looked at his hands and put them up to his face. "My fingers are ice cold."

"Closer than them?" Juliana screamed.

"Much closer. It's here." He looked up again, horrified, and pushed them all back from the edge and toward the spot where the door had been.

For a moment a large shadow blocked the light. The feather canopy shook hard as they looked up just in time to see two gigantic claws grab hold of the netting above them. They covered their heads as they backed away from the horrible claws.

Hank knew what it was before he opened his eyes. He had seen the claws just before the creature landed, and now the creature reached around the feather netting. And then there it was *the fifth finger of a pterodactyl.*

They moved quickly and pressed up against the closed door of the cave. The gold-flecked eyes of the pterodactyl stared at them through the netting. It moved its head, almost questioningly, from face to face. Hank stared back and wondered, if *this creature eats me, the last thing I'll ever see will be its gold eyes.*

But then the netting shook, and the enormous bird jumped into the air.

Below them, the battle continued, and they crawled back to the edge to watch. The smallest stegosaurus lay on its back. It was gasping, and blood was pouring out of a wound in its side.

The two T-rexes flanked either side of the larger stegosaurus. They ran one way, then turned and darted ahead for another grab at its flesh. One attack left a T-rex tooth impaled on its opponent's side. The stegosaurus bellowed, then swung its mighty tail, hitting the T-rex on the side of the head close to its eye. It fell hard and screeched, the sound bouncing up and down the valley. Blood spurted from its face. Hank could see flesh hanging from its teeth as its mouth opened and roared. Its head thrust upward, and Hank was sure the beast had looked straight at him.

The second T-rex hesitated. Its head swung back and forth like a searchlight, moving from the larger to the smaller stegosaurus. The injured beast still gasped for breath.

Never taking his eyes off the battle below, Hank pulled out his sketchbook and began to draw.

Oz looked up at the sky.

"It's gone."

"I *know* it's gone," Hank still watched the battle.

The injured Stegosaurus didn't move.

"It's not breathing," Oz said. "I think it's dead."

"I can't hear anything coming from it. Not even its heart-beat," Zebi's voice was calm.

The uninjured T-rex stood over its conquest, nudging it with its snout.

"It's over. They're finished." Hank gasped.

The two remaining stegosauruses moved away, sniffed, and called to their dead companion, a pathetic pleading that brought no answer. The larger of the two gave a howling cry before they turned and ran up the valley to the north.

The injured T-rex stayed on the ground, but the other

advanced toward the fallen stegosaurus. Before long, it had devoured most of its stomach. The air carried the sounds of tearing flesh and crushing bones. The smell of the creature's guts and bowels and blood wafted up to the ledge.

No one spoke. The only sound on the ledge was Hank's pencil scratching across his sketchbook. Below them the cries of the wounded T-rex filled the air as it struggled to stand. It couldn't, and Hank wondered if it would die.

"Zebi, do you hear anything from that T-rex?" Hank asked, rubbing his cold hands together.

"Yup. He's still breathing. I can hear his heart beating."

Ruby crawled over to Hank and Zebi and hissed. "We're trapped. We can't go back into the cave, and there's an injured T-rex right below us. What are we going to do?"

"First, we're going to catch our breath, and then we're going to use our powers and figure out a plan," Hank said quietly.

14
INTO THE SECRET VALLEY

Hank couldn't sleep. He stared out at the valley and listened to the others breathing. He knew Ruby would awaken first.

Moments later, Ruby opened her eyes. She looked first at Hank and then around at the sleeping faces. The sun had set, and he knew she was cold.

A low moan drifted up from the valley floor.

"The T-rex," she whispered, her green eyes widening.

Hank looked over the ledge. "It's still in the same place."

"We can't stay here forever. The door to the cave is still closed, and we need to find food and water. And I'm cold," Ruby said, wrapping her arms around herself.

Their voices woke the others.

"Oz, can you see any other caves or someplace we could take some shelter?" Ruby peered over the edge and shivered.

Oz rubbed his eyes as he stared across the darkening valley. "Nothing near us. It's almost nighttime, and the blue river is miles away. There *is* a cave on this side of the valley. It's not too far. I think we can get there. I can see it from here."

"I think we should stay on the ledge," Sam said, looking up at the North Star. "We're safe here."

"We need to get to shelter," Hank said.

Oz held up his hand for quiet and looked north again. "Over there," he said. "There's a kind of staircase at the far end of the ledge, and it goes down the cliff. If we take that, we'd be far away from the T-rex. I don't think he can stand. And Hank's right—we can't stay here."

"Remember what Mascan told us," Juliana said. "We need to work together. Let's check out everything nearby before we head off. I taste nothing other than that bleeding T-rex and the stegosaurus carcass."

Sam spoke next. "The only thing I can smell is the blood from the T-rex and some sap from those pine trees across the valley—and a lot of poo from a lot of animals."

"I hear nothing coming this way," Zebi added. "No animals—large or small. There's a fox hunting along the riverbank about twenty-five miles away. Everything else is quiet. That might not be a good sign. Maybe the other T-rex is at this end of the valley."

Ruby stared at Hank. "There's nothing much for me to

touch here other than these feathers. Do you think that ptero-dactyl will be back tonight?"

Hank looked out across the valley, right to the north and left to the south. "Nothing. I don't think the other T-rex is close by, and I'm not sure that pterodactyl is dangerous. She just stared at us through the netting. Did you see her claws? It would have been easy for her to tear through that."

"She looked right at me," Sam said quietly.

"She looked at all of us with those huge gold eyes, Sam. Almost as if she knew us."

"Or wanted to eat us!" Sam said.

"Maybe—maybe not." Hank took a deep breath. "Let's get going while there's still enough light. We didn't ask Mascan if our powers work in the dark, but I think they do."

At the far end of the ledge, Oz peered down over the staircase. "We're about fifty feet up. I count seventy-three stairs carved into the rock. Each step looks like it's wide enough to fit a large foot, but remember the rock is right beside us, so you can put your hand out to keep your balance."

Oz nodded to Juliana. "Remember, slow and steady. I'll go behind you, and—"

"I know. Don't look down."

Hank went first, then Zebi, Ruby, Sam, Juliana, and Oz. Just as Oz had said, there were plenty of places to grab hold. Nobody tripped or lost their footing. They could hear Juliana whispering, "don't look down, don't look down." A few minutes later, Oz took his last step, and they all stood on the valley floor.

The T-rex moaned. They turned back to look at him.

"He's lost a lot of blood," Hank sighed.

Oz squinted at the five-foot-long head resting on the ground. "I think part of his left eyelid is cut open."

"He won't last long here with only one eye."

"Hank don't worry about it. Are we safe? If we are, then let's go." There was both fear and anger in Ruby's tone.

They set off in single file with Zebi leading and Hank bringing up the rear.

Sam whispered to himself as he sniffed in every direction. "Remember our powers. Remember our powers."

"Stop!" Zebi said, spinning around. "Something's flying overhead, far up over the tops of the three mountains. I can hear wings flapping when it turns. It's watching us."

Ruby grunted. "*Of course,* it's watching us. *Everything* in this valley is watching us. Can you see it, Ozzie?"

"It's there, all right. I wasn't checking up there. It's circling and looking straight at us."

"Ozzie, you've got to look in *all directions*. I can't see anything up there. It's too dark now. How's your eye?"

"That ointment Mascan feels good. It takes the pain away. I think the stitches can come out soon."

"Not yet, Ozzie. Look at that pterodactyl!" Ruby pointed upward.

"I think she's watching to protect us," Hank said slowly.

"Don't think so." Juliana hissed. "That bird wants to eat us. *All* of us."

Hank shook his head. "She would have dive-bombed one of us by now. I think she's been up there since we left the ledge."

"How do you know it's a *she?*" Juliana asked.

"I don't know." Hank shrugged. "She looked at me. I just knew."

A second later, he put his hand over his heart. "Do you feel that?"

Sam, Oz, Ruby, Zebi and Juliana put their hands over their hearts, and their eyes widened. Six hearts began to pound in the same rhythm at the same time.

"Our powers!" Sam whispered; his eyes even wider through his thick glasses.

"The other T-rex is up ahead," Hank observed. "Maybe four or five miles. That's not far for a T-rex. He's traveling north, so we should be okay, but let's hurry."

"How much farther is the cave?" Sam asked.

Oz pointed to a tall pine tree about two hundred yards ahead of them. They started to run. "Over here!" He pointed to a stone staircase, like the one they'd just left.

They started to climb. These steps were carved more deeply into the rock.

Juliana whispered, "Slow and steady . . . don't look down."

"She's following us," Hank said, stopping on a step and looking up. "And she's flying much lower than before."

Juliana stopped climbing and pressed herself into the rock. She was in front of Hank, and he could hear her gasping and see her shaking.

"She's not going to hurt us, Juliana." His voice was quiet and calm. "It's not like with the grizzly." He reached up and patted her foot. "Everything is okay."

The pterodactyl circled overhead and was almost on top of the pine tree. Hank found her gold eyes gazing at him as she silently glided in circles not thirty feet away.

They scrambled upward, almost falling onto the ledge. The opening to the cave was about the size of a man. It was narrower than the ledge outside Mascan's cave and had a blackened space in the middle that looked like a long-forgotten campfire. It faced north.

Juliana took one quick look and ran in.

The bird landed on the far side of the ledge, folded her wings, and looked out over the valley. She was bigger by far than the model for their science project, especially her dangerous-looking claws. On the top of her head was a two-foot-long orange and yellow crest divided in the center by a red stripe. The crest jutted out and pointed backward. A gray membrane was draped over her skeleton, like an old piece of a tent and covered with short, black feathers. Her enormous wings had long black feathers that spread out perfectly when she flew.

With his heart beating hard in his chest, Hank moved a little closer to the bird. His eyes were drawn first to her claws and then to her remarkable gold eyes. He knew she had the power to kill him in an instant, but he remained completely calm. The fifth finger was separate from the other four, extending from her claw to become the outer edge of her wing, which ended at her short tail.

The bird turned her head and looked straight at him. Hank's heart was pounding and his whole body shook, but he stood still, waiting, watching, barely breathing.

She looked him over from the top of his head to his feet. Then she peered beyond him at the others. Juliana had crept out of the cave and was standing close to Zebi.

The giant bird banged her feet on the ledge like a soldier on parade. Left-right-left-right-left-right. She stared at Hank. A moment later, he realized she was stamping her feet to the rhythm of his heartbeat.

He looked back to the others.

"Our heartbeats," Zebi gasped.

The others nodded.

Hank met her piercing gaze. He thought back to Mascan's words: *Outside this cave, there are very dangerous beasts beyond anything you could imagine. But if you think and work together, you are almost invincible.* He looked once more at her enormous claws and sword-like beak. *If she'd wanted to kill us,* he left this thought unfinished, and meeting her eyes, whispered, more to himself than anyone else, *"Who are you?"*

The sound she made was a strange mix of exhaled air and blurred words pushed out through her needle-like teeth. Her enormous bill moved awkwardly.

"I have been waiting for you, for all of you. I am called Golden Eyes. I am here to guard you against our valley's beasts—you call us *dinosaurs.* Even using all your powers, you cannot protect yourselves against everything in this ancient valley, for there is good and there is bad."

From the back of the group, Juliana spoke up. "How can you protect us?"

"Ah, Juliana—the one who asks questions."

Juliana nodded. "Yes, I am. How can you protect us? You're only a bird. You don't have big teeth, and you're not nearly as big as them. What could you do against that T-rex?"

"I could pick you up and fly away."

"There are six of us!"

The bird's eyes were sharp and bright. "Indeed—six of you. Hank, you and your five friends have done well, but there is still much to do to protect this secret. Our valley is dying.

We need to remain secret to survive. And you can, no *must* help us. That is why you are all here." She looked at each of them as she spoke in her strange, wheezing voice. "Zebi, many centuries ago, my ancestors knew your elders. Do they still speak of our adventures? Sam, remind your friends of their powers because forgetting will kill them. Ruby, I see your red hair from the skies. Mascan was right—Oz's stitches are well done. And Oz, your power of sight is strong for one so young. You looked me straight in the eye when I was flying just below the clouds. Juliana, you will taste many things in this valley. Ask questions of yourself in the same way you do of others."

She remained quiet as she watched their faces. Then she took several breaths, filling her lungs with air.

"There are more in my army—twenty in all. They will be summoned and will respond quickly. We fly as fast as the traveling metal boxes on wheels you use. But you must summon us, or we cannot help."

"How do we summon an army of pterodactyls?" Juliana asked.

"You must all use your powers, but Hank, it is yours that will tell us where you are."

Without another word, the enormous bird spread her vast wings, leaped into the air, and was swallowed into the night's sky.

They turned back to the cave, and one by one, they squeezed in. A single candle on a ledge lit the space.

They looked around, gathering as much information with their newly heightened senses.

"There's something beyond this wall," Oz broke the silence. "Two somethings. I can see them through the rock, but they're fuzzy."

"I hear water dripping somewhere deep in the cave. And beyond that, running water. Maybe a river," Zebi said, turning his head from side to side, focusing on every hidden sound. "And something's scratching on the floor not far from us. Maybe someone is breathing slowly."

"When I touch these walls, the rock is smooth. Almost as if someone carved it or polished it," Ruby said. "Someone used a chisel to clear the stone. I can feel the small indentations. This cave is man-made."

"And it's only the first of lots of caves," Juliana whispered. "Taste the rock. It's bitter and salty. Maybe it used to be underground? Maybe we're near the second river—the one that comes from the ocean."

"I smell the salty air. Just like we're standing next to the ocean." Sam's voice was low and trembling.

"Hank, what was in the picture of the second river? Was it the one with the back of the animal watching the river?" Oz asked, looking off into the blackness at the back of the cave.

Hank pulled out his sketchbook and thumbed through to the drawing he'd done in Mascan's cave.

"Yes. I think we're near Ingemar, the second river."

Sam peered over the rim of his glasses and looked at the drawing. "Look at that beast. Now we know what it is: a dinosaur. So, if that's true, does it mean the rest of the drawings are true too?"

A voice spoke from the darkness: "That's exactly what it means." The back wall of the cave shifted so fast and so quietly, the candle barely fluttered. Mascan stood before them with Raif at his side.

Hank dropped to his knees as Raif leaped across the length of the cave and knocked him over.

"You've done well, my six young charges. You're safe, you've met Golden Eyes, and you've found another cave. You've proven to me that you can use your powers and, so far, at least survive in this valley. There is still much for you to do here, but I will teach you. Now come with me and see what the second river can bring you." He swept his arm toward a large cave, hidden behind the movable wall, and ushered them in.

There were no pictures, no writings, and no murals. There were shelves of books, with some containing large rolls of paper tied together with rope. Other shelves had leather-bound books, and others held stacks of small, thin books.

Most of the shelves were carved straight into the rock. Perhaps twelve feet tall, the highest shelf was wider than the rest and held a very long bone. Hank thought it was possibly the femur of a T-rex or a brontosaurus. There were what looked like recent drawings thumb-tacked onto boards leaning against another wall, and still more drawings spread out on tables in the center of the room, with smaller bones holding down the edges.

On every surface, candles flickered in large mason jars.

"Come and eat, and then you will sleep." Mascan led them through the books room and into a smaller room with a round table laden with food. Mascan sat beside Oz, his fingertips gently touching the skin around his stitches.

"Healing nicely," Mascan said peering down, "but it still needs time. Apply my ointment three times each day."

They ate voraciously and stuffed a few extra items into their pockets and backpacks for later.

"It's time to sleep," Mascan said. "You are tired." He led them into a pale-yellow cave where they found six hammocks, each with red and black blanket. A small shelf was cleaved out of the stone, holding a pitcher and six glasses.

They turned to thank Mascan, but just as before, he had disappeared.

Hank was tired and drifted off to sleep with images of an injured T-rex killing a stegosaurus, speaking to a pterodactyl, six rivers that each carry a secret, heartbeats that join us together.

Hank's heartbeat slowed, and soon he was in a dreamless sleep.

Hank woke at the touch of Raif's nose against his arm and wondered if it was still the middle of the night. He listened to the others' steady heartbeats as he lay in his hammock. Then Hank heard water running somewhere deep in the mountain. Mascan wasn't there. Looking over at the candle, he thought it strange that it hadn't burned down. How long had he had slept? Five minutes? Five hours?

Raif sniffed around the corners of the cave, interested in something. Checking that his Swiss army knife was still in his pocket, Hank left his hammock and wandered over to investigate. When his heart started pounding in his chest, he stopped. There, in front of him, was a narrow archway they had all missed. He looked back at his friends, still asleep, and then at Raif's eager face. When Raif stepped through the doorway, Hank followed. They made their way along a short passageway before arriving in another cave. The ceiling was low, and Hank was careful not to bump his head. Crouching down and cocking his head to one side, he listened. Water. He could hear it running beside him. He knelt to put it in his hand, but Raif growled, and he quickly pulled it back.

"What is it, Raif?"

Raif pulled at his pant leg and moved him back from the stream. Hank leaned against the rock wall and waited. Then he heard something big swishing through the water.

"Let's get a light and wake the others."

"Where'd you go?" Ruby glared at him from her hammock. "Someone . . . Mascan . . . left a bowl of apples for us." She bit into one.

"Raif found a passage leading to another room. I think there's something there."

Sam put on his glasses. "We don't go off on our own. We stick together. We use our powers. Remember Mascan's warning? Don't do that again."

Hank nodded. "You're right. Sorry."

"Did you explore the other room?" Juliana asked.

"A bit," said Hank. "There's water there, but Raif won't let me near it."

Sam looked at Hank. "Maybe we should stay away from it."

"I want to go and look at it. Juliana, I think you were right. We've found the second river: Ingemar—the one that comes from the ocean."

"Let's go," Oz said, peering into the darkness.

A few minutes later, they'd all gone through the passageway to the cave with the river. They stood just inside the entryway and peered into the dark.

"I don't like this," Hank muttered.

"Is that something in the water . . . swimming . . . with a long neck . . . I think it's watching us. It has teeth." Oz edged back toward the tunnel.

Zebi tilted his head. "I can hear it tearing something. It's not as big as that T-rex, but I still think we should stay away from this water."

Hank pulled his flashlight out of his backpack and shone it on the water. The river was about fifteen feet wide, and even with the light, they couldn't see the bottom. The water was moving quickly, and the creature was swimming against the current. It looked about seven feet long. One flipper-like limb briefly poked out of the water.

"It's a plesiosaurus!" Hank yelled. "Get back. They're carnivores!" Hank grabbed for Ruby just as the plesiosaurus rose to the surface and lunged straight at her.

For one horrible second, Ruby froze. Then, as she reached for Hank's outstretched hand, she slipped on the wet stone floor, and she fell to her knees. At that instant, the plesiosaurus opened its mouth and bit down on her backpack and a chunk of her red hair. She shrieked as her head was yanked backward. The plesiosaurus made a horrible sound, throaty and deep, that echoed around the cave. Hank and Zebi kicked at the beast from the shore, but it lunged again. Hank yelled for help. If they didn't do something fast—the plesiosaurus would drag Ruby under the water.

Then Hank saw the blurred image of Raif as he landed hard on the plesiosaurus's back. The creature let go of Ruby as its back flippers thrashed in the water. Its front flippers pushed it farther onto the cave floor as its long neck lunged again at its prey, and its gaping mouth showed rows of teeth as it grabbed the back of Ruby's head.

Raif bared his teeth, growled, and bit down on the back of the plesiosaurus's neck. The wolf tore into its slippery flesh, but still, it held on to Ruby. Raif moved his head and bit at the side of the plesiosaurus's face. An enraged roar came from the back of the plesiosaurus, and the screaming sound of the struggle bounced off the walls.

It folded its front flippers flat against its body and rolled sideways like a crocodile, carrying Ruby and Raif with it.

Hank pulled out his knife and waded into the ice-cold water. He stabbed everywhere: neck, throat, back, head, and eyes. Hank thrust his knife over and over again as it pierced its wet skin. Finally, the plesiosaurus's mouth opened, releasing Ruby. As Raif lunged at its head again, the plesiosaurus uttered a final rasping scream and slid back into the dark water. The last they saw was the tip of its mouth, still holding a large tuft of Ruby's curly red hair. Then it was gone.

Hank, Oz, and Zebi reached for Ruby, who let out a terrible moan as she fell into them. They half carried and half dragged her out of the water and out of the cave. Just before they entered the tunnel, Hank looked back at the bloody scene. The water was still, and he wondered if they'd killed the beast. *How many times did I stab it?*

They were silent as they stumbled back toward the cave where they'd slept so peacefully. Raif stayed at the rear, pushing them with his angry snout. His low, steady growl wrapped around them, slowing the frantic beating of their hearts.

Halfway along the tunnel, Sam stopped and threw up. Juliana dragged him back into the cave. Sam sat on his hammock and stared at the floor.

Oz examined the back of Ruby's head. The plesiosaurus's teeth had left deep scratches and had pierced the skin in three places. Hank thought the cuts looked deep—and there was a large bald spot on the crown of Ruby's head where it had pulled out her hair.

"How painful is it?" Oz was slowly examining her scalp.

"It feels strange," she said, still shuddering. "Like there's ice on my head."

Zebi pulled the amber egg from his pocket. The pungent smell hit them as he unscrewed the top. Stunned and cold, he rubbed Mascan's ointment over her wounds. "This will help."

Ruby sat still and stared at the wall.

Hank looked at his hands and saw the plesiosaurus's sticky blood covering his hands. His right hand still held the knife. He looked at it in his open palm and then tossed it onto the floor.

"What are you doing, Hank. Your knife saved Ruby." Zebi picked up the knife and opened the blade. He wiped off the blood on his pant leg, folded the blade back inside, and handed it to Hank. "Put it back in your pocket," he muttered.

15
VENGEANCE

Sam's voice was so quiet they almost didn't hear him. He sat on his hammock with his feet dangling over the side, staring at the floor. Then he spoke in short gasping sentences. "We screwed up. All of us, and it almost got Ruby and Raif killed. We didn't think because we didn't use our powers. We found another cave and rushed in. We were lucky this time. Oz, you saw something in the water, but you didn't see the danger because you didn't want to see it. Zebi, you heard the creature tearing something apart, but you didn't think beyond that. Juliana, you didn't use your power at all. Taste isn't just putting something on your tongue; it's sticking your tongue out like a snake and tasting the air. I could smell something, but I thought it was only the salt-water. That plesiosaurus lived in that cave. It stank of that animal, but I didn't notice. Ruby, never go out in front unless

you're touching something you know. And Hank, you said we should get back, but it was too late. You got excited about finding another dinosaur, and you didn't listen soon enough to what your power was telling you. We *all* screwed up."

"We can't ever do anything like that again. It will get us killed."

"Sam is right," Hank met everyone's eyes. "We were reckless. I don't ever want to go back to that cave, even if the plesiosaurus is dead. There could be another one. We're staying away."

Zebi nodded., "We need to move on and find the next part of the secret. We know there is more to this secret valley than dinosaurs. Ruby, are you okay with leaving this cave?"

Ruby's face glowed white in the candlelight. "I think my head is okay," she said. "Let's get out of here. Could a plesiosaurus make its way down that tunnel? How far can they come out of the water? We know seventy-five million years ago, they were water dinosaurs. Maybe they've evolved. Maybe they can live out of the water for longer than they could then. I'm not going to sleep and wake up to find another one in here."

They gathered their backpacks, drank their fill of water, and stuffed the rest of the apples into their clothes. The tunnel leading to the outside ledge brought warm, clean air into the cave.

As they arrived at the opening to the ledge, they stopped.

Oz stuck his head out and looked in every direction, including up at the sky. "The healthy T-rex isn't here, but the injured one is closer than Mascan's mountain. It's on the ground, almost right below us. I think there's something else coming this way, but not as big as the T-rex."

"Where is it, Oz? How close?" Juliana squeezed past him and looked out over the ledge.

"It's running across the valley, from the other side. I see it through those pine trees." He inched forward and leaned over the ledge. "I see the injured one now." He pointed. "It's behind that boulder with the stripe running through it. It must have dragged itself here. I think it's hiding from other predators."

"I can hear him breathing," Zebi looked over the edge. "He's fighting for breath, and his heartbeat is sort of fast, then slow, then fast again. His head is still on the ground, and his tail is flat against the side of the rock. He's having a hard time moving."

Hank closed his eyes. He felt as though the T-rex was right beside him. "Zebi, it can't stay here without being eaten by something else. The other T-rex isn't here to protect it now."

"It stinks!" Sam said, sniffing at the air and turning his head. "Can't you smell it? I think that eye is infected. And Oz is right. Something else is coming, but it's not anything we've seen before. It doesn't smell of blood and rotting flesh like this T-rex. It could be a herbivore."

Juliana shivered and pulled her sweater around her shoulders. "There's something else coming too—something I've tasted before. Could it be that pterodactyl?"

Oz turned and looked down the valley. "Whatever's coming is about a mile away. I can see the dust rising above the trees."

Hank motioned them away from the edge. "That beast is getting closer, and it's looking for something. It's coming for the T-rex; it can smell him just as well as Sam can. It's getting faster."

As the ledge began to shake, a shower of pebbles rained down on them. They pressed their backs against the rock.

"Maybe it's another stegosaurus!" Juliana guessed.

"No. Not a stegosaurus." Hank closed his eyes.

They could see three massive horns pointed upright and a large fan-shaped frill. Then a mammoth creature burst through the underbrush and stopped.

The magnificent twenty-foot-long triceratops stood before them. Hank figured the head alone measured eight feet. The triceratops snorted and puffed and wailed like a combination of a charging elephant and a lion preparing for an attack. The beast appeared surprisingly light on his feet. He galloped up to the T-rex, pawing angrily at the dirt. He moved closer and roared again, this time right into the side of the T-rex's head.

Hank wondered whether it smelled the blood. Was it threatening the fallen T-rex?

He pulled out his sketchbook and drew the single horn that rose from the triceratops's snout and the two long horns that grew forward over the tops of his eyes.

The two dinosaurs wailed and bellowed. The massive triceratops stamped his feet while moving closer to the T-rex's head. He roared and nudging the injured T-rex. At first, he looked to be playing with the T-rex, but then the nudging became more violent. He pushed the T-rex along the ground, even trying to roll it over. With each nudge, the T-rex howled. The triceratops's snout pushed harder as its middle horn jabbed at the T-rex's damaged eye. He stopped and sniffed the air and began again. He backed up several feet and ran straight at the T-rex, his feet stopping inches from its head.

Hank drew faster, barely looking at the sketchpad, his eyes fixed on the T-rex's face.

Then the triceratops did something curious. He moved away from the T-rex, went to a nearby pine tree, and rubbed his horns against the bark. Then came back to the boulder that the T-rex rested against and rubbed his horns along the rock. The sound grated and scraped in their ears.

"He's sharpening his horns on the rock," Hank yelled above the noise. "He's going to gore him."

The T-rex looked up the sheer cliff and into Hank's face.

"We need to save him."

"Are you crazy?" Ruby almost spit out the words."

"By using our powers to call an army," Hank said quietly.

Sam smelled the blood and dust and pus. Zebi listened to the T-rex's gasps and its heart pounding. Juliana tasted the rage in the air as the triceratops prepared for its kill. Oz looked down into the T-rex's eyes and saw the pain of the dying beast. Ruby focused on the T-rex's skin and the cut on the side of his face. Hank's eyes stayed on the T-rex's imploring gaze.

At first, the sounds of the approaching pterodactyls made them feel as if they'd stuck their heads out of a car window at high speed. The air banged into their eardrums, and the wind pulled at the skin on their faces.

Oz smiled. "They're almost here."

The sky darkened and became a shifting black kaleidoscope of gigantic wings over an alliance of deadly red claws reaching downward. Then Hank could hear voices and flapping wings.

"Save him of ten thousand battles! Kill the three-horned monster!"

They stared unblinking as the flock of pterodactyls

synchronized their attack. The black cloud of wings circled the triceratops.

Oz pointed out the leader with its distinctive yellow and orange crest and red stripe down the middle.

"It's Golden Eyes," Hank shouted.

The T-rex twisted his head and looked up at the sky. The triceratops seemed unaware of the flock's imminent attack.

Oz pointed. "Look! The T-rex has seen the pterodactyls, but the triceratops hasn't. How can he not see or hear those wings? Watch their tails spread open as they practice their dives. Look at those killer claws!"

Hank sketched as the rest of them watched in horror. Finally, the triceratops turned his massive head and saw the flock forming over his head. He burst out with a frenzy of bellows.

Hank looked up from his sketching and watched the circling pterodactyls. "If they're going to win this fight, they'll have to avoid the horns and ridge around his head." He pointed as the lead pterodactyl dove, its tail spread wide, and its wings folded back. As it charged, a scream sliced the air. The triceratops reared his head and knocked the bird hard with his snout. The second pterodactyl flew down with its claws spread wide and seconds later was digging into the back of the triceratops's neck. It ripped a piece of hide and flew off. The triceratops bellowed and thrust up with his horns.

Then two pterodactyls swooped down, one from either side. The first was knocked away by a horn, and the second found another piece of flesh, ripped at it, and took off. The next one landed on the triceratops and started to dig with its beak and claws. Despite his injuries, the triceratops remained on his feet and whirled around. The triceratops threw the pterodactyl off as it landed against the sheer rock.

The flock gathered again in aerial formation. Hank felt sure he had spotted Golden Eyes. She had flown close to the ledge and glanced at Hank.

The T-rex had not moved. Still on the ground, his eyes never left the wing-filled sky.

Oz moved forward to lean over the ledge, but Ruby grabbed his belt and pulled him back. "Ozzie, the last thing we need is for you to fall over the side."

He pointed to the group circling over the valley. "They're dividing into two synchronized formations for their next attack, one close to the mountain and the other farther out into the valley. Look at the one at the front." He watched the birds' actions closely. "I can see them speaking to each other. The one in front is giving orders. Some of them are younger birds, and they're listening to their leader. I think she's looking at us, Hank. She's the same one who spoke to us."

Hank nodded. "It's Golden Eyes. She wants us to know she's here."

"I wonder where they'll strike next," Juliana said as they watched them gathering speed.

"I'll bet they'll try to rip out its eyes," Oz stated. "Then it's defenseless. The one it threw into the mountain hasn't moved yet. Do you think it's dead?" No one answered.

"Are you drawing this? Who would believe this battle?" Sam looked over Hank's shoulder at his second sketch, showing a pterodactyl flying away with strings of flesh in its claws.

Golden Eyes circled and came so close to their ledge; they could feel the rush of air from her wings.

The attack resumed as the two groups sent one bird from each group at the same instant. The pincer movement confused the triceratops, and it swung its head back and forth, trying to choose which one to gore. He couldn't avoid both attackers as they dove at him simultaneously. His footwork began to slow.

Zebi yelled. "Look at Golden Eyes! She's between the two groups and giving orders like an Air Force general. *Now the left eye, open the middle of the back, dig deeper.*"

After a series of rapid attacks, the triceratops stumbled, now covered in blood.

Golden Eyes made a long, slow pass beside the ledge, then gathered speed and became a dark, blurry line as she drove her red claws into the triceratops's eyes. He dropped to the ground and lay still.

"His heart is skipping beats. Now it's slower," Zebi said. Then several seconds later, "Nothing. He's dead."

The pterodactyls glided overhead, watching the bloody carcass. The triceratops had fallen several feet away from the T-rex.

Sam's voice was shaking. "Will they eat him?"

No one spoke.

Moments later, Golden Eyes landed on their ledge. She took several long breaths and looked directly at Hank.

"You summoned me just in time, my young friends. This triceratops has brought much death to our valley. He was not hungry. He just liked to kill."

Hank looked into her eyes. "Now we know how to bring you to us."

The great bird cocked her head to one side. "We know our battle plans. We know how to kill when we need to." She looked back at her flock. "We fly up to where the great white bears roam. We practice how to kill."

"Will you eat him?" Sam asked.

She turned her massive eyes onto Sam. "Yes, we will eat him for two reasons. We are meat-eaters, and we are hungry after that battle. His meat will be a welcome meal, enough for all of us. Do you want any?"

Sam pulled back from her. "We are not hungry."

"What's the second reason?" Juliana asked, pushing herself nearer to Golden Eyes.

"Rex is our king, and he is injured."

They looked down at the injured T-rex, then back to Golden Eyes.

"King?" Juliana asked.

Golden Eyes made a blowing sound that must have been laughter.

"You think we are just a valley full of prehistoric beasts? That we don't have laws and traditions? How do you think we are all still here? There is much that is evil here. And so, Juliana, the second reason is that our old king must be protected. He has led us well through many battles, and we do not want the smell of the triceratops blood to attract other predators."

"But your king is injured, and the smell of *his* blood will attract predators too, won't it?" said Hank, looking away from Golden Eyes and down at the carnage below.

"Exactly. The six of you did not arrive here by accident. You were all chosen for your skills. You are here to help us. Today, you have done much good. But you must do more."

She studied each of them in turn and nodded her approval.

"You are the leader of the pterodactyls," Oz said. "We watched you leading that attack, Golden Eyes."

Once again, they heard her laughing sound.

"My eyes are golden because, like you, Oz, I have the gift of exceptional sight. Can you see what is on that riverbank next to the snowy owl?

Oz stared and shook his head.

"Come here—closer to me."

She opened her wing slightly and nudged him next to her until their heads were inches apart.

"Your powers can go farther, Oz, even beyond that northern river. Look further, many miles farther than that polar bear and her cubs. What else can you see?"

"A dog sled with two men. They're carrying something big."

"And what is it?"

"Crates of something. Machinery? Drills? And there are some small bags tied with rope on top of the crates."

"What's in the bags, Oz?"

"Diamonds," he whispered. "Many diamonds."

They heard another laughing whistle, and Golden Eyes pulled her wing tighter around Oz as if hugging him.

"We have work to do here." A moment later, she leaped into the air. They watched her glide slowly across the valley. One by one, the other pterodactyls formed a line behind her. Their procession made a dark moving shadow across the floor of the valley, then landing next to the carcass, they began to rip it apart and eat.

Within seconds the triceratops was covered by red claws and stabbing beaks. The valley was silent but for the noise of the feeding frenzy.

16
A GOOD DEED

The triceratops's carcass was picked clean. Blood covered the pterodactyls' heads as they prepared for the flight over the valley. In a whoosh of flapping wings, they took off.

Hank leaned over the ledge and watched the birds fly off in different directions. He wondered how their army had gathered so quickly. Once they'd disappeared, Hank looked back to the valley. He had drawn the final moments of the feeding when the bones of the triceratops had emerged from the black wings and red claws. Now they lay heaped in a pile on the ground—the skull, seven feet long, four massive legs, and the rest were fragmented pieces.

"We have work to do," he said, standing up. "I'll go first." His foot was already on the first step of the staircase that led down from the ledge. He knew the others were using their

powers, just as he was using his own. If there were danger approaching, they would know.

Once they reached the bottom of the stone staircase, Hank and Raif took the lead. They approached the T-rex slowly. When he was about ten feet away, Hank knelt. He looked at the beast's extraordinary face and felt each breath exhaled from his nostrils. There was a long gash under its swollen eye. The creature groaned in a voice lower than Hank had ever heard.

"You are Hank?"

"I am."

"And Raif?"

The wolf growled and backed up a few feet, showing his teeth.

"Your group has done well today. I saw you watching our battle."

"You are injured," Hank said quietly. "The skin below your eye is cut and infected. Can you see?"

"Only light, nothing else."

"We are afraid of you."

The T-rex snorted, which Hank took for a sound of laughter. *You should be.*

"But you need our help."

"I do."

"If we help you, will you hunt us or hurt us when you are well?"

"What do you think, young Hank?"

"I think we can't rely only on our powers. We have to use our brains. You are the most incredible, terrible creature I've ever seen. Can we trust you, or should we let you die here?"

Just then, Golden Eyes landed beside the T-rex. Her eyes were blazing. "You have to help him, young Hank."

"But he's a huge dinosaur—king of the valley. The most dangerous of all," Hank exclaimed. "He could kill us in a blink."

"Yes, he could. So, could I. But we need you, here, now."

"Can we trust you?" Hank said, staring hard, not blinking.

"You think that because I am so different from you that I cannot also be the same as you? That I don't have feelings, only anger, and terror? Do you know why we killed the triceratops? Because he hunts our nests, steals our eggs, and kills our young. He killed my youngest male. He would have been strong, like me. Now we need to repair the T-rex's wounds. Mascan used to do this, but now his hands are weak and shake, and he can barely see."

"There is a play they teach us in school called *The Merchant of Venice*. A man named Shakespeare wrote it," Hank said quietly.

"What is a play?"

"It's a kind of story." Hank half-smiled.

"And what happened in this play of Mr. Shaking Spear?"

"One of the characters was from a different tribe than the others."

"We have many tribes of creatures here," the T-rex nodded.

"Mr. Shakespeare wrote: 'If you prick us, do we not bleed?'"

The T-rex made a long, deep sound of disgust. "Perhaps we are not so different. You can see that I bleed, just like Oz's eye and Ruby's head. Because I kill for meat, does that make me evil? I am a meat-eater, and so are you. You can trust me, young Hank. I will be true to you, as you will be true to me. Perhaps this Mr. Shaking Spear knew something about different tribes."

The T-rex moved his enormous head and moaned. "I need someone to repair my eye."

Hank turned and motioned to Ruby, who crawled up behind him. "Are you crazy, Hank?" she hissed. "You think I should *stitch him up?* Me? Ruby Basher, *stitch up a live T-rex?*"

"Yes, Ruby. Stitch him up and put Mascan's ointment on him. You have the power of touch, and you need to use it."

"I may have the power of touch, but it's for *humans,* not beasts. Anyway, there's hardly any ointment left. Ozzie needs it for his eye, and I need it on my head. Did you think of that? What happens if our injuries become infected and we've given all our ointment to the T-rex?"

"He needs it, Ruby."

"So do we. And Mascan gave it to *us not him.*" She hissed.

Oz crept up beside them and looked into the eyes of the T-rex. Hank could see the color fade from his face.

"That's a pretty big cut, Hank. He'll need all the ointment that's left."

"Ruby doesn't want to give it to him. She says the two of you need it."

"I think I'm getting better." Oz shrugged.

"What about her?" Hank said, gesturing to Ruby.

"I looked at her scalp. She still needs some of it."

"*Of course*, I need some of it. What's the matter with the two of you? This is a *beast*. Why would we help him when only yesterday he would have killed us?"

"Stay here," Hank said.

"Why? What are you up to?" She looked over her shoulder, horrified, as Oz and Hank moved back and left her facing the T-rex with only Raif by her side.

They watched her stand and face the T-rex. The dried blood spread down the side of his face, but she only stared directly into his one open eye.

"You are Ruby?"

She ignored him and focused on the cut. Leaning in a bit closer, she could see the redness and swelling around his eye and the bleeding had not stopped. They could all see the T-rex watching her.

"I don't have a needle that will go through your skin. It will break."

The T-rex sighed deeply and closed his good eye.

She felt Hank beside her. "I have my tent repair kit. It has thick needles."

"He'll kill me, Hank."

The T-rex sighed. "Remember Mr. Shaking Spear."

"What's he talking about?"

"If you prick us, do we not bleed?" the T-rex murmured.

"I told him about Shylock in *The Merchant of Venice*. Remember—Mrs. Blatherfield's class," Hank whispered.

She made a face. "I remember."

"He's trying to show we're not so different. Will you do it? You're the only one who can."

"I thought that being attacked by a plesiosaurus would be the most extraordinary thing that would ever happen to me. And here I am, on the same day, ready to stick a needle into a T-rex's face."

"How many stitches do you think you'll need?"

She looked at Hank out of the corner of her eye. "You can't always get your way, but this time maybe you will."

Oz's hand appeared, holding the egg of ointment. She grabbed it, gave him an angry look, and started to crawl forward. When she reached the T-rex's head, she stopped. The beast stared at her with his injured eye. She winced as she saw his injury.

His lower eyelid was sliced in half with an open and bleeding gash that continued another twenty inches downward.

There was congealed blood around his swollen red eyeball, surrounding the wound site and down the side of his face. The skin was puffed up and pink.

"Can you see anything out of this eye? Light? Partial vision?"

"Some light. Blurry images."

"Your breath stinks."

"That's because I'm a meat-eater. The flesh sticks to my teeth."

She leaned closer and slowly pulled back his eyelid.

"What do you see, Ruby Basher?"

"Your wound is infected. The deepest part is closest to your eye. The stegosaurus's spike hit you, and it punctured the skin close to the side of the eyeball, but not the eyeball, which is good. But the cut extends down to here"—she touched his cheek, covered in dried blood— "which is not good."

"What will you do?"

"It needs to be cleaned. Is there any water near here?"

"Only in the cave of the plesiosaurus."

"I'm not going back in there." She turned to Raif.

"Come here, Raif." She patted the ground.

"Why the wolf?"

She ignored him and continued to pat the ground. Raif crawled toward Ruby, never taking his eyes off the T-rex.

"Good boy." She pointed to the dried blood around Rex's eye. "Clean him up, Raif."

The wolf began to lick the end of the wound. His first licks were gentle, only using the tip of his thick tongue. He looked up at the T-rex every few seconds. Then he licked harder and pulled at the skin. They could hear the rough scraping as the hundreds of projections covering his tongue gradually removed the dried blood, pus, and grit. Then he placed his giant front paws over the top of the eye and licked under the eyelid.

When he finally stopped, he looked back at Ruby. This time, it was Ruby giving the commands.

"Good job, Raif." She almost smiled. "Stay here in case it starts to bleed again when I stitch it up."

She spread Mrs. Plunkett's tent repair kit on the ground. There were straight and curved needles, strong thread, and a small pair of pliers.

Ruby picked up the largest curved needle, moved around to the T-rex's good eye, and held it up. "This is what I'm going to stick into your face."

The T-rex made his low bass moan. "Get it done."

"I'm starting at the bottom and will work my way up to your eye. I'm keeping the stitches separate, so they don't pull out. I don't know how long this will take."

Rex remained quiet, watching her with his good eye.

"And you can't move, or I could make it worse."

Ruby could hear Juliana whispering to Oz. "Is this what she did to you?"

"The same thing, only these stitches are going to be bigger."

"Did it hurt?"

"Yes."

The five friends watched in silence.

Ruby talked to herself. "Okay, Ruby, get a good grip on this needle with the end of the pliers and find the best spot. Yes. Good. Stick this end of the needle in here, pull the needle under the skin, and come up on the other side of the gash about the same distance as you did when you went in. Now leave some thread hanging out on this side so you can tie it. Don't go in too deep. Yes. That looks okay. Now tie it. Hold this first end of the thread and bring it over to the second end. Wrap it around the end of the pliers and make a knot, maybe a double knot. Don't pull the thread too tight or leave it too loose. I guess that's not bad for a first stitch."

Hank watched Raif as he followed Ruby's hand, pulling the thread through. She knelt close to the T-rex, her face still, her fingers moving slowly and carefully, stitch after stitch. Several stitches later, the flesh started to bleed.

"Raif, clean up this blood." She sat back and watched the

wolf lick at the trickle of blood. The bleeding stopped, and she began again.

"You are doing well, young Ruby. I will not forget your good deeds."

For once Ruby was silent as she kept on stitching.

When she knotted the last stitch, she sat back on her haunches and surveyed her work.

"Okay, Rex, you're done. Move your head a bit. Slowly. How does it feel?"

He lifted his head off the ground and turned slowly to each side. "It feels different. Like I've got something holding me," he said.

"Does it feel too tight?"

"No."

"Good."

Ruby took the amber egg of ointment out of her pocket. She blinked and stared, turning it over in her hand, and then held it out for the others to see. In the darkened cave, they hadn't noticed the details on the outside of the egg. It was carved out of amber and depicted the walls of Mascan's cave in miniature. Ruby turned it slowly in the light. Hank had to squint to find every detail. He saw the separate ridges of the waves from the second river, the three mountaintops of Ladon, the fourth river, and the polar bears along the banks of the fifth river Alme Tulah. He wondered how so much detail could be in something so small. Who had carved it, and when?

Unscrewing the lid, Ruby stuck her index finger in and took out a small amount.

"The most dangerous part is next to your eyelid. It will get the most movement and moisture from your blinking." She slowly spread the ointment over the wound. The T-rex remained very still. She scraped the last bit from the bottom of the jar when she reached the last stitch.

"Okay, Rex, you're done. Nothing left."

"I owe you my life, young Ruby."

"Yup. And Raif. You owe him your life too."

He sighed and raised his head to look over at Raif.

"You have more work to do yet, my young friends." Golden Eyes said as she watched with the others.

Hank nodded to Golden Eyes and walked over to the triceratops bones. "We need to get these away from here. They'll attract other predators."

"You think we can carry that any distance?" Zebi asked, looking over at Golden Eyes. "Tell us what's coming up or down the valley."

She leaped off her perch, spread her wings, and shouted back to them as she climbed higher. "Use your powers."

"I hear small creatures a couple of miles away, weighing maybe fifteen to twenty pounds," Zebi said. "Still, they could be nasty. I don't hear the plesiosaurus anymore. Maybe he *is* dead. Mascan is not near us. I think there's something big about twenty miles down the valley. It's walking slowly. Wait. There's more than one of them. A herd, but they won't be here for a while."

Oz squinted up to the sky. "Golden Eyes is up there close to the clouds watching over the valley. She's catching the air currents, so there's nothing dangerous, or she wouldn't be doing that."

"I can taste something peculiar," Juliana said. "Not animal or vegetable. I've tasted it before, but I don't know where. I remember being with my grandmother. I think it's dangerous, but I don't know why."

Sam spoke up next. "I don't smell the T-rex's infection the way I did before. But those bones will attract something soon, so let's get rid of them and then find someplace safe."

Ruby sounded tired and impatient. "My fingers are numb from digging the needle into his tough skin. My power tells me nothing."

They all looked at Hank. "I don't sense anything," he said. "Let's go. Raif, stay here. Bark if something happens."

Hank whistled softly and walked over to the skull. "Do you think we can carry it?"

"It's not going to be as easy as the hollow bones of the pterodactyl. This dinosaur can't fly, so its bones will weigh a lot." Sam said, tilting his head as he sized up the weight.

They all grabbed hold of the skull and lifted it.

"It's heavy," Ruby screwed up her face in disgust.

"It stinks," Juliana said.

Golden Eyes appeared suddenly overhead.

"Follow me! Bring it over to the other side of those rocks. The farther away we get, the better his chances."

Oz squinted at the rocks in the distance. "Even if we don't see anything, keep your powers working."

The skull bones were heavy and difficult to carry, still having muscle and skin hanging off them. They walked for fifteen minutes and followed Golden Eyes to an indentation in the earth on the other side of a tall boulder.

"Drop it there, and go back for the rest," she said.

It took five more trips to move all the bones. Their last effort made for an unlikely picture of six figures carrying the spine of a triceratops, Hank positioned at the front, supported by Zebi, Ruby, Sam, Oz, and finally, Juliana, holding the tip of its tail. They were all covered in blood.

They dropped the spine onto the pile of bones and hurried back.

Rex was standing as Golden Eyes and her flock stood nearby.

"I am feeling a little better. Stronger." Rex said. "Ruby did a good job. But I can't stay out in the open. I must get my strength back after that battle and keep moving. I still have enemies in this valley."

Hank looked up into the extraordinary face.

"Your eye is looking better. The bleeding has stopped. Can you see out of it yet?"

"Slowly, young Hank. Time will heal it."

Hank nodded. Rex would live. Their work here was done, for now. Hank stifled a yawn as the others straggled into the clearing.

"Rex?" he said, looking up into the dinosaur's enormous eyes, "where can we be safe tonight?"

17
INTO THE TREES

"**W**hat do you mean we're going to sleep in the trees?" Ruby asked. "That's what he said? *Trees?*"

"Not much farther, according to my map," Hank moved quickly, leading the group. "I trust Rex. If he *were* going to kill us, he'd have done it instead of sending us to find shelter."

Oz, half running and half walking, looked back impatiently at Julianna. "We need to hurry. It's going to be dark in about an hour."

"My legs aren't as long as yours, Oz," Juliana muttered.

"We can't slow down, do your best."

Hank read the notes in his sketchbook out loud as Raif trotted beside him. *Beyond the large round boulder with a thick stripe of quartz running through the middle, past the cluster of pine trees, half of them lying dead on the ground. Walk toward Three-Top Mountain for five hundred large steps and find the*

small water that bubbles up a few inches out of the ground. Stay back from the mountain and don't go near any cave openings. On the other side is a small forest of lodgepole pine trees; the largest is in the middle—it's about ninety feet tall. The treehouse is twenty-five feet from the top.

It was beginning to get dark when they entered the small forest. The trees had grown so close together that it was hard to walk. They felt their way forward, on the lookout for one tree taller than the rest.

"Here it is!" Sam was pointing at a massive tree; the trunk alone looked about five feet in diameter and eighty feet tall. He walked around to the other side and called out to the group. "Over here. There are steps carved into the trunk."

Oz peered straight up. "Looks like the treehouse is supported by these four trees. It will get us off the ground and away from predators."

"Let's go," Hank ran forward. "It's getting dark."

Hank eyed the trunk. The bark was thick and riveted, so you could almost grab a hold of a piece of the bark to help you climb. Hank listened to Sam quietly counting each step and smiled. His oldest friend took in every detail.

Hank and Zebi grabbed Raif and started lifting him up the tree. Zebi stood behind him and pushed from below. Hank watched from below. Seventy-six steps later, Zebi, Hank and Raif reached the treehouse.

Once inside, they stood still and stared. They were in a large room with a vaulted ceiling that reached up to a dome some twenty feet across. Polar bear rugs covered much of the floor, and there were four round windows cut into the walls. Compass directions—north, south, east, west—were written in black ink over each one.

A tree's massive trunk grew straight through the middle of the treehouse and out through the ceiling. On one side was a stone sink with a faucet. Towels and six hammocks with Hudson's Bay blankets hung around the room. A wooden table stood in one corner, along with two benches made from branches. There was a bowl of fruit and a large, blackened pot in the middle of the table. Pitchers and drinking glasses were on a nearby shelf.

"What's in the pot, Sam?" Ruby said, yawning.

"Vegetables and meat."

Hank pointed at the top of the walls. "Look! It's the same rivers that we saw on the walls of Mascan's cave."

"The same," Zebi nodded, eyeing them carefully.

"Whoever made this treehouse knew Mascan's cave," Ruby said. "Maybe it's a copy of the mural, in case something happened to the other one?" She looked at the polar bear rugs on the floor. "These were stitched together with porcupine quills. Look how long it took me to stitch the T-Rex, and that was using proper thread." Her fingers prodded the minor details. "Each skin is undamaged. Nothing should have survived through winters and open windows. But it has. I wonder how?"

"Maybe winter doesn't come here," Juliana said. "Maybe it's always like this." She touched the tip of her tongue to a small spot on the wall near the drawing of Alme Tulah, the fifth river. "I don't know why this treehouse is here, but we're safe for now."

Sam spoke up. "I'm hungry." He removed the cover of the big black pot and smelled the meat, carrots, celery, and onions. "Sit down and eat."

"What kind of meat do you think this is?" Ruby squinted into her bowl.

Hank shrugged. "It could be just about anything."

They ate in silence, each mulling over some piece of the day as they stared at the painted ceiling. They staggered into bed. Within minutes, they were all fast asleep.

In the middle of the night, Hank awoke with a start. Bright moonlight shone through the east-facing window and settled on his face. He stepped out of his hammock and tip-toed to the window. Squinting up at the stars, it took him a few minutes to wade through the constellations. He could see the same sky from his backyard. How was that possible? There was nothing about this secret valley that was the same as 39 Ranger Road. He searched the sky and remembered Mrs.

Plunkett's star-gazing rule, shared during many conversations in the field behind their houses.

Always look for the Big Dipper first, boy. Then, from the bottom star of the handle, go northeast in a straight line and find Polaris. A very important star. It stays in the same position in the sky throughout the entire year. It's also called the North Star, and it marks the end of the Little Dipper handle.

"Found that one easily, Mrs. Plunkett," he whispered into the dark.

Look for Draco the Dragon. It curves around the south of the Little Dipper and then comes back again. It's hard to find Draco because the stars are usually faint.

"I think that's Draco. Am I right, Mrs. Plunkett?"

This one is easy, boy. Lyra is just south of the head of Draco and has a very bright star called Vega.

"Got it."

East of the Vega star and southwest of Draco's head is Hercules, the Strong Man. Look for the three stars going north to south and then continue south.

"Got that one, too."

Then he stopped. And there, clear as day, was a constellation that shouldn't have been there at all. Orion the Hunter belonged in the *winter* sky, not the summer sky. He stared harder, but it was there. But weren't there three stars in Orion's Belt? This one had six.

He thought back to Mrs. Plunkett's remark about Orion's Belt being a constellation in the winter sky. She'd been helping him pack the night before he left for camp. She'd stopped and taken him outside and looked up to the sky. He remembered her naming the three stars in Orion's Belt and then saying they looked like notches in a hunter's belt. Hank wondered why she had pointed out so much about Orion's Belt. Was there something about this constellation that he should know? Maybe it was a warning?

Would she be surprised at what was happening to him, to all of them?

Were the six of them in some way connected to the six stars of Orion's Belt?

Then he remembered the newspaper article—the one he'd seen on his way to school that morning. "Constellation Missing from Galaxy," the headline read. The first lines described Orion's Belt and stated how unusual it was that it was missing from the night sky—especially since its star patterns were the brightest in the winter.

Stop it, Hank. Too many questions and hardly any answers. Go back to sleep.

As he returned to his hammock, he heard Sam talking in his sleep. Ruby's head rested on the edge of her hammock. He could see her scalp in the moonlight; the skin looked raw, and the long lines of the plesiosaurus's teeth marks were visible from the crown of her head down to her neck. He thought about the amber egg and wondered if he'd made the right decision, giving the remaining ointment to Rex.

Climbing back into bed, he shivered in the cool breeze. What would this day bring? And how were they ever going to get out of this valley? He drifted off to sleep listening to Sam: *Remember your powers . . . remember your powers.*

The morning started with a loud explosion followed by a rumbling sound. It shook the treehouse violently, and for a few seconds, they all wondered if the entire structure would collapse.

"I don't think that sound is the dinosaurs. It's something else," murmured Zebi.

"What else do you hear?" Hank asked.

"A lot of high-pitched screams. Rocks are falling and crushing things. Maybe underground? It's kind of muffled and far away. And men are yelling. Someone is shouting orders, and someone else is arguing. I hear metal sliding into a hole." He fell silent, and his face was still.

After several seconds, Zebi whispered. "It's a gun—that sound is someone loading a gun."

"Are you sure?" Hank asked. "Where? In what direction?"

Zebi closed his eyes and slowly tilted his head. After a moment, he opened his eyes and pointed out the west-facing window, straight across the valley. "There. To the northwest.

That's where the sunsets. Across the valley and maybe two miles farther north."

Oz jumped up and ran to each window in turn. "We're too far down. I can't see anything. I'm going to climb farther up this tree."

"Wait!" Juliana snapped at him. "I can taste something that wasn't here last night. It's not that far away. My grandfather used to work for the railroad in the blasting department. I can taste dynamite in the air! Someone's blasting in this valley."

"Blasting? Are you sure?" Oz stared at Juliana. "Are there other humans here? Maybe they have powers too. I have to get a better look." He was at the door and scrambling up the tree with Zebi, Hank, and Juliana right behind him. They were much higher now, and the tree swayed under their weight.

"Steady now. Nothing fast. Careful where you place your feet." Hank whispered from above.

"Sam and I will stay here," Ruby hissed. "Six of us shouldn't be climbing to the top of the tree. It's not safe."

The tree was enormous, and it began to sway with its weight. Hank, Oz Zebi, and Juliana held on until it stopped.

"Climb back down a bit. There's too much weight this high up, and it won't hold us all. I'm going up farther. I need to see where the blasting is coming from."

"Slowly, Oz." Hank's voice was low. "Hold on."

He and Zebi and Juliana inched back down the tree.

They each found a stable branch to stand on and wrapped their arms around the trunk. They watched Oz's feet find a sturdy branch, then another, and then another.

"What do you see?" Juliana asked.

"Keep your voices down," Sam hissed from below.

Barely a minute later, Oz climbed back down.

"Back to the treehouse," he jerked his head. "And keep quiet."

Once inside, they gathered around Oz.

"There's blasting farther up the valley, about two miles from here. Three men. One of them is wearing a floppy brown hat, just like in the picture." He pointed to the ceiling and the drawing of Adamas, the third river.

No one spoke.

"The man with the hat was waving his arms and pointing at the ground. And something else. The whole area has a kind of wire netting over it. Maybe it's to keep Golden Eyes and her army away? There's also a wall of boulders, about thirty-five feet high, surrounding that side of the mountain. One of the men looks like he's chained. He walks as if he's dragging something. And the third man has a rifle aimed at something in the valley."

"I need to go up and listen," Zebi stood up.

"Zebi, this could be just as dangerous as the dinosaurs. Don't take any chances." Hank warned.

"Look at this!" Ruby held up the amber globe of ointment.

"I just took off the lid, hoping I could scrape out a bit more for my head. It's full again!"

Juliana peered over to look. "How?"

"Maybe the same way that we mysteriously found hot food when we needed it," Hank said. "Someone's looking out for us."

"Where was that person when we were in the plesiosaurus's cave?" Ruby snapped.

Hank looked out the east window through the trees and knew Mascan was somewhere nearby. *He felt it.*

Zebi was out the door and starting his climb. The tree began to sway again with his weight, he stopped and held on to the trunk. Hank watched as Zebi stared out in the direction of the explosion. After several minutes, he climbed back into the treehouse.

"I could hear their voices clearly," his voice was low. "One man shouted, 'Forget about the tunnel; we'll make another tunnel. Just remember your quota.' What do you think that means?"

"No idea," Hank shrugged. "Quota of what?"

"I think Oz is right," Zebi said. "There's at least one person, maybe two, walking in chains. When they move, I can hear the metal dragging." Zebi tilted his head again and then held up his hand. "I hear water dripping, and what sounds like metal tools chipping away at something, and voices. Little high-pitched voices—it almost sounds like children's voices."

"Mascan was right! It's a mine! People—and children—are prisoners," Sam said quietly. His nose twitched. "And Juliana was right, too—they're using dynamite. I can smell it."

"Maybe they're making some kind of prison, so the miners can't get out, and the dinosaurs can't get in," Ruby muttered.

"I don't think even Rex could get through that wall of boulders. And the netting Oz described would keep Golden Eyes out. I hear something else, but I can't tell what it is. A moaning sound—like people are in pain. Does that make any sense?" Zebi asked.

"No, I only saw those three people. But two of the men have pale faces, and they squint when they look at Floppy Hat. I can't see Floppy Hat's face, but he's definitely in charge."

Ruby turned the amber medicine ball around. "They never see the daylight because they live in a mine."

"But why would someone have a mine in a secret valley of dinosaurs?" Juliana asked.

"Maybe because they have something so valuable it has to be kept secret." Ruby squinted at the amber egg. "Mascan thought it might be diamonds."

Sam reached for the ball and turned it slowly in his hands. "But how do they get it out?"

Hank looked out the south-facing window toward the other end of the valley.

"What is it?" Juliana whispered.

He remained still, staring beyond the walls of the tree-house. Raif stood beside him, his ears raised and alert.

Zebi looked in the same direction.

"What do you hear?" Hank asked.

"It sounds like an earthquake. It's a long way off but getting louder."

"Any guesses?" Juliana asked.

"I think it's a herd of something," Zebi said. "Maybe they're migrating from one end of the valley to the other." He moved toward the door.

"Wait a minute!" Sam snapped. "What about our powers? What about working together?"

"I'm going up to get a better view" Oz was already out the door.

"Is that the plan? Climb the tree and wait?" Sam sounded annoyed.

"Sam is right. We gather whatever information we can and make a decision." Hank said.

Oz climbed to the same branch he'd stood on earlier and looked in the opposite direction from the blasting. The trees were so close together that their branches were intertwined, allowing Zebi to scramble onto the next tree and climb to the same height as Oz. Hank climbed over into one of the trees at the forest's edge while Sam followed Hank onto the same tree. Juliana and Ruby climbed onto the same tree near the south window of the treehouse. They balanced themselves on two separate branches.

Zebi spoke first. "They're different weights. The smaller ones are running; the larger ones are walking. They're not two-legged like the T-rex. They walk on four legs, but they've stopped now. Maybe they're eating or drinking. The adults are calling to the younger ones. Not a roar like the T-rex or the triceratops. And they might be rubbing themselves on tree bark. And I can hear a small river and more drinking."

Oz clutched at his branch and tried to stand on his toes to get a better look. "I don't believe it! I can see heads and parts of necks over the trees—long, long necks. Brontosaurus— four, five, seven, ten, twelve of them! Wow, Zebi's right. It's an enormous herd. They're staying close together, probably for protection.

"I don't taste anything bad," Juliana said. "No blood, no pus—just some dirt. I think one of the bigger ones is tired. I can taste her breath; she's panting as she's trying to keep up with the herd. Maybe she's sick or very old."

Sam clung to his tree and peered through the branches. "They're not frightened. They're just walking. I don't smell fear in any of them."

"I'm glad they're not close enough to touch," Ruby said. She swayed slightly in her tree.

Hank had climbed up to the highest point of his tree.

"This isn't an attack. They're traveling slowly. The adults are watching for danger. Maybe there aren't any predators nearby, or the size of the herd frightens them away. The leader is out in front, and he has excellent eyesight. I think he can see us. He's looking straight at me now. I want to stay and watch them from here."

"You're too low Hank," Sam said. "If you have to get back to the treehouse in a hurry, you might have trouble."

"They're not looking to fight. This is a peaceful herd of herbivores."

"Maybe," Sam said, cleaning his glasses and squinting.

They watched and listened and hung on to their trees. The sound of the herd grew louder.

"I can see the leader now," Oz said. "He must be seventy-five feet long. More are walking with him, but he's the biggest, and he's in front. He's looking straight toward these trees. I think he sees me. He's stopping now and waiting for the rest of them to stop. They're changing direction—coming straight for us!"

"Why would they come to us?" Sam stammered.

No one answered. The herd cleared the underbrush and walked into the open area just beyond the edge of the forest. Mostly hidden by the thickness of the branches and thick trunks, the six waited and watched.

Hank watched as a shadow moved across the ground and

toward the herd. *Golden Eyes.* Moments later she flew close to the brontosaurus and circled.

"Zebi, are they saying anything?" Juliana asked.

"No. She's just staring at them. I wonder why?"

The leader gave a trumpeting call, sort of like an elephant. The herd started to walk again; their tails raised off the ground. They all stayed on their branches and held on to their trees. Hank noticed the calves were watched constantly.

The herd stopped fifty feet away. The leader looked at Hank and bellowed loudly, and the rest followed. It wasn't the angry roar of the T-rex's battles; Hank couldn't understand it, but somehow, he wasn't afraid.

Sam began to shake.

"Hold on, Sammy," Ruby screamed over the noise. "Don't let go of that tree. Everything is fine."

The extraordinary sound stopped abruptly, and the leader turned his enormous neck and eyes again toward Hank. The leader walked forward and extended his neck until his face reached twenty feet up the tree. He stared at Hank. His head was small compared to the rest of him, but he put his snout up against the trunk and pushed. The tree began to sway, and for a moment, Hank thought he might be trying to throw he and Sam off. But they held on, and the tree soon stopped swaying. Next, the brontosaurus stopped at Ruby's tree, looked at her, and pushed the tree into a swaying motion. He went to each tree and repeated the action. Then he looked back at Hank and Sam and made a strange noise. His mouth was close enough for them to see the worn-down teeth of an herbivore—nothing like the flesh-ripping teeth of Rex or the plesiosaurus.

He turned his head to face his herd and gave another loud call. Then he marched his herd away.

When all the trees stopped swaying, the group returned to the treehouse.

"Why did he do that?" Juliana asked.

"Were you afraid?" Hank replied.

"No! I don't know why, but no! It was just like looking at a huge beanstalk."

"I wonder where they're going," Zebi said.

Sam peered out the window as the dust settled and the noise lessened. "What I don't understand is what these dinosaurs are doing here. Why *here?* Why not Africa? Or South America?"

"They're here because they can't get out of the valley," Hank said. "And if they got out, how long would they last? There's something special here—something that keeps them alive."

The six of them watched from the treehouse windows as the enormous creatures slowly walked out of sight.

18
ATTACK AT THE MINE

Hank turned to face his friends. "I think we should get out of the trees and stay close to that herd."

"Why?" Juliana asked.

"Because the brontosauruses aren't going to hurt us, and I think we should get closer to where Floppy Hat and the other men are. We can stay on this side of the valley and keep hidden behind some bigger trees and rocks."

He closed his eyes and concentrated for a few moments. "I don't feel anything near us. The valley is quiet."

"Great. Let's get out of these trees and head north." Hank was at the door and starting to shimmy down the trunk. The others followed, with Raif jumping from branch to branch until they were all on the ground. Moments later the entire group was creeping through the thick forest.

Once they were out in the open, they ran behind the trees and boulders scattered along the valley floor.

A minute later, they stopped and crouched near the ground behind some tall grass. "The brontosauruses are heading straight for that side of the valley," Hank whispered. "I wonder if Beanstalk knows there are people over there. Let's head for that boulder, directly across the valley from Floppy Hat."

It took them several minutes of half running, half walking to get to the rock; as they peered across to the area where they'd seen Floppy Hat, they could see the entrance to a cave.

Hank locked eyes with his friends. "Now we use our powers. Zebi, what do you hear?"

"Talking." Zebi's eyes widened. "One man is saying, 'I'll take those chains off while we have a bit of fun. You'd better be good shots!' Now he's laughing. I can hear the key going into a lock. And another one." A moment later, he gasped. "They're going to use the brontosaurus herd as target practice!"

"Why? They're not bothering anyone!" Ruby almost spit out the words.

Hank glared at Ruby. "Keep your voice down."

Oz crouched down and peeked out from behind the boulder. "I think Zebi's right. I can see something moving under that netting—and something is poking out toward the valley."

"Is it a gun?" Sam asked.

"I think so" Oz whispered.

"Zebi, we need you to listen. What are they saying or doing?" Hank practically hissed the words.

Zebi closed his eyes and moved his head back and forth. His expression gradually changed from one of concentration to one of terror.

"Many guns," he said quietly. "Big rifles. And they've just placed a bigger gun on a stand. I think it might be a machine gun." He tilted his head to one side. "They're loading ammunition."

Juliana's eyes widened. "We need Golden Eyes and her army—now!"

Hank closed his eyes. Oz stared wide-eyed into the cloudless sky. Juliana's lips parted slightly, and the tip of her tongue prodded the air. Zebi continued moving his head to find the faintest sound. Sam inhaled deeply through his nose. Ruby rubbed her fingertips together and looked up to the sky.

Hank shook his head. "It's going to start. We're too late."

"Beanstalk sees nothing. He's leading them right into it," Oz moaned.

"No matter how bad this gets, we need to stay behind this boulder," Hank said. "A stray bullet could hit us —and the machine gun might be able to reach over here." They pressed their backs into the boulder as a burst of rapid shots pierced the air. Moments later, Beanstalk's deep bellow echoed around the valley. The next gunshots were almost deafening, and the bullets sprayed around the herd as it turned to flee farther up the valley. A flock of small birds burst out of a nearby tree and shrieked as they looked for more cover.

Oz took a quick look around the edge of the boulder. "Two of them have been hit." The guns started up again, and Hank pulled his head back, his face angry and stunned.

"The first ones were smaller; now they've hit a huge one," Hank said as the ground shook and the great animal landed hard and lay silent. "I can't see how many more are injured."

Hank wanted to close his eyes, to block out the sight of the enormous animals bellowing and then falling.

As suddenly as it had started, the gunfire stopped. The valley was silent except for Beanstalk moaning.

Juliana jumped up and took a few steps toward one of the fallen brontosauruses. Oz grabbed her, pulling her back behind the boulder. Deep cries of pain and the higher-pitched squealing from the smaller brontosauruses filled the valley.

Hank's voice was low and quiet. "They're reloading their guns. I think they've hit three, at least. Maybe four or five."

"Beanstalk?" Ruby whispered. "Is he hit?"

"Can't tell yet," Hank whispered and then held up his hand. "Keep your voices down. The sound will bounce off these rocks, and then they'll turn the guns on us."

"Wait—I hear a clicking sound," Zebi said. "Maybe the machine gun is jammed?"

But the rifle fire continued.

Zebi leaned out a few inches from behind the rock.

"One of the shooters doesn't hit much, but the other one is a crack shot. He's picking off the closest ones. Beanstalk is up against the wall of boulders with some of the others. The wall is too thick, and the guns are too far back to reach them."

"No . . . wait!" Hank said, his voice shaking. "I can see one of the shooters coming out from under the netting. He's going to shoot down on them from the top of the wall. He's laughing and waving at the two men under the net. And he's looking for the right boulder to prop up his gun. Beanstalk is trying to reach him, but his neck isn't long enough, and he's batting his head against the rocks."

Then Hank's eyes widened. "Wait—they're coming."

"Golden Eyes?" Juliana whispered, looking up at the sky.

"There! Right at the top of the mountain, coming down." Hank's eyes followed the giant birds descending toward the netting.

"Golden Eyes is out in front," Hank's voice was low. "I can see the red in her crest. She's skimming down the side of the mountain like a fighter pilot. The rest of the flock are right behind her in V formation. They're gliding down, straight at the shooters, heads leaning forward, and those huge claws spread open and ready to grab them."

The guns shots kept booming throughout the valley as the men's laughter sounded high and excited.

Hank looked away from the massacre and up at the sky. "Two will attack the shooters under the net, and the other one the guy on top of the wall. Their wings are black, and tail feathers fanned out. Look at their claws. They're almost there."

He gasped loudly. "One of the birds is pulling and ripping at the first shooter! The man under the net can see what's going on, and he's trying to crawl away. Golden Eyes is circling overhead, giving out her orders. 'Get his head . . . rip his eyes out . . . he's getting away . . . stop him . . . use your claws or hit him with your wing . . . throw him down the other side of the wall . . .'"

Hank fixed his eyes on the flock's attack. "They're flying around and turning in mid-flight. They've attacked the first shooter under the net, and now he's not moving. The shooter on the wall is fighting and trying to duck, but there are too many diving at him. The man's pretty fat, and I don't think he can run very fast. Now he's batting at them with his gun. He hit one, but they're still coming at him. Golden Eyes just knocked the gun out of his hands."

A terrible scream echoed across the valley.

"What happened?" Ruby gasped.

"The man is sliding down the wall," Hank said, "and he's landed right in front of Beanstalk. He's trying to sit up. Beanstalk has his head in the man's face. He's staring right into his eyes."

Zebi listened. "The man's heartbeat is banging in his chest like a hammer. He's starting to choke. But Beanstalk's breathing is slow, and his heart is beating once every several seconds."

"I see Beanstalk opening his mouth. I think he's going to rip the man's head off. He's putting his mouth around the man's head." Hank's voice was flat and emotionless now.

"Why?" Sam stammered.

No one spoke, but they knew that their hearts were pounding in the same rhythm at the same instant.

"Maybe he's not going to rip his head off," Ruby said quietly.

"The man's heartbeat sounds like that machine gun. How can his heart go that fast?" Zebi said, turning to look at Ruby.

"I don't think it can," she said. "I think Beanstalk is doing something else to this man."

"What?" Oz didn't take his eyes off the man.

"I think he's trying to scare him to death."

"Is that possible?" Juliana asked.

"If his heart doesn't slow down, I guess it is."

Zebi held up his hand. "I can't hear it anymore. All I can hear is Beanstalk's heartbeat."

"Now the man's just lying on the ground—Beanstalk let him go," Oz said. "He's not moving—I think he's dead, probably from a heart attack."

They heard another mournful bellow from Beanstalk, rippling around the valley and up the sides of the mountains.

"He's leaving the man there and going from one brontosaurus to another, pushing them with his snout, but they're not moving. I think there are five dead. The others are coming back from the other side of the valley."

Golden Eyes startled the group when she landed beside Hank. She looked at him and cocked her head.

"Whose idea was it to call?

He pointed to Juliana.

"You're very clever." Golden Eyes said. "Let me tell you what you've done, Juliana. This is our last remaining herd of brontosauruses. We had more, but most of the older ones have died. We are grateful this attack wasn't worse."

She stared intently at Juliana, then nodded before once again leaping up into the sky.

For a moment, they all stared after her. Then Juliana spoke. "What's going to happen to the dead ones?" she asked.

"They'll be left there," Hank replied. "Predators are probably nearby right now."

He rubbed his eyes and slumped against the boulder. "What was that other sound you heard, Zebi? You said it was high-pitched and farther away."

"I can still hear it," Zebi said, "but it's faint. I can't tell where it's coming from."

Sam sniffed the air. "Are they small animals or birds?"

"Zebi—concentrate!" Ruby sounded impatient. "Is it possible there are other people over at Floppy Hat's place?"

Hank gestured for *quiet*. "I can't find it. I *feel* it, but it could be anywhere."

"I hear it again," Zebi said. "It's louder now, and I think it's coming from under those nets at Floppy Hat's."

"Maybe it's the other shooter," Hank said, "the one who got away? We know there were three men."

"Nope. There are two voices, and they're not as deep as the shooters."

"Oh no," Oz gasped. "Two children crawling out from under the net. Where'd they come from?"

Zebi spoke quietly. "I think they came from the mine. I could hear higher voices, like small children, but I couldn't figure it out." His voice was angry now. "I couldn't hear them properly because they were underground. What are they doing, Oz? Are they getting away?"

"They're trying different ways to climb down the wall, but they're holding their hands over their eyes. Maybe they're having trouble seeing in the sunlight. They look hurt, but what will they do when they get to the bottom of the wall and find themselves in the valley?" Oz looked at the movements below.

"The children are hiding behind the wall, so they're safe from any predators. Five brontosaurus bodies are lying dead, and that smell will attract predators. All that meat won't just stay there and rot." He lifted his head and motioned with his chin. "Look! They've climbed down the wall. They've stopped and are looking at the dead man. Now they're running."

"Where? Which way? Toward us?" Sam asked.

"No. They're running in circles as if they don't know what to do."

"We have to help them!" Ruby pleaded. "It's not safe for them in the valley."

"She's right," Hank looked at Sam. "We can't leave them there. Whatever we decide to do, we have to do it now."

Sam nodded in agreement. "We need a plan. We've seen enough death in the valley today."

"Oz, Zebi, and I'll go," Hank said. "We're the fastest runners. Raif will stay here with you for extra protection. Stay behind this boulder."

"Okay, Hank, but no yelling out to them, or you'll attract something. And you know how fast some of the dinosaurs can run." Sam looked at their uncomfortable faces. "What's the backup plan?"

"We'll keep our powers on alert," Hank said, "and try to see and hear and feel anything that's coming. If we run into trouble, we'll head for the mountains on either side of the valley. According to Mascan's cave drawing, this is the narrowest part of the valley so that we could run in either direction."

Sam nodded. "Not a brilliant plan, but it's a plan."

Hank was the fastest of the three. His strides were long, and he used his arms well and knew how to breathe efficiently. He turned around now and again to make sure Oz and Zebi weren't lagging too far behind. After they'd covered some distance, Hank raised his hand, and they all slowed to a trot.

"Something's coming," he said. "Not fast, but in this direction."

"How big?" Oz asked, breathing deeply.

"Not as big as Rex. It's coming up the valley toward the treehouse. Maybe something's following the path of the herd?"

"Let's make tracks," Hank said, and they sped off at full speed.

Several seconds later, they neared the mountain. They could see the dead brontosauruses now. Three of them looked young, one looked old, and the last looked like an adult. There were pools of blood on the ground around them. Glancing back over his shoulder, Hank watched for other dinosaurs. *Good. Nothing so far.*

"Where are they?" Zebi yelled. "Something's coming our way. We can't just wait here."

At first, they saw nothing. Hank stopped beside the old brontosaurus and looked at the blood that was draining out of him. They each looked in a different direction: Hank looked up toward the netting and then up the wall. Oz looked back down the valley beyond the treehouse. Zebi walked around the boulder and then cocked his right ear in the direction of the netting up above.

"Over there!" Oz said quietly. "Look."

At first, all Hank could see was the dead man lying on the ground where Beanstalk had left him. But then he saw them: two dirty-looking boys cowering behind the body, their hands over their eyes. Hank took a few steps toward them, knelt on the ground, and pointed to himself. "Hank," he said, patting his chest. "These are my friends, Oz and Zebi."

The children remained still as stone. Then the taller boy raised his head and stared.

Once again, Hank pointed to himself. "Hank,"

The second head came up.

"52," the taller boy said, pointing to himself.

"31," said the smaller one, squeaking out his words.

Hank, Oz, and Zebi stared. The children were skinny—they looked like they were starving—and they had dark circles under their eyes that stood out against their pale skin. They wore dirty rags and were barefoot, and their shaven heads showed the occasional tuft of dark hair.

Hank smiled and motioned. "Come with us."

The boys looked at each other, then up the wall, and then at the dead man lying at their feet.

Zebi spoke softly to Hank and Oz. "Something's coming up the valley. Faster now. We have to go."

But the two boys ran in the opposite direction, back towards the stone wall. The smaller one—the one who'd called himself 31—yelled as they ran: "33, 28, 44." The older boy—52—ran alongside him, also calling out numbers: "36, 10, 17, old 99." Hank tried to make out the other things he was saying, but his language, if that's what it was, was gibberish to him.

A few seconds later, the two boys were scampering like mountain goats up the stone wall.

"You're going the wrong way," Zebi yelled after them. "Come with us! We can help you."

"You'll be safe with our friends and us," Oz yelled.

But the boys kept climbing. Hank was about to run after them when, all at once, his heart started to pound in his chest. "Move! Now! Whatever's coming is just about here!"

He took one last look at the two boys, who were almost at the top of the wall, and then turned and ran. Across the valley, they could see Ruby, Sam, Juliana, and Raif starting up the mountain. A few scrubby trees were at the bottom, and giant boulders covered the hill, perhaps left behind after an old rockslide. Hank could tell those boulders were making the climbing easier. *Good. They used their powers, and they know what's coming.*

He glanced back to Oz and Zebi. "Faster!"

Hank felt his chest tightening.

Zebi pulled up even with Hank. "They're not as big as the T-rex or brontosaurus, but they're fast." He shouted. "FAST."

Then Oz was beside him too. "They've seen us," he yelled. "They're heading straight for us."

"How far?"

Zebi screamed. "JUST RUN. DON'T TRIP."

Hank watched Ruby, Sam, Juliana, and Raif climbing to a hole in the mountain. It was about the size of a pumpkin. *Was it big enough?*

Oz took a quick glance. "Two . . . maybe three minutes. I can see the dust they're kicking up."

Hank looked over his shoulders. At first, he saw nothing, then—

"Raptors," he screamed, almost tripping over his own feet. "Big ones!" They were about six feet tall. Their beaks were open, ready for attack. Even from a distance, Hank could see their enormous claws he knew would tear them apart. There were three of them and they were heading straight in their direction.

Up ahead, he saw Sam and Juliana disappear into the hole, then Ruby and Raif. *At least they made it.*

Finally, they reached the bottom of the mountain and began scrambling up the boulders. They could hear the raptors grunting and screeching angrily. Hank looked back and saw the lead raptor staring right at him. He had to move even faster! He knew they were no match for these dinosaurs.

Hank used his last bit of strength to jump from one boulder to the next. His total concentration was not tripping, not falling, but making it alive to the pumpkin hole. He could hear Oz and Zebi gasping a few feet behind him and Ruby screaming from up above: "Don't look back! You can make it!"

Hank sensed they were about two hundred feet behind them. He could hear their enormous feet smacking onto the rocks, and he knew they were closing in. Ghastly screeching sounds ricocheted off the rocks as the raptors maneuvered their way up, leaping several feet at a time.

Oz yelled. Hank glanced back and saw him climbing. Blood was running down his legs. The raptors turned toward Oz. They were about twenty feet from the hole. Ruby was screaming. "Pick him up—get him in here!"

Hank and Zebi grabbed his arms, and they half dragged, and half carried Oz. Ruby's outstretched arms reached out of the hole and grabbed Oz, and in an instant, he was inside. Zebi dove in next, and finally Hank dove in as Ruby and Sam yanked on his arms from inside. Suddenly he felt a sharp clamp like the raptor was tearing his foot off.

"IT'S GOT ME! HARDER!"

They all grabbed Hank and pulled hard. The raptor let go to get a better grip. Suddenly Hank was barreling head first and landed in a heap against the wall on the other side of the cave. They were all shaking as they pressed their bodies against the wall, staring wide-eyed through the hole at the angry screeching raptors stamping around near the opening.

An angry beak and part of a head, eyes bulging, pushed into the hole. The raptor looked straight at Hank as it snapped and spit, trying to stuff itself farther into the cave. With a final angry shriek, the raptor pulled its head out.

Inside the cave, no one made a sound. They sat still, barely breathing as they listened to the raptors clambering around on the rocks. Finally, the screeching stopped, and the sounds of claws on rocks faded away.

"They're gone," Hank sighed.

"They're not gone until we know they're gone," Oz whispered. He crawled over toward the opening.

"Don't you dare stick your head out," Ruby grabbed the back of his shirt.

Oz got as close as he could and peered out at every angle. "I see them," he whispered. "They've found the brontosauruses, and they're tearing them apart. I hope Beanstalk isn't watching."

Zebi crawled over next to Oz. "They're devouring them. I can hear them crushing their bones."

"They'll stay there until they're gorged. We're not taking any chances. We're staying here." Hank gasped, still catching his breath.

"What happened to the two kids? You left them there." Ruby asked angrily.

She started to say something else, but Sam held up his hand as if to say, "let them speak."

Hank tried to explain. "Two boys. We only saw them for a minute. Not long enough to ask them much." He glanced at Oz and Zebi, who nodded. "They were dirty and skinny and wearing rags. They squinted as if the sun was too bright, but it wasn't bright. And they didn't speak much English, but they seemed to understand what I said."

"Did they talk to you?" Ruby asked.

"They sort of spoke gibberish. When I asked their names, the bigger one pointed to himself and said 51. The other one said 31. Then they ran away. We tried to get them to come with us, but."

Ruby's voice was almost a whisper. "You couldn't, could you? Because of the raptors?"

Hank shook his head and stared at the floor.

"I watched them climbing up the stone wall," Juliana said.

"We just ran out of time." Hank sighed.

Sam took off his glasses and rubbed his eyes. "If you'd taken the time to go get them, none of you would have made it back alive."

"Their names were 31 and 52? Are you *sure* that's what they said?" Ruby asked. "What kind of names are 31 and 52?"

"Prisoners' names," Oz said quietly.

19
A QUIET NIGHT

The exhausted friends explored the new cave. It wasn't nearly as big as some of the other caves they'd been in, and Oz couldn't detect any stalagmites or stalactites. He figured humans might have made it.

"There could be other passages," Zebi looked at each of them, "but we have to stay here. At least until they leave."

"Sit down, Hank, so I can look at where it bit you," Ruby said, taking Mascan's amber egg out of her pocket.

"You're lucky. Barely a scratch and no broken bones" Ruby smiled for the first time since the attack. "You've got a bit of a cut here, and it's swelling. Keep still while I put on this ointment."

"Have you noticed that all the dinosaurs have been heading north? Why do you think that is?" Hank asked.

"Maybe it's just another one of this valley's mysteries," Sam said cleaning his glasses on his shirt.

"Are the raptors finished yet?" Juliana peered through the hole. "Have they left?"

Hank took a quick look out of the pumpkin hole and sighed. "Not yet. They're still picking at the bones."

"What about that man's body?" Juliana's quiet voice came from farther back in the cave.

Oz poked his head out. "Completely gone and Beanstalk is watching from farther up the valley."

Hank's heart sank as he leaned his back against the wall. He wondered how Beanstalk felt, watching the gory feast. Did he have feelings like a human? "Who would believe it?" he said quietly.

"Who would believe *any* of this?" Zebi muttered.

"I think there are people who *do* know," Hank said. "Think about the mine. There were men there, and at least one of them is probably still alive. And what about 31 and 52? Who are they, and how did they get there? Were they born here, or did someone bring them into this valley?"

Zebi sighed. "We have to wait here until those raptors leave. The sun will set soon, and there's no way we're going into the valley at night. We're sleeping here tonight."

A while later when everyone else was asleep, Hank sat with Raif, watching the raptors. It was their third day in the secret valley. He remembered the thunderstorm and the bear, meeting Mascan and Golden Eyes, Ruby stitching up Rex's eye, the treehouse, and the brontosauruses. He remembered how fast they'd run across the valley and the sound of the raptors' roar and the pounding of their feet. He yawned and thought about the science fair judge, and the eggs in Mrs. Plunkett's basement. As he drifted off to sleep, he wondered how it was all connected.

He awoke with a start at some point in the night and sat up quickly. Raif was beside him in an instant but remained quiet. Pulling out his flashlight, Hank checked around the cave. Everything seemed the same. His senses were on high alert, and he had no idea why. What had awakened him?

The back of his neck felt cold, and he shivered slightly.

He got up soundlessly, tiptoed to the opening of the cave, and stuck his head out. All was quiet. There wasn't a wisp of breeze, but the stars were bright, and they lit up the valley. He looked over toward Floppy Hat's: no lights, no noise. He looked north and listened for Beanstalk but heard nothing. Then he looked up at the sky, filled with bright stars, and found Orion's Belt. The six bright stars were precisely where they had been the night before. He crooked his neck and gazed up at the moon. It was three-quarters full, and along with the stars, it lit up the valley. A giant, black silhouette glided overhead. *Thank you for watching us Golden Eyes.*

He returned to his spot on the cave floor and shone his flashlight over the walls and ceiling. Nothing was out of the ordinary. Ruby's eyes blinked open.

"What's wrong?" she whispered, sitting up.

"I don't know. I feel something, but I don't know what it is, and it's bothering me. I think I'll go outside."

Seconds later, Sam, Oz, Juliana, and Zebi were awake.

"He wants to go outside," Ruby hissed . . . watching Hank.

"Not without the rest of us." Sam stood up and put on his glasses.

Moments later, they were all on the ledge outside the cave.

Hank closed his eyes to let his powers find any danger nearby. He looked at the rest of them and shook his head. *Nothing.*

They all sat cross-legged with their backs against the smooth rock, still hot from the day's sun. No one spoke.

Hank thought about 31 and 52 and their odd way of speaking. He remembered how the children had squinted at them as if the sun was too bright, and how skinny and dirty they were. But he couldn't forget the last, panicked looks on the two boys' faces.

But at that moment if Oz had used his power and looked over at Floppy Hat's, he would have seen the glint of the moon on the lens of someone's binoculars as a man hid under the broken netting. He was the only one who hadn't died in the pterodactyl attack, and now he was looking out across the valley. Oz would have seen the man's thick, dirty finger adjusting the binoculars' focus as he looked at each one of them. He would have seen the man's chin jut out in anger when his binoculars found Raif; he was afraid of Arctic wolves, and he knew this one would be a problem.

"I'll stay away from that beast it'll kill you for sure."

Oz would have seen Floppy Hat's binoculars studying Ruby, Sam, and Juliana. He would have seen him spend several seconds looking at Ruby's skull as she turned to speak to Oz and wondering what had injured her. *Too bad you're still alive. I'll meet you again one day.*

If Zebi had been using his powers, he would have heard the man crawling out of sight, dragging his legs, and cursing the horrible pterodactyls. And he would have heard him pulling the hidden door to his cave open and disappearing inside. The cave was his family's secret, and Floppy Hat, like all his relatives before him, was very good at keeping secrets.

But Oz wasn't looking, and Zebi wasn't listening. None of them were, not even Golden Eyes.

One by one, they crept back into the cave and went to sleep. Not one of them had used their powers.

At exactly midnight, Hank was jolted awake. He stayed

still for several moments listening to everyone breathing. Then he shimmied out of the pumpkin hole with his sketchbook in his mouth and sat quietly against the wall. A moment later, Raif wriggled out briefly nudged Hank with his cold nose. Hank watched the wolf's white coat as the animal moved rapidly down the mountain and continued running through the valley. He thought about whistling for him, but he knew Raif would come back. He always did.

He looked up, found the North Star, and followed it to Orion's Belt with its six bright stars. *Still safe.* He wondered when the stars would start to fade and when they would ever get out of this valley.

He looked at his sketchbook, remembering Mrs. Plunkett's advice the day he'd left for Camp Big Bear. *Keep it with you, boy. You never know when you might want to draw something.*

He flipped it open to the first page, with its drawings of the secret cave. It seemed like something from months ago, rather than a few days. He remembered looking at the sketches of teeth and claws in the first cave. He never imagined that he'd see a live plesiosaurus, T-Rex, stegosaurus, brontosaurus, and raptors in real life. He'd drawn them in great detail except for the raptors. He also knew that except for Mrs. Plunkett, and Oz, Sam, Ruby, Juliana and Zebi, he had to keep his sketches secret.

Hank rifled through the pages until he found the sketch of the rivers and his transcription of the ceiling writings in the second of Mascan's caves.

The purple will touch the crescent moon before the six entwine.

Purple? So far, he'd seen nothing purple in the valley. And how could anything touch the moon? And what six? There were six of them and six rivers. And six stars in Orion's Belt. It was a strange and difficult riddle.

The sky will rain with claws tipped with blood when danger follows close.

Could this be about Golden Eyes? He had drawn the pterodactyl's claws, blood-stained after the attacks on Floppy Hat's men and the battle with the triceratops.

Beware of knowledge not completed before you drink from the valley's nectar. They knew more now than when Zebi and Ruby had stumbled onto the first cave after the grizzly bear attack, but Hank knew there was still much to learn about this secret place. And what was the valley's nectar? Was there was a magical fruit or something that grew nearby?

Thundering rocks will charge from the ground and not the air above.

Were they going to have an earthquake or rockslide?

He flipped the pages back to the sketch of the third river—Adamas—the one he'd drawn quickly, without including some of the more minor details. They hadn't seen a waterfall yet, but there was one in the picture. Floppy Hat and his guns were keeping something secret. Could it be that they were hiding Adamas somehow? But if so, where was the waterfall? That would be hard to hide.

He heard shuffling inside. Sam popped out of the hole and sat down beside him.

"What are you doing out here all alone?"

Hank handed Sam his sketchbook. "Just looking through this and trying to figure some things out."

Sam held the book up to face the moon. He peered through his glasses. "You're good at this, Hank. I think we won the science fair because of your drawings. You just get it right. Look at this," he said, pointing to a sketch of a stegosaurus with a whirling tail and boney plates along its spine. "Now we've seen them with our own eyes, and we know these drawings are perfect."

Hank shrugged. "We won the science fair because of our whole project. You did some excellent building Sam and Ruby's research made it believable. She sure is good with her hands—she built some of the best details on the face. It all held together perfectly. And Mascan was right about your dad: he is a good engineer." He laughed softly. "When we were following you to the fair in our car, I thought one of the wings was going to break off."

"That truck ride was something else," Sam said, smiling.

"My mother yelled at my father the entire way, saying he was going too fast and that he was going to dump the whole project on the road."

"At least you have a mother and a father." His words hung in the air.

"You have your grandmother."

Hank took a deep breath. "She's not my grandmother, just some strange old lady who lives next door. She cooks for me and watches out for me. It keeps the Children's Aid Society away; they'd never let me live by myself because I'm too young. She stays in her house, and I stay in my house—by myself now that my mother's gone."

He'd finally said it. He stared off over the valley, waiting for Sam to say something. When his friend finally did speak, it wasn't what Hank had expected to hear.

"Do you ever think that maybe she's *not* just some strange old lady who happens to live next door? Maybe she's *meant* to be there." Sam took off his glasses and rubbed them clean with the corner of his shirt, squinting up at Hank.

"Yeah, maybe. But she *is* strange. You know, she never calls me anything but *boy.*

Sam shrugged and put his glasses back on. He smiled. "You think I don't have strange people in *my* family?

As Hank's laughter echoed across the valley, he thought he might tell Sam about Mrs. Plunkett's secret basement.

Then he decided that even with Sam, some secrets stayed secret.

"One more thing," Sam said. "I don't know how this is going to end, but I do know that you have to keep your sketchbook secret. No one can ever see it. You've made a record of what we've seen so far, and for some reason, I think that could be dangerous. Keep that book hidden, okay?"

Hank nodded. *Sam always was smart.*

20

A COLONY OF BATS

Long before the sun began to rise, a faint noise stirred Hank from his sleep. He kept his eyes closed, listened, and took several deep breaths to control his racing heartbeat. Then he concentrated and used his power. Was there someone else nearby? He thought about his sketchbook and then remembered that he'd put it in his secret pocket before he and Sam climbed back into the cave. That had been Mrs. Plunkett's idea. "Certain things you keep safe, boy," she had said. "Keep your secrets tucked away. I've sewn a pocket down the side of your left pant leg, just above your knee."

He opened his eyes into a slit and squinted. But he was sure someone was nearby.

He remembered Mascan's cave and how he'd opened that stone door leading out to the valley. Was there a door here they hadn't found? The early morning light came into the

pumpkin hole as Hank crawled around the perimeter of the room, peering into dark corners, and looking for any cracks in the cave wall. He heard Raif's paws land on the rock as he returned to the cave from his nighttime hunting. The wolf sniffed at the sections of the wall, his snout jerking in small movements. Hank watched him move eagerly from one area to another until, after a few minutes, Raif stopped and raised his head.

Hank crouched down and placed his hand exactly where Raif's nose had been. *There!* A loosely fitted square rock in the stone wall. As tempting as it was to open it, Hank knew he had to wait. Everyone needed to be a part of the decision. The last thing they needed was another disaster like they'd had with the plesiosaurus.

He sat with his back against the wall and waited as, one by one, the others woke up.

"I think I heard someone on the other side of this wall last night." Hank said quietly.

There were gasps of "what, where, when" as they looked around the cave.

"Raif heard it too. I started searching for a door, but he sniffed it out." Hank put his hand on Raif's head.

"Why didn't I hear anything," Zebi sounded surprised.

"Where is it?" Ruby looked around.

"In the corner over there, right behind where Zebi was sleeping."

"Is it safe?" Ruby whispered.

Juliana stuck her tongue out as her eyes swept back and forth across the walls. "I taste nothing."

Oz put his hand up. "Before we do anything, we need to agree on a plan."

Only Sam stayed quiet, his big brown eyes looking from one to the other. Hank watched him listening.

Hank stood up and walked over to the spot Raif had found. "There's probably a lever or a handle or something behind this square rock. But even with Raif here, I'm still afraid of what might be behind that wall."

Sam finally spoke up. "So, we know what we have to do, right?"

Oz was the first to answer. "Use our powers."

Sam nodded. "Always."

Sam motioned for them all to gather into a circle. One by one, they called upon the powers Mascan had given them.

Zebi spoke first. "All I hear is silence, or maybe a slight hum, but I can't be sure."

Oz squatted down and peered at the square rock. "I think I see a faint light." He reached out and wiggled a slightly loose rock but then pulled his hand back and shoved it into his pocket. "I can see the light in the crack but nothing more."

Sam inhaled and stared at the stone.

"Anything?" Ruby asked.

"I smell something," Sam answered, "but I can't tell what."

Juliana poked her tongue out and closed her eyes. "Is it like what I could taste in the air at Floppy Hat's place before they shot the brontosauruses?"

"No, I don't think so," Sam replied. "It doesn't smell like dynamite."

"Why would anyone dynamite something in the valley?" Ruby asked. "There's nothing here but dinosaurs."

"I sense something on the other side," Hank said, "but nothing dangerous. I don't feel another big dinosaur there. Maybe something much smaller? We can go in and look. If we don't see anything, we turn around and come back here. Everybody agrees?"

They all nodded.

Hank pushed the square rock, which slid away effort-lessly. Reaching into the dark, he brushed his hand along the right side of the rock and gasped. "Found it." He gently pushed on a lever, and it clicked softly. The door slid open. One by one, they stepped through the opening. They stood still and waited, allowing their eyes to adjust to the dark. Six short, thick candles stood burning in a circle on the floor. Raif growled softly.

"Mascan!" Hank whispered into the stillness.

Complete darkness began a few feet over their heads and ended who knew where. Twenty feet? A hundred? Hank shone his flashlight and shone it upward. On the right side of the cave, perfectly chiseled into the stone wall, a staircase rose on a slight curve, its upper reaches lost in the blackness.

Hank shone the beam around the cave's walls. They were plain rock—no painted murals of meandering rivers here, no bloody claws and teeth, no sayings written in an ancient script, and no names of forgotten strangers.

Ruby ran her hands over the wall at the bottom of the staircase. "I can feel each chisel mark. I wonder where this staircase goes."

"Are we alone in here?" Sam whispered.

"I don't think so." Zebi tilted his head. "I hear something breathing, short breaths as if it's small. Maybe mice? Or rats?"

"Something's flying up there," Zebi jerked his chin upward. "Probably bats."

Something swooped over their heads, and the sound of flapping wings echoed in the air around them.

"They're huge. Definitely bats!" Zebi shouted. He ducked and grabbed Ruby, covering her bare head with his jacket. "They're huge!"

"How many?" Hank yelled over the noise of wings and a strange clicking sound that was becoming louder and faster.

"A lot of them. Probably hundreds. Maybe thousands," Zebi said, still holding onto Ruby's head.

Oz screamed above the din. "They're enormous! Bigger than any bat I've ever seen."

Ruby yelled from under Zebi's jacket. "Are they attacking us? What's happening?"

"They're trying to figure out where we are. Bats use sounds to find food, but I don't think they attack humans." Zebi said.

"Maybe the small ones in *our* world don't, but who knows what these will do."

"Do you think they could be giant vampire bats?" Juliana peered at them sideways. "They suck your blood."

"How much blood do they suck?" Ruby was shouting now.

Hank tried to sound calm. "I don't know what a vampire bat looks like, but I don't get the feeling they want to suck our blood, Ruby. Calm down."

"How much blood do they suck?" Ruby yelled, stamping her foot as she burrowed her head deeper into Zebi's jacket.

"Stop it, Ruby! No one is being attacked." Hank muttered.

Hank watched as the bats' glided closer. The flickering candlelight showed hundreds, flying down toward them. He motioned to the others to form a circle around Ruby; heads tucked down onto their chests and arms around each other's shoulders. They stood completely still. One by one, the candles flickered out.

After a few minutes, Oz looked up. "Do you think they're slowing down now?"

Hank pointed his flashlight straight up and watched as a bat dove into the glow. Its mouth was wide open, with teeth bared, as its leathery wings and furry body flew straight toward his face.

Hank dropped his flashlight and threw his arms over his head a split second before the bat turned in mid-air and vanished. He heard his heart pounding—along with five others.

He raised his head and watched the bats more closely. Their bodies were at least a foot long, and many of their wingspans were up to four feet, he figured. So many were flying around that escape wasn't an option. They had become wrapped in a living, moving wall of black wings and hideous mouths.

As the bats pushed in closer, Hank could feel the rough tips of their wings as they passed. He stared in wonder at the agility and accuracy of their flying.

Each time a bat flew past, it turned its head toward him and bared its fanged teeth.

After a few minutes of watching, Hank picked up on a pattern. The bats would fly down one side of the cave, circled them, and then fly up the center before disappearing into the darkness. There were so many of them, that the movement was constant. Then, as suddenly as they had appeared, the bats vanished.

"Everyone okay?" Hank asked as the last bat disappeared, and the clicking sounds faded into a space somewhere high above them.

Ruby screamed. "Something just fell on my head!"

"I think that's bat poop," Oz said. He reached over and examined her bald spot with Hank's flashlight.

"It's called guano. It's got a lot of nitrogen in it," Sam said gently.

"I don't care *what* it's called or *what* it's got in it. Get it *off* me." Ruby shook her hair violently. "What *is* it with my head?"

Oz ripped his shirtsleeve off, spat on it, and wiped the top of Ruby's head.

"I think most of its gone," he said. "I could spit on your head and try to rub off the rest of it."

"Never mind, but thanks, Ozzie. I'll spit on your eyebrow when I take out your stitches."

"Get the candles," Hank said, pointing his flashlight at the floor. Zebi and Juliana shoved them into their pockets.

They headed back to the door. The cave with the pumpkin hole was more appealing than one filled with giant vampire bats. But when they reached the wall, the door was closed—and the release lever was gone. Hank lay on his stomach and felt around the base of the door and to either side. Ruby ran her fingers lightly over the rocks, prodding the smallest crevices. Oz searched for a glimmer of light, and Raif sniffed and pawed at the rock. *Nothing.*

"Even our powers aren't helping," Hank said.

"We have to stay in this cave, filled with swarming bats?" Juliana sighed.

"Maybe" Oz said.

"We never should have left the trees. We were safe there, and Mascan brought us our food," Ruby whined. "Even the raptors couldn't get us."

Hank smiled at her. "Maybe there's a reason we left the forest."

"We have nowhere to go but up those stairs," Sam said. "Maybe they'll lead us back out again."

Together, they inched their way back to the center of the cave, stopping and listening every few feet. Hank looked up into the blackness and then at Zebi, who shook his head. "They're quiet," Zebi said. "I only hear them breathing. Probably thousands of them."

They climbed the stairs single file with their right hands touching the wall as Sam quietly counted eighteen steps before they came to a landing. Hank aimed his flashlight up the next flight of stairs. There was no end in sight. He whistled softly, and they heard the bats start their clicking sound.

"Hank! Never whistle around a cave full of vampire bats!" Juliana hissed.

"Sorry." He shone his light around the landing. Embedded in the cave wall was a large wooden door, intricately carved with a mural of flowers.

"I don't feel anything like a handle," Ruby said, running her hand over its surface. "But the stairs lead up here, and it appears to be a door, so we have to figure out how it opens." She continued to run her hands over the carved flowers on the door. "Maybe it's a kind of puzzle, and we have to figure out how to unlock it? I've read about secret doors in castles."

Ruby leaned her forehead against the door. "Zebi, I need you to listen to the wood sliding to make sure I'm not jamming it."

Their two faces were pressed into the door as Ruby's finger tips touched and moved small bits of different flowers. Zebi listened, whispering quiet instructions:

"Not yet . . . no, that one won't work . . . yes, that will slide." Hank and the others watched as she twisted, pushed, slid, and pulled every petal, stem, or stigma, sometimes lightly, other times with more force. She moved carefully and silently from one flower to the next as Zebi whispered directions.

Hank cast his eyes upward to the dark emptiness. He

wondered how high the cave went. And how did they get out? He knew they had to leave to feed, usually at night or dusk.

As Ruby continued to prod at the door, Hank pulled out his sketchbook and started to draw the face of the bat that had dived straight at him. Juliana peered silently over his shoulder. Hank tried to remember every detail—from the length of the bat's fur to the curve of its fanged teeth. The creature appeared to lift off the page as it came to life. Hank looked over his shoulder and smiled at Juliana.

"Do you draw?"

"Sometimes," Juliana said, studying the bat carefully.

Hank flipped over to a new page.

"Are you going to draw them . . . the boys with the numbers?" she asked, leaning closer to Hank, and holding the flashlight.

"I'm going to draw the older boy first." He knelt with the sketchbook on the floor.

Juliana peered over his shoulder. The only sounds in the cave were the moving pieces of the door's flowers, Zebi whispering to Ruby, and Hank's pencil.

Hank muttered quietly as his pencil started a single line. "I start with the head shape. I use the head's outline as a kind of map. Next, I *find* the shape of the eyes." His pencil brought each detail to life. "Both boys had large, black eyes, with dark circles under them. They popped right out at you. Once I get the eyes, I can see the face in my mind. Sometimes, when I draw the eyes, I have to change the head shape." He took out his eraser and made the head shape smaller. Then he tilted his head and drew in the nose, mouth, and cheekbones. The face slowly appeared. "The ear lobes need to sit a bit lower than the end of the nose, and these dark circles need to be even darker."

His pencil worked furiously on the smallest detail. "He didn't have much hair. It was short and black, and it stuck straight up in short spikes." He squinted and moved away from the sketch. "Yes. Better."

Oz leaned in closer. "That looks just like him. Yes. That's 52!"

"Do the other one." Juliana whispered.

Hank flipped over another page. They watched as 31 gradually appeared on the page. "He was a little smaller but similar looking." He put down his pencil. "That's how I remember him." He flipped back the page to 52 again.

They stared at the two faces.

Juliana whispered, "They look kind of the same. Like brothers."

Hank's eyes widened as he turned to her. "Maybe they are." He slowly closed his sketchbook and slid it into his pocket.

Hank felt a tingly sensation on the back of his neck and knew something was watching him. He looked up into the blackness. His vision reached far enough to see a lone bat hanging upside down.

You're not the same as the others. You're so much bigger. Your wings probably reach six, maybe eight feet across. Your eyes are bright red like they're on fire. Why are you watching me?

The red-eyed bat opened its mouth, showed its fanged teeth, and emitted a series of loud, rapid clicks—*Bang-bang, bang-bang, bang-bang.* Hank peered into its mouth and shivered, and his heart hammered in his chest.

Oz, Ruby, Zebi, Juliana, and Sam looked around to see what was wrong. Ruby gasped as she followed Hank's gaze and saw the giant bat looking down on them. "It's not going to attack," Hank kept his voice calm. "I'm sure of it. It just scares me."

"We're *all* scared," Sam murmured slowly. "Now, we need to open this door."

Hank looked away and focused on Ruby. A few minutes later, she said, "Yes!"

One of the door's wooden petals made the slightest sound as it slid, wood on wood, and then stopped as it reached the end of its slide. Ruby shifted it back into its original position.

Ruby began to move her fingertips over each flower. She pushed, prodded, twisted, and pulled every piece of every flower of the door, whispering, "Here . . . yes . . . got it."

Juliana whispered to Hank. "Write down what she's doing! We may need to remember it."

Ruby's tiny, nimble fingers flew over the flower door as if she were a concert pianist running over a keyboard. With each newly discovered piece of the puzzle, she whispered, "Got it!"

Petals slid, stems turned, stigmas twisted, and leaves pushed into place.

Hank frantically drew the location and order of each piece of the puzzle.

No one bothered to look up at the single bat that had flown closer and was now hanging upside-down from a nearby wall, watching over Hank's shoulder.

The last secret flower piece was in the center of the door. Ruby pressed and twisted, and a satisfying *clunk* echoed through the cave—she'd unlocked the door.

Hank counted each step in his sketchbook. Ruby had moved at least thirty-six petals, stigmas, and stems. He looked up and held his breath as Ruby and Zebi put their fingertips on the door and slowly pushed it open.

21

THROUGH THE FLOWER DOOR

Light entered the cave on the other side of the door through a series of apple-sized holes in the ceiling. Hank thought they were ventilation shafts just like the ones in Mascan's cave. As Zebi held the candle over their heads, they stepped in, one by one.

Inside long, metal shelves were lined up and held large glass bottles with ground plants and tree bark.

"Someone's in here. I can hear breathing," Zebi whispered.

"I can *feel* them," Hank murmured back.

Raif leaped out in front of them and growled as a figure emerged from between two shelves and walked toward them.

"Well, well, here you are," Mascan's voice croaked softly.

Raif growled low and menacing.

"Raif, you are formidable indeed," Mascan smiled.

"Did I hear you near our cave last night?" Hank asked.

Mascan brushed his fingers against a row of bottles as he came closer.

"No, no. I am an old man and need my sleep." There was laughter in his voice. "And Hank, you know that I am almost completely blind. Why would I come to look at you when I barely see?"

"But Hank felt someone near us," Juliana said. "Who was it?"

"Ah, Juliana, there you are. An old friend of mine came to look in on you. I *felt* that you were all right, but I just needed to be sure."

"This is someone we can trust?" Juliana asked.

Mascan nodded. "He has helped me greatly over many years. He knows every secret tunnel in this valley and how they are all connected. His name is Drem." As he spoke, Mascan moved jars of what looked to be eggs farther back on the shelf.

"And what do you need to do now?" he asked, still moving the jars.

"We need to see the night sky and find out what Orion's Belt is saying," Hank said. "If it still says six stars, we can stay."

"But don't rush, Hank. The young are always in such a hurry, no matter what the century. There's still time to get you outside."

He walked toward them haltingly.

"Light another candle. I know my way around all my caves in the dark, but a few shafts of light from my ventilation holes isn't enough for you."

"Ruby, come here and let me feel your poor head. It *has* been taking quite a beating."

He raised his claw-like fingers and moved them gently over her hair and scalp. "It's healing well but watch this part near your neck. Perhaps a little more ointment," he said, moving his fingertips over the base of her wound. "It might give you some trouble just here. But your hair will grow back, dear Ruby. If you ever shave your head, you'll be the only person in the world with a plesiosaurus scar." He chuckled to himself.

"Remember, the ointment in my amber egg has cured many—some with small cuts and others with serious injuries." He turned to the group, his blind eyes staring. "You must keep the egg safe. Do you understand? It carries extraordinary powers and is valuable to all who hold it. It's the only one of its kind in the world. Some will try to steal it, but it may save your life one day, so keep it secret. You do know how to keep a secret, don't you?" His smile had vanished.

"How is my friend Rex?" Ruby asked. "How's his eye? No infection? I put a lot of ointment over his injury."

"Ah, poor Rex. He's old and tired like me, but I'm happy to report, he's getting stronger. That was an extraordinary battle, even for our valley. Imagine, first the stegosaurus attack, and then the triceratops almost goring him, and, in the end, Golden Eyes and her remarkable army."

Mascan slipped his fingers inside his long, flowing shirt and absentmindedly pulled out a ragged leather pouch on a braided cord. Hank saw him take a shiny stone, about the size of an egg, out of a pouch. He held it for a few seconds before sliding it back into the pouch, which fell back beneath his clothing.

"Ruby, you did Rex a remarkable service," Mascan smiled through his beard. "He will be your friend for life. You gave up all the ointment to help him, even though you and Oz still needed it. I'm proud of you, Ruby."

She looked at her shoes. "It wasn't quite like that. I'm glad Rex is getting better. The amber egg never really runs out of ointment, does it?"

"It *is* a bit of a mystery. But it hasn't ever run out, which is rather a good thing, considering your injuries."

"Where do get this ointment? Who makes it? And why is it so secret?"

"I make it—and that's all you need to know. As long as I am alive and the amber egg is in your possession, it will always contain my ointment." His voice became lighter. "Your stitches! What precision and evenness! Each stitch is spaced perfectly from the next one. Think of it. Both Oz and Rex needed stitches in a matter of hours."

"There's no infection? And Rex is getting stronger?" Ruby prodded him.

"Much better," Mascan said. "How right I was to give touch as your power. I wonder how I knew that *you* would have such talents."

Oz shivered as Mascan leaned toward him.

"Now, let's have a look at that eyebrow." Mascan closed his eyes and ran his fingertips lightly across the arch of the brow. "Excellent work, Ruby. The stitches can come out soon. There's no infection, and the two sides are holding together perfectly."

Raif jumped up and bared his teeth. The fur on his neck stood up, and his head and tail pointed stiffly. His growl rolled through the cave.

Mascan held up his hand. "It's Drem, bringing our meal. Hank, control your wolf."

Hank thought Drem was as old as Mascan, but as the man came closer, Hank saw a younger face and eyes that were not blind.

Zebi and Oz helped Drem carry the meal to the table. There were bowls of fruit and platters of steaming fish, dishes of hot potatoes, and pots of stew. A long plank of wood held different cheese and bowls of jams.

Mascan stood over them as they ate.

"Were my bats too disruptive? They gave you quite a greeting," he said, as he walked slowly around the table. Once again, Hank caught a glimpse of the leather pouch hidden in the folds of his robe.

"How can they be *your* bats?" Ruby asked. "They scared us!"

"Bats are quite friendly," Mascan replied. "They won't attack you. They're rather interesting creatures and much maligned. This particular group has been in the cave for hundreds of years, since long before I came to the valley."

"Why were they swarming us?" Sam asked.

"I suppose it was a kind of bat swarm. But remember, you were in *their* cave. My bats were seeing whether *you* were going to hurt them. They didn't hurt you. Perhaps they were just saying hello rather enthusiastically!"

Juliana spoke up. "Are they vampire bats?"

"Always so inquisitive," Mascan smiled. "Perhaps they are, although I've never seen them suck a human's blood."

"What about *the* bat? The one with red eyes who stared at me and looked three times as big as the rest?" Hank asked.

"He's *my* protector—just as Raif and Solvor are yours. This remarkable bat was born the same day I was—403 years ago. I can't remember the last time he killed anyone."

"What's his name?" Sam asked.

"Sometimes the years melt together, and it's hard to remember the details. My bat's name is very complicated, so I never use it. I have always called him INK. A few weeks after

I was born, someone gave him to my mother as a companion. He's been with me my whole life."

"And he looks out for you?"

"He does. He's fierce and loyal and clever—like Raif and Solvor." He turned his gaze toward Raif, and Hank wondered how this blind man seemed to know where they were. "It's a shame Solvor couldn't fly high enough to get over the mountains and into our valley."

"Where is Solvor now?" Hank asked.

"With Mrs. Plunkett. He stays in the big tree by the shed, watches her house, and follows her when she drives. He's a very good watchman."

"Solvor flies all around the property and keeps watch at night. Sometimes he leaves during the day, but that's when Mrs. Plunkett is studying downstairs in her secret room. Then Solvor flies off to see his community of owl protectors. He's ancient and needs to train some of the younger ones."

Hank lowered his voice, even though he knew everyone was listening. "And the eggs in Mrs. Plunkett's basement— did they hatch?"

"Of the six eggs, only one hatched. The rest never came out of their shells. We had hoped for at least three, but no, just the one. A female. Quite a good-sized and healthy one."

"When?"

"Just before you left for camp. She's getting quite big

now. Mrs. Plunkett will have to move her soon. She can't learn to fly in a basement now, can she?"

Hank stared at Mascan. "Who's eggs were they?"

"You know whose eggs they were."

"Golden Eyes?" Hank whispered.

Mascan nodded.

"Why couldn't they stay in the valley?"

"Because for many years now, one family has known a secret passage into this valley. They do terrible things here, one of which is to kill the pterodactyls. I used to think they shot them for sport, but I realize they do it to protect themselves. The pterodactyls are the only predator that can reach that place of darkness where this family does its business. The family's real name is Erebus, which means *darkness*. But they've always used the name Foster."

Foster! Hank's heart thumped—the science fair judge, the one with the three birthmarks under his eye. The one Mrs. Plunkett had warned him about. Was he connected to this man in the valley? Hank had many questions for Mascan, but he decided just to listen.

"The pterodactyls are important," Mascan continued. "They provide valley news and fly beyond the valley to find this secret. With all our powers, we cannot find how this family sneaks into the valley."

Mascan shook his head. "The damage they do here is bad enough, but the Foster family also controls something else, something deadly—maybe even more deadly than the dinosaurs."

Everyone stopped eating and stared at Mascan.

"There is a flock of giant prehistoric hummingbirds here. Their beaks are about eighteen inches long, and their wingspan about four feet. They can kill almost anything by stabbing their long, pointed beaks straight through the eyes. I've seen these hummingbirds swarm a brontosaurus and go into a frenzy of stabbing, killing in a few seconds. They only come during the hottest days of summer when the sun is bright. Nobody's seen them in years; however, several days ago, I thought I heard their distinctive humming sound."

"The eggs," Hank said.

"Exactly. The Hummers have stuck their beaks into our pterodactyl eggs in the past, and now, Golden Eyes' group is our last flock. There are twenty of these remarkable birds, and each one is precious."

"I may have heard the Hummers down the valley yesterday," Zebi said quietly.

Mascan stopped behind his chair and looked in Zebi's direction. "Perhaps you did."

"It's rare for Golden Eyes to have any eggs, but she did last year. We decided to move them one night to keep them safe," Mascan said. "Getting them over the mountains was quite an operation."

"And the fledgling?" Hank asked.

"She will stay outside our valley for a while longer. Then we will bring her back."

"How?"

Mascan said nothing. Hank waited, but Mascan didn't reply.

Ruby broke the silence. "Were 31 and 52 living in a mine at Floppy Hat's?"

Mascan nodded. "That's a good name for him. But I knew him years ago as Erebus. He would have brought them there when they were about three. Only children that small can crawl into the narrowest tunnels. Before long, the children are so traumatized and abused and starved that they forget everything, even their language."

They stared at him, horrified.

"When the children grow too big for the narrow tunnels or cause trouble, Erebus takes them out at night and throws them over the edge of the mountain. The fall usually kills them. If they survive the fall, it's a race between the sabre-toothed tigers and Golden Eyes. If Golden Eyes and her flock get there first, she carries them to caves further up the valley. However, sabre-toothed tigers prowl the valley at night, and they often get to the children first."

"What is Erebus mining?" Sam asked.

"Diamonds, his family has been doing it for about two hundred years."

Mascan retreated to a chair in the corner of the alcove. Moments later, his chin was resting on his chest, and he was asleep.

Hank couldn't stop thinking about Erebus—Mr. Foster—and their meeting at the science fair. He'd been so interested in Hank's drawing of the fifth finger. Had he somehow known then that Hank would end up here, in the secret valley?

Moments later, Mascan jolted himself awake. He looked directly at Hank.

"How did you get here, to this cave?" Hank asked.

Mascan smiled and spread his hands out. "Through one of my tunnels. This distance between this cave and the one where we first met, when you all fell through my ceiling, isn't so far. I have books with ancient drawings. I like to read with my magnifying glass." He chuckled softly. "No . . . I am not completely blind. And INK likes to be near his colony. Also, I come here if I feel I am in danger and cannot get out to the ledge or the valley. It is my sanctuary."

"It's time to visit Orion's Belt," Mascan said abruptly, drawing a compass out of the folds of his robe. "I will show you my passage through the mountain caves. There are many, but some have collapsed over time. The passage will bring you to a small, sheltered ledge on the side of the mountain. Hank, you must take notes, or you will never find your way back. Even I can get lost in these tunnels. Then INK finds me," he smiled.

Mascan turned to Ruby as her hand clutched at his arm.

"Are there any plesiosauruses?"

"No, Ruby. No plesiosauruses."

They left the dining alcove, past the flower-carved door, and toward the back of the cave. Then once again, the bats started their distinct clicking sound.

Juliana whispered, "I don't understand. We're getting farther away from them, and their clicking is getting louder. Mascan stopped and turned to the door. His old face was still and pale.

Hank watched as Mascan's hand reached into his robe, opened the pouch, and clutched the egg-sized stone. This time, Hank got a good look at it. He didn't know anything about rocks, but he could see many colors reflected in the light from ventilation holes above.

As the clicks and squeaks swelled, Hank could sense more and more bats whirling past the other side of the door. Zebi backtracked and, still holding the candle, pressed his ear against it. At the exact moment, Mascan grasped his chest. His mouth opened, and his eyes bulged.

Ruby grabbed cushions and a blanket. "Lay him down! Carefully. Here." She leaned over clutching his hand.

"What's wrong with him?" Juliana's voice was shaking.

Mascan's eyes closed. Sweat covered his face, and his lips had a bluish tinge. He clenched his fists.

"Someone's after INK," he gasped. "They know that if they find him, they'll probably find me. They're in the cave," he said, pointing a crooked finger toward the flower door.

Ruby whispered. "Quiet, Mascan. Breathe slowly. Don't speak. INK will help you."

He nodded weakly as the bats raged on the other side of the door. The sound reached an ear-splitting pitch, even louder than when the bats had swarmed them. Wings hit the door, and chattering teeth stabbed at it. Their frenetic movements continued until a shattering boom pierced the air. Moments later, the smell of dynamite drifted into their cave.

Mascan put his hands over his face. Zebi left his post by the door and knelt beside Mascan, his ear to his chest. Ruby gripped his wrist and took his pulse.

"His pulse sounds like fingers drumming on a table," Zebi held his fingertips over his wrist. "That can't be good."

Mascan lay on the ground, mouthing words in a peculiar language.

From the other side of the door, they heard a scream, loud and angry at first, then less so until all they could hear was a pathetic whimpering. Raif gave a low growl and sniffed at the door.

"How many people do you think are in the cave?" Zebi asked quietly.

Hank closed his eyes and whispered. "Only two, and one of them isn't moving now. But the other one is climbing the stairs. I think he's going to try to open the door."

They froze as a voice spoke to them from the outer cave—it was a deep bass voice, getting louder as the man climbed the stairs.

"You're in there—I can hear you. And now your loathsome bats are all dead." He laughed.

On the door, one petal slid from the locked position to the open, and then another.

What if he has a gun? Hank thought. *He could shoot Raif in a second, and we'll be unprotected.* He looked at Ruby. She eyed the door as, one by one, the man on the other side, was unlocking its secrets. She returned Hank's glance and nodded. She tiptoed over and silently slid the second petal back into its locked position. After every second or third move from the man on the other side of the door, she silently, slowly undid his work.

They all watched Ruby's nimble fingers. *Would it work?*

"Here I come!" The deep voice was laughing. The wooden door shook as the man leaned into it, trying to push it open. But it held firm. He tried it again; the door shuddered against his weight. "What?" he screamed. "How can this be? I *know* the secret to this door! And you cannot change the secret. Why isn't it working?" He banged on the door with his fists and kicked it hard. But the door didn't move.

Then his angry screams changed. "Get away from me!" he shrieked. "No! No! Get back. Get away from me. Stop! No!"

Then, silence.

Hank looked at Mascan. The color returned to his face, and he smiled weakly. "INK has found him."

"What is INK doing to him?" Ruby asked.

Mascan spoke quietly, "we will not open this door, Ruby. Do you understand?"

She nodded, still waiting for his answer.

"What do you think INK is doing?" Mascan answered softly. "He's a vampire bat. They have two chemicals in their saliva. One that prevents the blood from clotting so they can suck faster, and the other numbs their prey to keep him asleep. INK will finish soon. The man will never bother us again."

22
AFTER THE BATS

INK finished his work on the other side of the door. Mascan walked slowly stopping several times to catch his breath. He led them out of the cave and into the tunnels. Raif stayed at the rear growling softly.

Hank watched Mascan navigate turns in the dark tunnels, fingertips brushing the walls, each step slow and careful. He used no cane, but he knew exactly where to grab hold of every bit of rock that would help him through the maze. Each time Mascan stopped, he reached into his robe and held the mysterious stone. After each stop, Mascan's wheezing and coughing lessened. He stood a little straighter, and for the first minute or two, walked a little faster.

No one spoke as they found their way through the winding dark tunnels. Even Mascan was quiet. His expression was sad, and his shoulders drooped. When he finally did speak, his voice quivered.

"How could they have done it?" He sighed. "One stick of dynamite kills a colony that has lived in that cave for centuries. My bats rarely bothered a human, and they had the most organized life! I admired them. Such interesting creatures, and such good companions, once they got to know me. They had extraordinary skills. How I will miss my bats."

Hank spoke quietly. "But they didn't kill INK. He's still alive. We heard him on the other side of the door."

Mascan's old eyes twinkled. "My old friend," he chuckled.

"Did I tell you that INK and I met Napoleon Bonaparte once? What a marvelous time that was! We visited him on Elba Island in 1814 after the French had sent him into exile. Of course, I refused to call him Emperor, which annoyed him, but he was fascinated by INK. He would come and watch INK fly around Elba's shores at night. He was desperate to escape and return to France, and he thought INK might carry him off the island." He laughed. "INK stole one of his rings—gold with a magnificent ruby. INK has always liked shiny stones."

They continued through the tunnels, listening to Mascan's labored breathing.

"Does INK ever come through the tunnels with you?" Hank asked.

"Sometimes. INK is too big to fly through, so he sits on my shoulder. Most of the time, he flies out through the bats' escape tunnel at the top of their cave." He stopped and leaned against a wall, gasping and coughing.

"Have you ever been up to the top of the cave?" Hank asked.

Mascan's voice was grave and forceful. "Don't *ever* climb to the top of that staircase. Never. You must promise me." He shook Hank's shoulder.

"Why? What's up there?" Hank asked. "That might be the only way for us to get out one day."

Mascan turned and spoke to all of them. "There are things in this valley you don't need to know. Terrible things. You must all promise me you'll stay away from that staircase." He started walking again. "INK wouldn't ever allow it."

"We've seen you several times now," Juliana said, "but this is the first time we've seen INK. Why?"

"He has his haunts. He loves to go out at dusk, just after the sun has set, and flies for hours. Sometimes he's not with me. But if I'm in harm's way, his powerful wings can bring him back in seconds."

From the back of the line, Sam's voice rang out. "Bat!" In a rush of air, something flew past; it happened so fast that Ruby couldn't even cover her head.

"There are more coming through the tunnel," Zebi yelled as bats zoomed by them.

"Isn't this marvelous! Bats! I wonder how many survived." Mascan voice seemed stronger, and he started walking faster.

Sam spoke up from behind. "I smell the fresh air. We must be close to a way out."

"Yes, perhaps a hundred feet, Sam. Watch now, Hank, two more turns; this one's easy to miss. Remember to listen for the waterfall. It's somewhere over to the right, deep in the rock. You must hear the waterfall before you go outside. If you don't, you're following the wrong tunnel."

"I hear it!" Zebi said. "It's small, probably only a few feet wide. Where does it come out?"

Mascan stopped and clasped his stone. He fought for breath and gasped heavily. "No one knows. I've never seen any evidence of a river in this cave, but there must be one. That waterfall has been flowing as long as I can remember, but we've never found the source."

"You shouldn't be in this tunnel. This air isn't good for your lungs," Ruby said.

Mascan's coughing stopped as Hank watched him once again transform himself and wondered. *What power does that stone have?*

"Hank, help me climb this last bit." Hank almost carried him the last few feet. Then, all at once, they were outside on a ledge overlooking the valley.

Overhead Orion's Belt shone like a beacon.

"It still has six bright stars. We're safe here for now."

"Well done, Oz," Mascan said. "You use your power well. Remember to watch for even the slightest dimming of any of the six stars. If one of them is gone, you *must* get out of the valley before the sun sets on the following day. I am going to leave you here now. I must return to my work and check on INK. He'll be missing his colony."

Mascan put his hand on Hank's shoulder. "The next cave is just along this pathway, beyond that boulder." He shook his raised hand as Ruby started to speak. "No, Ruby. There are no plesiosauruses. I would take you there myself, but I'm afraid I must return to my cave now. I need to rest."

With a final nod to the direction they were to walk, Mascan turned and re-entered the tunnel. For a few moments, they watched as he walked away until the darkness eventually swallowed him. Once again, they were on their own.

23
TIME TO FLY

Hank peered down the ledge toward the boulder Mascan had pointed out. He could hear faint voices coming from that direction.

"There are other people in there," Hank said. "Perhaps four or five. Zebi, can you hear them?"

"They're speaking a combination of English and what sounds like the language 31 and 52 were speaking.

"I see a faint light," Oz said. "Maybe from a campfire?"

"Ozzie, can you see any guns?" Ruby asked.

"Nope, no guns."

Everything seemed quiet as they looked down into the valley. The darkness stretched out a few hundred feet beneath them.

"How is it that it looks so peaceful and normal now, and in the daylight . . . who would believe what's here?" Sam said.

A bat flew past and then veered off in another direction.

Juliana gazed across the darkness. "Do you think there are other places with secret valleys of dinosaurs? If this one exists, why can't there be more?"

No one answered. Hank couldn't imagine another place like this anywhere, but then he would never have imagined this place either.

"Should we head over to the cave? It's where Mascan wants us to go."

Everyone nodded. As Hank took the lead, inching along the ledge with Raif at his side, he could see Golden Eyes circling overhead. As the single-file line drew closer to the boulder, the voices got louder. Hank wished there was a way to warn them they were coming, but he didn't want to call out. Who knew what that might attract? And so, he slipped quietly around the boulder—and came face to face with five people, standing in the entrance to the cave, seemingly waiting for them. They wore oddly fitting clothing, most of which looked too big. A fire blazed behind them.

"I smell meat roasting," Sam murmured.

Raif growled and bared his teeth. All five of the people stepped back behind a wooden table.

A tall woman with few teeth and bright orange hair spoke. "You are the six? Mascan says you have come."

"Who are you?" Juliana stepped forward.

"Our cave." She gestured to the back of the cave, full of crude furniture and clotheslines heavy with old blankets.

"Celia." She pointed to herself. "You must eat," and gestured for the others to offer them their stools.

A short man stepped forward. "Joe. Come—sit and eat. We cook beast." He took out six misshapen wooden bowls and crude wooden spoons.

The friends sat down, eagerly digging in. Celia smiled.

Hank looked closely at each one and turned back to Celia. "How old are you? When is your birthday?"

"What is birthday? I am nothing old; I am nothing young. I stay in between."

"Where is your family?" asked Sam.

"What is family?" The man who answered sat farther back in the cave. He had a nervous look and was sucking his thumb.

"Mothers, fathers, sisters, brothers, sons, daughters, grandparents, cousins."

"We do not know these people. We know only us and others in the valley." He jerked his head north, up the valley. "We stay here. Our cave. Safe here. Mascan here. INK watches. Beasts don't come up here. Rocks too high."

"How many others in the valley?" Hank asked, scraping the last bits of stew from his bowl.

"Live in many caves on the highest mountain. Beasts

come near to them. They fight with beasts. Sometimes fight with others." He stopped and looked nervously at the others as if he might be saying too much.

"Do you go to Mascan's tunnels?" Juliana asked Celia.

"Mascan looks at plants. We don't know these things. Sometimes others look to find Mascan. He hides in cave. Mascan smart."

"Why do they look for Mascan?"

"Mascan carries Stone of Life. Much wanted. INK watches for Mascan. INK kills bad ones who look for Mascan."

Hank asked her if they knew where the waterfall in Mascan's cave led. She stared at him and shook her head.

"No waterfall. Much danger. Only Mascan go into tunnel." She pointed to Joe and another woman. "Now Joe has broken sleep. Much danger before. Must sleep to chase away bad."

She led them all farther into the cave, where a fire blazed. A small tunnel pulled the smoke up and away from the main living area. Long bones, a large set of teeth, and tree limbs lined the shelves on the walls. There was a piece of meat on a spit. Hank peered at it closely, then looked at Ruby. *T-rex?*

There were many other types of teeth, too, some threaded onto a necklace and others carefully arranged into their piles. Ruby pointed to a jawbone that looked like it came from a raptor. There was a hide with feathers threaded through it.

Behind the fire was a small, pile of sandals made of woven grass. The five strangers moved to the back of the cave. Suddenly, Raif bolted out of the cave, a white blur flashing past them. Hank rushed out and looked up.

Golden Eyes circled overhead, accompanied by many of her flock. She landed on the ledge just outside of the cave.

"Call off your beast. He is unwelcome."

Hank signaled for Raif to move closer to him. "Hello, Golden Eyes. How did you know where we were?"

She snorted and made her usual gasping sound. "We always know where you are, all of you."

Hank looked over his shoulder. Oz, Ruby, Sam, Juliana, and Zebi had crowded around him.

"Why are you here, then?"

"It is time for you to see more of our valley. Many of our walking beasts are traveling north. You must see this migration, each mountain, and how the rivers run above and below the ground. And you must also see our waterfall. It holds many secrets."

"When do we leave?" Hank smiled.

"Only you, Hank. The others in my flock fear they may be unable to carry a human. We like to fly high and with great speed. Sometimes, as you know, we fly above the clouds, but most of all, we like to fly over water. You will come with me, and my army will fly with us."

"What are you going to show me?"

"Are you afraid?"

"Of course, I'm afraid! I don't know where we're going or why. I don't even know if you can carry me. What happens if you drop me?"

She expelled several short breaths. "Why do the young ask so many questions? We will leave at daybreak and fly in a zigzag pattern up the length of the valley. I wish you to see it from above. You cannot understand this valley if you only see it from the ground. And yes, I can carry you. I have carried others bigger than you."

"Are you *sure* you won't drop him?" Sam asked.

"No, I'm not sure, but I believe it will be fine as long as he doesn't move too much or lean over too far. We have protected many in this valley, and most have lived to speak about it—although usually in secret."

Hank studied Golden Eyes. "How will you be able to take off with me on your back? I weigh more than you do.

"You weigh more than my actual body, but not when combined with my wings. I take off in a low glide. You will run beside me, and as I gather speed, you will jump on my back."

That night, the five cave dwellers gave up their beds for the visitors. They slept on furs spread on the floor in front of the last fire embers, while Ruby and Juliana shared the bed closest to the fire.

Hank tossed and turned. Golden Eyes' instructions had been simple enough, but he shivered as he thought about what he would do. *I'm going to run along beside the queen of the pterodactyls and then take a giant leap, fling my left leg over her back, and we'll take off. What would Mrs. Plunkett say?* Somehow, he knew the answer. The beating of his heart promptly sped up, and he felt a thump in his throat. The others woke and looked at him as they rubbed their eyes.

"It's okay," he said. "Go back to sleep." He gave them a half-hearted smile and a thumbs-up. They went back to sleep except for Sam, who got out of bed, put on his glasses, and sat beside Hank.

"Look at what we've done here in the last few days," he said quietly. "Mascan wouldn't have brought us to this cave or introduced us to Golden Eyes if it wasn't safe."

"Are you sure?"

Sam squinted at Hank. "I don't know why, but I trust her. Don't you?"

Hank shrugged and raised his eyebrows. "Would you ride on the back of a pterodactyl?"

Sam chuckled. "Remember when we were building our science project in my garage? Remember all of Ruby's research and your drawings? We thought it was so big! Who'd have thought we'd be here tonight on the side of a mountain, sharing a cave with strangers, looking out over a secret valley of dinosaurs, and talking about riding on a pterodactyl's back?"

"You haven't answered my question. Would *you* ride on Golden Eyes' back?"

Sam rested his chin on his fist. "Yes and no. Yes, because I *do* trust Mascan, but no matter how extraordinary Golden Eyes is, she's still a predator." Hank's eyes widened, and his heart started to pound again. Sam patted his arm. "Mascan will not put you in danger. Just don't mess with her. Do what she says. If she says she's carried bigger people than you, then it should be okay. But as for me, no, I think I'd be so nervous that I'd probably lean over and drop my glasses or, even worse, fall off."

Over on her mat, Ruby sat up. "Think of this as a big test, Hank. You need your sleep before every test, or you can fail. Both of you, be quiet and go to sleep." She lay back down and pulled Zebi's jacket over her head.

Hank could hear her deep, low, shrieking voice—*EEEE*—in that hazy state between slumber and consciousness. The night air had been cold on the mountain, and he was finally comfortable. The bed's warmth pulled him gently back into sleep, but she called to him again, this time more insistently—*EEEEEEEEE . . .*

He crawled out of bed, wondering again what was ahead of him. As he pulled on his clothes, one thought lodged in his mind: *Time to fly.*

Standing on the ledge just outside the cave, he watched

as Golden Eyes flew low over a small patch of grass on the side of the mountain where the cave people planted root vegetables. The first sliver of the sun rose behind her, and for a moment, her immense wings eclipsed its bright orange rays. Her flock flew higher in two lines, waiting for her.

Hank wondered if Mascan knew he was about to fly. *Of course he knows.*

Golden Eyes circled wide and glided slowly into her landing. Looking at him with her piercing golden eyes, she said, "Ready?"

It was more of a command than a question.

"Now we fly." She ran a few steps, with Hank running alongside. When she gave a slight nod of her enormous head, Hank slung his left leg over her back, and she jumped into the air. No one saw them take off except Raif.

It had rained overnight in the valley; the ground was softer, and the colors were darker. For just a moment, Hank wondered if Golden Eyes might drop him somewhere over the herds of beasts below. He shook his head. *Bad thoughts are dangerous.*

The rest of the flock flew on either side of them. Hank noticed their beady eyes and the way they looked at him, as if they were hungry. Why had he agreed to something this dangerous? Was this a mistake? Not for the first time, he wondered if he'd ever make it out of the valley alive.

He looked back down at Raif, who was watching him lift off into the morning mist. The sun was burning off the dew on the grass, and his bare feet felt cold and wet in the chilly air.

The sensation of moving silently and weightlessly away from the ground was astonishing. The earth was receding beneath him, leaving him feeling both elated and terrified. At first, he didn't move a muscle—he was too scared. But eventually, he dug his knees into Golden Eyes' sides, trying to hold on.

"Don't hug me so closely with your knees!" Golden Eyes shrieked. "You'll push the air out of my chest. Tuck your head down behind my crest. Your hands are too tight around my neck. Listen to me, young Hank!"

He did his best to follow her directions. Loosening his hands and relaxing his knees made his heartbeat even faster.

So, *this* was flying! He took several deep breaths.

The pterodactyls' wings made a kind of *whoomph* sound as the air passed by, creating small bits of turbulence around them. Golden Eyes navigated easily, and little by little, Hank began to relax. Finally, he worked up the courage to look down at the land below. The sun hit the western side of the mountain range and almost blinded him. As he adjusted his legs, Golden Eyes threw him a quick look over her right-wing. He knew he would never forget her large, wise eyes—eyes that could so quickly fill with kindness. It was unlike anything he'd ever experienced.

Hank noticed no other birds were flying. *Probably because the pterodactyls were predators.* The thought made him nervous: the last thing he wanted right now was an air fight. For an instant, he thought about the Hummers, but he forced that thought out of his head.

Golden Eyes and her flock glided in two lines over the valley, and Hank could see their long shadows skimming over the land. He noticed a few rabbits ahead of them, racing to avoid the pterodactyls. Golden Eyes stayed a hundred feet above land, but the rest of the flock flew low, their wingtips almost touching the ground, claws outstretched, and heads thrust forward, their eyes locked on their prey. One of the rabbits dove into a hole between some rocks, but two others kept running. Two pterodactyls adjusted their wings, reached down, and grabbed them as they ran for their lives. They did it effortlessly, and Hank felt a little sick to his stomach as the hunters swallowed the rabbits quickly and in mid-flight.

"They are hungry, young Hank," said Golden Eyes, somehow sensing his discomfort. "You have seen much worse in this valley of ours."

"Yes, but it's just . . . I've never killed anything." He tried to push the images of the kill out of this head.

"Others of your kind do this without feeling. We rarely kill except for food."

"How many others of *my kind* are in the valley?" Hank asked. "Celia said there were more of us, further down the valley. Will we see them?"

"Perhaps. One never knows when *your kind* will leave their caves. We do not fly too close to them because they have guns. They have killed some of our flock before."

After gliding for several minutes, they arrived at the valley's west side and landed on a wide ledge jutting out from the mountain's sheer face. It was the same fork-topped mountain where they'd seen Floppy Hat, but further to the north.

Hank jumped off Golden Eyes and stretched his legs. The other birds were landing, and he watched as they slowed down and navigated the air currents. He noticed no signs of the dead rabbits other than a bit of blood on the beak of one of the birds.

"Why are we stopping?" he asked. "Is it safe?"

"There is no place truly safe in this valley," Golden Eyes said. "Not even Mascan's cave is safe anymore. But I need to rest. Humans are heavy, and it is not natural for us to be beasts of burden. As you saw, we usually eat anything we carry."

Hank felt a chill run up his spine, and his heart thumped in his chest as the flock of pterodactyls gathered around him.

Golden Eyes glared at him. "Stop it, Hank. We will not

hurt you, and you are disturbing *your* group with your pounding heart."

Hank nodded and took several deep breaths to slow his pulse.

A pterodactyl approached Golden Eyes and opened her beak. Inside lay the bloody hind portion of a rabbit. Golden Eyes looked pleased and snatched it, swallowing it whole.

She turned and addressed the flock.

"A good morsel so early in the morning. Perhaps there will be more rabbits to fill our stomachs. You must fly like the owls we see when above the clouds. That is how you become a great hunter. Owls have serrated feathers, and wings for funneling the air. They fly silently. We do not have those advantages, but we have other things: our strength and ability to glide on our great wings. We must try to be silent. That and our claws will be our greatest weapons."

She glanced over at Hank. "Are you hungry?"

He was fighting the urge to throw up. He wanted to get away from these dangerous birds and their dead rabbits and return to the cave. All at once, coming with Golden Eyes and her flock felt like a terrible mistake.

"We have flown low and stayed away from the clouds," she said. "I know I can hold on to you, and you can keep your balance. It will be different than your first ride. We will fly higher and closer to the clouds. Remember, I flew slowly and was gentle. There is much to see in our valley, and while we'll start slowly, we'll soon fly faster and higher. The sun is rising, the sky will be clear, and the man with the gun has disappeared again. Are you ready?"

He met her gaze and nodded. She started her peculiar movement across the small ledge. Looking over her shoulder at him, she began to pick up speed.

"Run now!" she screeched, half running and half jumping toward the edge of the cliff.

He sprinted after her, pushed off with his right foot, slung his left leg over her back, and grabbed her neck. He was on. At that same instant, she leaped off the edge of the cliff and flapped her enormous wings. Once again, they were airborne. Behind him, he heard a rustle of wings as the rest of the flock took off. As Golden Eyes flew higher, Hank looked down and saw things on the ground become smaller. He didn't know why, but this was not as frightening as the first time they'd taken off.

After several moments of climbing, he turned and saw the flock struggling to keep up.

Golden Eyes also watched them as they flew.

"Concentrate on the power in your wings! Use each movement to force the air down. Harder . . . harder . . . fast er! Push the air away!" She screeched as she flew higher. "I carry this heavy boy, and still, I am faster than you. Maybe

I'll make one of you carry him next time. You will sink like a stone into the mouths of the beasts below! *Now fly!*"

Hank could hear them, breathless and panting, uttering the same *EEEEEEEE* sound that had roused him from his sleep, all the while staring up at Golden Eyes and then at him. Gradually, the gap between them lessened. He could hear them grunting and the sound of the air moving through their wings. Finally, after several minutes, they caught up.

"We will climb slowly, young Hank," Golden Eyes instructed. "I don't want you lacking in oxygen and getting dizzy. You might fall off."

He took a deep breath and held on a little tighter.

"What did you bring with you?" she asked.

"Nothing."

"Don't lie to me! I can feel something in your left-rear pocket. The air is not moving as well off that side of me. What is it?"

"I forgot—it's my book. I always have it with me."

"I know it's a book. I can feel it. What *kind* of book?

Sam's warning rang in his ears. *Just don't mess with her. Do what she says.* But Sam was back in the cave, and Hank was riding on Golden Eyes' back. She could drop him anywhere at any time. And she had told him twice not to lie to her.

"It's my sketchbook."

"What do you draw? Paintings like in Mascan's cave?

"Sometimes," he said. "I just draw what I like, what I find interesting. Mrs. Plunkett gave me this book just before I left."

"How is Mrs. Plunkett?"

"She's old, but I think she's okay. She told me that I might find something interesting to draw."

Golden Eyes made a hiccupping sound that Hank took for laughter.

"Imagine!" she said. "Something to draw in this valley!"

Hank reached back and put his hand protectively over his sketchbook. Remembering what Sam had said, he did up the button to his pocket and felt a little better. He was supposed to keep his sketchbook a secret and now he had told Golden Eyes. The least he could do was to keep it safe.

They flew in silence for several more minutes

"Will you show me your drawings?" she asked.

Hank thought about her question. What could he say to a pterodactyl who carried him over the secret valley of the dinosaurs? She could drop him, and he'd break his bones. Or perhaps she'd drop him over a herd of ferocious raptors. Hank wondered where the raptors were. He shivered, remembering their race to the pumpkin-hole cave. He tried not to think of the raptors' horrible, gaping beaks pecking at them inside the cave.

"I'm waiting for your answer, young Hank." Golden Eyes

wiggled her body as if she were thinking of throwing him off. But he didn't believe he was in any danger.

She won't throw me off. I'm part of something here, and she wants me to stay. She wants me to live! The idea that she might like him made him smile. *Imagine having a pterodactyl as a friend!*

"You are laughing, young Hank. Are you not afraid of me? Do you not think that I will throw you off?"

"No, I don't," he replied. "Why would you go to all this trouble and then kill me? You want to show me something just as much as I want to see it."

"You are wise. Wisdom is to be cherished and used sparingly, not as a sword in a fight." They flew for several more minutes in silence.

"Did you ask me about Mrs. Plunkett because you wanted to find out more about the six mysterious eggs?"

Golden Eyes kept flying and remained quiet.

"Because if that's why, I can tell you what I found in her basement."

The only sound was the flapping of her wings as they soared across the valley. The other pterodactyls were far behind them again, and it seemed as if they were alone.

"I went downstairs looking for food. My mother was gone. I was alone. Mrs. Plunkett went to a clinic and was supposed to be back in three days. But she was away for longer. Then I twisted my ankle. Then I ran out of food."

"And Raif and Solvor found you and became your protectors," she finally spoke. "How fortunate, young Hank. It is not safe to be young and alone. Even we beasts here in the valley know about protecting our young."

He shivered as they got closer to a small herd of raptors.

How did she know these things? The earth beneath them fell out of focus as his thoughts distracted him, and he struggled to recover his balance.

"Hold on, young Hank! Concentrate. I am not so good at catching things in mid-flight. I could not see what was inside the house on that night," she said. "I circled high, watching, and waiting. I knew you had gone to the basement, and I wondered what you would think of the things you found there. Mrs. Plunkett has kept it secret for too many years."

She stopped talking, waiting for Hank to speak.

"When I first opened the door into the secret room, I thought the filled shelves were with fossils. But when I looked closely at them, I realized they were bones. They hadn't been alive 75 million years ago; they had been alive much more recently. My ankle was sore, and I was afraid I'd fall, and then no one would find me, so I was careful. I got to the back of the room and heard a buzzing sound. That's when I found the hidden room. And that's where I saw them."

"The six eggs?" Her voice was softer.

"Yes, but only one of them was moving—rocking back and forth. I wanted to touch it, but I didn't. I was afraid I'd hurt it. I watched it for a long time, wondering what it was. Last night Mascan told us these were your eggs."

"Yes. My six eggs and only one of them lived. I hoped more would hatch, but it was not to be. Tell me, young Hank, was the rocking strong or weak?"

"I don't know. The egg moved in a rhythm. Back and forth, and then a stop, and then back and forth again. I didn't see any cracks in the egg, and I didn't hear any sound coming from it. When I was thinking of touching it, I put my hand out, but the rocking stopped. Almost as if whatever was inside the egg knew I was there. I drew a sketch of it."

The even slow rhythm of her wings changed, and she spun her head around to look at him.

"You drew a picture of my egg?"

Hank grabbed her neck and instinctively squeezed his knees into her sides. His heart raced, and he thought about the others in the cave.

"Show it to me," Golden Eyes demanded. "I must see my egg."

She flew faster, almost recklessly. Hank watched them fall even farther behind. Then she headed for a large, tall boulder in the middle of the valley.

We can't land here! But the boulder got bigger and nearer, and they landed with a soft thump.

"Is this safe? We're out in the open. What happens if something finds us before we have a chance to take off?"

Golden Eyes said nothing.

The flock approached the boulder. "Stay near, in your line formation, like I taught you." Golden Eyes screeched. "Alert me if anything comes near."

He knew what she wanted. With his hands shaking, he pulled his sketchbook out of his pocket. She stood close to him, breathing heavily, and peering over his shoulder. He flipped it open to the first page, where he'd drawn the egg from memory. He'd wanted it with him on his trip, and Mrs. Plunkett had taken his original. His sketch caught the sunlight perfectly. Golden Eyes gasped, and he turned to look into her eyes as she gazed at the page.

"Did it have those rough bumps, just as you've drawn? And where those brown spots around the bottom?"

"Exactly like that. I drew it as accurately as I could. What does this drawing say to you?"

She ignored his question. "How many brown spots were around the bottom of the egg?"

He closed his eyes. "I could see four—exactly what I drew. I didn't move the egg. There might have been more underneath it. What do the spots mean to you?"

She looked out over the quiet valley, still and silent.

He stood beside her on the top of the boulder and waited. The sun had fully risen over the valley; the colors were bright and the air warm. He looked up at the flock, still divided into two groups. Like good sentries, they flew in expanding circles over the boulder.

As Golden Eyes stared into the distance, he began to wonder if he was right to tell her about the sketchbook. But he was pretty sure she'd known about it long before she had sensed it in his pocket. He left her to her thoughts and looked at the boulder where they were standing. Peering over the edge, he figured it was about ten feet high. His eyes followed the black stripes that cut through the surface, and he wondered if it was molten rock left here after the Ice Age. It was strange to have a boulder sitting alone in the middle of a valley, wasn't it? But then, what wasn't strange in this valley?

He glanced over his shoulder at Golden Eyes. There were no screeching orders, no insults, no demands.

Finally, she turned to him. "The spots tell me that my fledgling is strong. She will be a good leader."

Up above, one of the smaller pterodactyls broke the formation and flew off down the valley, screeching loudly. A moment later, the entire flock changed its course. Hank looked around. At first, he saw nothing. There was grass, smaller rocks, a few trees, and what looked like a dry riverbed.

But the screeching continued, and the pterodactyls continued to fly in the same direction.

And then they heard it: a roar that ripped through Hank's chest and blocked his ears. This wasn't a T-rex or a triceratops, or even a stegosaurus—Hank already knew those sounds—and it certainly wasn't the high-pitched shrieking of the raptors. No, this was a big cat. He knew what mountain lions sounded like at night behind his house, back on Mrs. Plunkett's piece of land. But this howl was much louder and deeper as if it came from a much bigger animal. There was more than one animal and they were coming up the valley, straight toward them! Hank shoved his sketchbook into his pocket and squinted into the sun, waiting.

The sound jolted Golden Eyes from her thoughts.

"She turned quickly and peered at him. "We are in trouble—those are sabre-toothed tigers—three of them. We need to get off this rock *now*; they can easily jump up here. We have one chance: I take three steps, and you jump on. Remember?"

Hank nodded, his knees trembling so hard they knocked together.

As the tigers roared into view, bounding toward the boulder, Hank couldn't imagine moving at all; he felt as though his throat had closed and his legs had turned to rubber.

"Concentrate!" Golden Eyes screamed. "One, two, three—jump!"

It wasn't a good jump. As Hank clung to Golden Eyes' back, half on and half off, she struggled to hold him up. She frantically flapped her wings but couldn't fully lift them. Hank's heart pounded as she seemed to lose her strength.

They half flew, and half fell off the end of the boulder and dropped like a stone. Golden Eyes hit the ground with her claws, digging deep ruts into the earth as she skidded to a stop. Hank looked up at where they'd been—nearly ten feet above the ground. One of the tigers jumped to the top of the boulder; the other two followed closely behind. The cat crouched, his tail swishing back and forth. *This one will attack first.*

The tiger's two incisor teeth were massive, and his jaw was open wide, like a snake.

"Hold on!" Golden Eyes screeched again, running forward then hopping several steps.

Hank wanted to close his eyes, but the tiger's open jaws and long teeth transfixed him. Golden Eyes flapped her mighty wings, and they rose a few feet off the ground. Roaring and showing his teeth, the cat leaped high into the air.

For a moment, Hank thought they were clear, but then he felt it—a downward tug that threatened to pull them back to earth. The tiger's incisors caught the tip of Golden Eyes' tail.

Enraged, Golden Eyes fought harder. Each flap of her wings propelled them another few feet, but the tiger held on, its teeth piercing her tail. Somehow, she was carrying Hank as well as the enormous tiger. When Hank looked back, he could see Golden Eyes was bleeding. Still, she fought and flew higher, and still, the tiger held on.

From out of nowhere, two of the smaller pterodactyls flew beside them and dove into the tiger's neck. It roared and batted them away with his front claws while its jaws clamped onto Golden Eyes' tail. The pterodactyls circled and hit him again, ripping at his fur and stabbing their beaks at his eyes.

Far below on the valley floor, Hank could see the other two cats running after them, flicking their tails, and waiting for their bloody meal to drop from the sky. He wondered how far Golden Eyes could fly carrying such a heavy load. The tiger roared again as one of the pterodactyls drew blood. The flock struck from below, tearing at the tiger's stomach. The tiger roared and batted at them as he continued to swing from the end of her tail.

"He's letting go!" Hank screamed. But even with its mouth wide open, the tiger wasn't falling. Hank looked closer, and his heart froze: the tiger *couldn't* let go—its foot-long incisors were stuck in Golden Eyes' tail like two long spikes. The tiger twisted frantically, trying to release itself, but its spikes stayed attached to her tail.

Hank knew each time Golden Eyes flapped her wings, she was getting weaker. He knew she couldn't land or fly for much longer. He also knew they would both die if the tiger continued to hold on.

The sounds of Golden Eyes' screeching jolted him. "Turn around and kick the teeth. Hard!" she screamed. "The teeth will break."

Hank stared at her, speechless. *Kick a sabre-toothed tiger in the mouth and knock out its teeth?*

"Do it *now!*"

Hank turned around on Golden Eyes' back, so he was facing backward—eye to eye with the giant cat. He looked into its angry face with its eyes gleaming and curled upper lip. Its front paws were no longer swiping at the other pterodactyls—they were clawing up Golden Eyes' tail. Hank could see the blood on its fur and the spit oozing out of its mouth. He didn't have much time.

Hank leaned back, holding onto the giant bird with both hands. He clenched his jaw, aimed his right heel directly at the tiger's incisor, and kicked hard. His heel hit the tooth but not hard enough to break it.

The cat snarled and roared. Hank was so close that he felt the spray of the cat's bloody breath.

"Again! Harder!" Golden Eyes' voice was raspy, and her breath came in gasps. Even without looking, Hank could tell that they were dropping.

Once again, he focused on the teeth. He heard and

saw nothing other than the two-foot-long incisors piercing Golden Eyes' tail. He took a deep breath and smashed his heel into the tooth. The second his foot hit, he heard a loud, cracking sound: the tooth broke in two. The tiger blinked and roared, its spittle landing on Hank's face.

"Kick the other one! Faster—I'm falling!" Golden Eyes screamed again.

Hank kicked and struck a second time and a third. Each kick was harder and faster than the last. Finally, the second tooth broke and released the tiger's bloody jaw. Just before it fell, the tiger's eyes widened, and it roared and sprayed more spittle directly into Hank's face.

For a split second, Hank felt safe. The tiger was falling, and Golden Eyes was still flying with him still on her back.

But the next instant Hank saw his sketchbook tumbling through the air toward the tiger's face. It flipped open to the page with the six rivers. Then it hit the tiger's face and kept falling, turning over and over, as different sketches appeared and disappeared in the air.

The tiger landed, and the sketchbook smacked him right on the side of its bloody jaw. The tiger looked up, roaring and pawing the air as it struggled to its feet. A few moments later the three tigers were prancing and roaring beneath them.

The next instant, Hank stared at his sketchbook, now red with blood, lying open on the ground. A light breeze flipped the pages. He held his breath as he and Golden Eyes flew farther and farther away. A few moments later, he could no longer see it.

Golden Eyes panted and gasped as the blood still bled from her tail. Hank watched as it dropped in strange red patterns, hitting the ground in splats. The tigers ran after it, jumping into the air and snapping at the drops of blood.

"I cannot fly much farther," she screeched. "We are near that cliff. Turn around carefully and slowly. We are still not out of danger. Do not lose your head and make a mistake."

He did what she told him and slipped his arms loosely around her neck.

The great bird turned her head to face him. "What is the matter?" she asked. "I can feel that something is not right with you. Are you hurt?"

"No, I'm OK. I dropped my sketchbook. It must have come out of my pocket when I was kicking the tiger."

"I cannot go back," she said, turning to face the cliff. "I am too weak. You will make another sketchbook."

For the first time since he'd arrived in the valley, Hank could think of nothing to say. In an instant, as he'd watched his book drop to earth, he'd realized that it was his most important possession. And now it was gone. He remembered every sketch. How could he ever replace all of that?

"I can't make another sketchbook. I can't."

"It's a book, young Hank." Golden Eyes continued to fly slowly toward a narrow ledge about halfway up the mountain next to the one where they'd seen Floppy Hat.

"It's *my* book, and I drew those pictures. It's the one thing I'll take out of this valley with me—the one thing I want."

"What are you saying?" Golden Eyes' voice was weak and irritated. "You want me or one of my flock to risk our lives to go after your book? It's a *thing*. It does not breathe. It cannot fight or fly or eat or mate. And how do you know you're getting out of this valley? Are you so sure?"

"Yes, I'm sure. Mascan won't let us down, and you won't either. We'll leave when Orion's Belt changes in the night sky."

"Remember what I said about wisdom, young Hank: it is to be cherished more than things. My kind carries no *things*. Your kind will fight and kill for *things*. We will only fight for food or our young or a good mate."

"I still want it back. Not because it's a *thing*, but because of my drawings. I don't know if I'll ever return to this valley. That sketchbook is my only connection. I won't sell it for money or trade it. I'll keep it hidden from everyone."

"Even Mrs. Plunkett?"

He stared at the back of her head. "That might be difficult. But I'm pretty sure she's filled with secrets that she'll never share. She gave me that sketchbook knowing I'd come to this valley."

A few minutes later, they arrived at the other side of the valley. Golden Eyes landed hard on the top of a cliff three hundred feet above the valley floor. Hank climbed off, noticing her body was shaking, and blood was still dripping from her tail. He looked more closely at her wound. The tiger's tooth stuck to her tail. Easing it out gently, he slid it into his secret pocket and buttoned it closed.

"You need shelter," he said, pointing to a patch of dirt under a rocky outcrop. "You need to rest and get strong again."

Golden Eyes hopped over to the spot and leaned her head against the warm rock. Almost instantly, she was asleep.

Hank sat down next to her and stared at the dirt. He was tired and hungry and empty inside. Why had they ever left Celia's? He looked over at Golden Eyes injured tail. The bleeding had finally stopped, but there were two big holes where the tiger's teeth had pierced and ripped her tail. He wondered if it would ever heal. If only he had the amber egg. He had no idea what to do for the first time since he had come into the valley.

He closed his eyes, exhausted and desperate for sleep.

He had just started to drift off when he felt a familiar thrumming in his chest. He opened his eyes and jumped to his feet. The others were in trouble.

24

RAIF THE PROTECTOR

Raif had known what was going to happen long before his boy ran those few steps and jumped onto the pterodactyl's back. Even now, he couldn't get the image out of his brain. *Why are humans so stupid? Why do they do such reckless things?* The wolf waited outside the cave and listened across the valley as Golden Eyes and his boy, and the rest of the pterodactyls fly. The sound of their wings was so identifiable, the bigger the pterodactyl, the lower the sound. Since Golden Eyes was the biggest in her flock, she was easiest for his ears to find.

He had worried as he heard them flying into the first sliver of the morning sun. Although it was a feat few would dare, the even and continuing rhythm of her wings told him his boy was still safe.

The sound of the boy's even heartbeat had calmed Raif.

At first, it had been a hammering sound, uneven and rattled as Golden Eyes soared over the cliff. He willed his boy to calm himself and listen to her instructions. Moments later, he heard the boy's heartbeat slowing down. *Good.*

Several minutes after they had flown away, the small one called Sam ran out of the cave.

"I missed him," he whispered, clutching the fur around the wolf's neck. "Will he be, okay? Which way did they go?"

Raif growled and looked due northwest. Sam sat beside him, staring off into the valley. The wolf wondered where this small boy with the glasses was looking. He would not be able to see them. The last bit of morning mist was sitting stubbornly on the valley's floor, and the small one did not have the power of sight. He could see nothing so far away.

"Keep an eye out for anything we don't know," Sam had said, yawning and leaning the side of his face into the wolf's shoulder.

Juliana had been the next to run out of the cave.

"Hank's gone!" she gasped, staring across the valley as the red ball of the sun rose over the horizon. "Is he still flying? Did he fall off? Is he safe?"

Mascan was right: this one asked too many questions. *Of course, he's okay.* He licked her hand. *Do you think I would be sitting here with you if my boy had fallen off?*

Soon everyone was awake. The cave dwellers kept their

distance from him, but they gave their guests warm food. Knowing they were safe, at least for now, Raif ran several hundred yards straight up the mountain. He was hungry. Starving. He caught his first rabbit—a small one that he tossed in the air and swallowed in one gulp. He hadn't been hunting on his own since they'd left the other side of the mountain. Living in the tunnels with only scraps of food thrown his way had left him weak. But his job had been to protect his boy and his friends.

At least I can hunt. The wolf breathed in the clear morning air and at last felt free and alone. Lapping clear, cold water from the trickle of a spring was a welcome treat. He needed to remember this spot where the pure water flowed. The rock next to the spring jutted out in a familiar shape. On one of his more daring ventures into the boy's town, he had peered into the back of a store where meat was sold—the smell was spectacular. A man in a white apron had been cutting slabs of meat on a counter with tools that looked something like the thing Mrs. Plunkett used to cut her firewood: it had a wooden handle and a shiny blade. This rock reminded him of that blade.

Sniffing the ground for more game, he glanced over his shoulder for his old friend Solvor. It had been their habit to look out for one another, and he would forget, now and again, that Solvor hadn't made the trip into the valley. *Where are you now? Probably perched half-hidden on the oak tree beside the oldest woman's shed.*

The wolf hunted for several hours, and after swallowing four more fat rabbits and several field mice, he felt stronger. He stood still and listened, trying to sense if the boy's friends were safe. When he heard nothing, he was worried and headed farther up the mountain to see if he could hear them or spot his boy and Golden Eyes.

All at once, the wolf sensed it: his boy's heart was pounding. He leaped from rock to rock, anxious to see what was happening. *Had the boy fallen? Was he lying on the ground with broken bones?*

Moments later, standing on a narrow ledge, he had his answer. Somewhere over the valley, Golden Eyes and his boy were mid-air, fighting off a sabre-toothed tiger.

His boy's heart sounded like a machine gun. How could this have happened? Most of those tigers were killed years ago, and the few remaining were rarely seen in the valley during the daytime.

I remember that battle. I thought it would kill me. She was waiting in a tree and jumped onto my back and tried to dig those horrible fangs into my back. She was strong but I finally rolled and threw her off. She was strong and screaming through the whole attack. It took a long time for my broken ribs and that slice through my back to heal.

He cocked his head and listened to the ferocious growls he remembered so well. *Who are you biting now? My boy or*

Golden Eyes? This is a mighty fight; Will Golden Eyes and my boy survive? She is a mighty fighter, but is that enough to win against this tiger?

She's the biggest and bravest pterodactyl he had ever seen. Maybe she can win, maybe not. Then his boy would be killed as well.

He cocked his head and listened to the strange mid-air battle. His boy was brave and clever and would do his part, but still, he was only a boy. Mascan is probably in his cave and listening as well. He will want to hear every bit of the news, good or bad.

It's stopped. Are they dead or are they injured?

He took a deep breath and waited for Golden Eyes to get to a safe place. Snippets of their conversation floated to him on the breeze that ruffled his fur.

This cannot be. They are arguing. Golden Eyes can be demanding, and his boy could be stubborn. He's lost his sketchbook during the battle?

The wolf growled to himself. *What was she thinking? Of course, his boy wanted his sketchbook.*

He listened further. *Golden Eyes is refusing to risk her life for a thing?* The wolf looked out over the valley. *Watching my boy sketch—the jut of his stubborn chin, his narrowing curious eyes, and a steady hand—had been fascinating to watch. You are wrong, Golden Eyes. His book is much more than a thing.*

The wolf spotted a small group of misshapen dots far in the distance. He could see them now. *Golden Eyes is hurt, flying erratically, and failing to keep her flock in formation. He watched them until they reached the mountain ridge, where his boy almost fell off her back. They were tired and hurt, but for now, they were safe.*

Raif had been so keen to find his boy that he'd forgotten about the others. Then he felt something trembling underneath him. *A rockslide? Was something powerful shifting within the mountain?*

Had the ancient tunnel system that ran beneath these peaks somehow weakened the structure of the mountains?

He heard it again: a muffled rumbling from deep inside Mascan's mountain, accompanied by a slight shaking beneath his paws.

He looked down the mountain and found the children.

The small boy is breathing quickly and cleaning his glasses. The loud girl, the one who'd stitched up Rex, is stamping her feet and shouting angrily. The girl who asks too many questions is screaming back. The hearing boy is listening to Mascan's tunnel entrance and motioning with his hand for silence. And the one with the stitched-up eye was looking directly at him without blinking.

Raif bounded down the mountain in leaps as he went over boulders and outcroppings of bushes. Landing on the ground and pushing off with his enormous paws, he knew he was going dangerously fast, but he didn't slow down. They could see him now. He counted five of them. At least they were all there. The cave dwellers could take care of themselves.

He landed from a twelve-foot drop in front of the entrance to the tunnel. He smelled the dust at the entrance and knew it was what he'd feared. *Something has collapsed deep inside this mountain.*

The loud girl was the first to speak. "We haven't seen Mascan. The cave people ran away."

"I think I hear a heartbeat," the hearing boy said, pointing toward the mouth of the cave. "It's faint, but it's there. It might be in the room with the flower door, but I can't tell for sure."

The wolf wasn't worried about INK. The giant leader of the bats will have heard the beginnings of the shift many seconds, possibly minutes, before the collapse. INK was clever. He will have used his strong red eyes and found his way out as the rumbling had started. And if INK had been there, he would have warned Mascan. But perhaps he'd been hunting. And if Mascan had been in there without INK . . . well, this was bad news indeed.

The wolf stood at the entrance to the tunnels and alerted all his senses. The dust from the rock still floated in the air. He cocked his head and listened. And there it was, just as the hearing boy had said: a faint heartbeat. It was time to get to work.

The wolf started down the tunnel slowly, waiting for the

dust to settle, waiting for the heartbeat to grow louder. Inch by inch, he followed the path they'd taken the previous day. The air was thick with black dust. The sound of water, first dripping and then flowing more steadily, led him to the turn where Mascan had pointed out the fork in the pathway. He stopped for a moment to rest. The light from outside had faded, and he gave his eyes time to adjust to the tunnel's gathering darkness. His breathing felt tight, and his steps became smaller and slower.

"Raif, are you there?" he stopped. The small boy called to him. He growled loudly—a warning to stay where he was. The wolf kept going.

He crept forward for several more minutes, and then he heard the heartbeat again—a bit stronger now. He sneezed out the dust and crawled inch by inch through complete blackness. A wall of fallen rocks stopped him, but he sniffed his way around it and climbed up the mound before stopping again. There was no way through—and he couldn't stay here much longer, breathing in this thick, deadly air, or he would choke. He'd have to find another way.

The hearing boy walked a few feet into the tunnel before Raif managed an angry growl, telling him to go back outside. By the time the wolf had made it to the entrance of the tunnel, flecks of black had covered his coat, his eyes were red and running, and he was spitting black bits of blood. The children crowded around him as he lay on the ledge, breathing in the fresh, cool air.

The loud girl brought a dish of water from the cave and put it in front of him.

"You can't return to that tunnel, Raif," the small one said.

You are right.

Voices from behind the boulder down the ledge told them the cave dwellers had returned. Raif nudged the small boy, indicating that he should go back to the cave dwellers. They needed food, and he needed rest—and time to figure out what to do next. As the children made their way along the ledge, Raif found a spot a few yards from the cave, a place where he could think and continue to watch his boy and Golden Eyes.

A few hours later, INK landed on the ground beside him.

"Mascan is alive," the giant bat reported, his red eyes staring at him. "But the fool will not leave his medicine room. He says his medicine is secret and is more important than he is."

The wolf stared into the distance but listened to every word.

"The air in the room is good," INK continued, "but he's afraid the dust is going to ruin his herbs. As soon as the sun goes down, I will fly into the forbidden passage. Mascan cannot stay there alone without food and water. Drem is gone, perhaps buried in the rock or another tunnel. Or perhaps he ran out through the bottom of my cave. Wolf, are you listening to me?"

Raif's sore eyes glistened, and he growled softly in response.

"You will do what you must, wolf. I will eat and gather my strength, and then I will go after Mascan." INK hopped a few awkward steps, jumped, and then in a moment, was airborne.

As Raif watched him go—a black streak across the sky—he realized the air smelled like rain. He looked at the dark sky and wondered if the rain would come. Water running through the collapsed tunnels would only make his job harder. And if the old man had fallen or was trapped, rising water could drown him.

Watching the clouds accumulate above the mountaintops to the west, the wolf thought the rain would come sometime during the night, perhaps early in the morning. He would sleep now and then make sure his humans were safe in the cave before he left.

He awoke sharply and without warning. *How long have I been sleeping?* He pricked up his ears. *There are no sounds from the cave.* He looked at the sky, found the brightest star, and searched until he saw Orion's Belt. Six stars. *Good, they're all there.*

I will drink water from the stream, see what I can hear at the tunnel entrance. I will just go inside a few steps and listen for the heartbeat. It was weaker than before but still there. The old man lived, though barely. Look after him and keep him safe from any trembling rocks. That's your job, INK, not mine.

I will check the humans' cave. Everyone sleeping except the loud girl. Somehow, I expected that. She is sitting up in her bed, and she is staring at me across the sleeping bodies. He blinked at her, turned, and ran down the mountain. *I have work to do.*

This is dangerous and I will have to be careful every second. Those tigers hunt at night, so I must be careful. Remember they lay on the lower branches of trees, watching and waiting for unsuspecting prey to wander underneath them. Their eyes shine in the moonlight as they can moved silently and almost invisibly through the long grasses and small trees.

Raif slid effortlessly onto the floor of the valley. He had one thing to do, and he had to do it quickly: find his boy's book and bring it back.

His paws were strong but not as strong as the tigers. Although he'd heard only one tiger growl during that midair battle, he knew the tigers hunted in groups. His fur shone in the moonlight, making him easy to see. He could only hope that his boy and the pterodactyls had inflicted enough damage on the tiger.

The first several minutes were silent. A gray blanket of

mist covered the valley. Nothing moved. Not the slightest breeze.

The wolf was glad he had rested. He ran silently toward the area where the battle had taken place. Avoiding the trees and using his peripheral vision, he was getting there quickly. He knew the book was halfway across the valley, in a straight line from the cliff to Mascan's mountain. Running long distances had never bothered him, and this night was no exception. He ran so fast; he started to feel as if nothing could catch him, as if he was completely safe. But he was wrong.

The minute he slowed down to look for the book, the wolf felt the quick, hard bite of a snake on his left hind leg. He felt its teeth jab straight through his leathery skin. The wolf jumped high and kicked his leg so hard the snake flew through the air. *Good. At least I won't get a second bite.*

He ran for several minutes, leaping over a small stream without even touching the water. Then he began to feel the pain. A short time later, his leg was collapsing, and he could no longer feel the ground with his paw. His vision blurred, and his breathing became difficult. It was a rattler! He knew there were Diamondbacks in this valley. The worst thing he could do was to keep running; that would spread the venom faster. But he had no choice: he had to find the book.

Moments later, he could smell it, coated in the scent of the boy, the tiger's spit and blood as well as Golden Eyes' blood and feathers. He was getting close. He tried to run straight to it, but he could not keep moving in a straight line. *Keep your eyes on the book. Keep going. Don't stop.*

There it is! Right in front of me. Grabbing it in his mouth, he could taste the tiger's blood. As he turned to make his way back to the safety of the ledge, his leg buckled, and he fell. The pain gnawed at him, and then he started to tremble and wretch. The wound was wet, and he knew that soon some animal would smell the blood seeping from the bite. If the tigers found him, they would kill him quickly. Now he had no strength left to fight or even to run.

He had watched his boy think through two fights: with the grizzly bear and the plesiosaurus. His boy had thought of a plan and followed it. Now, he had to do the same, and he instinctively knew just what his plan should be. *You need to stand up and find some mud—fresh, wet mud.*

He headed to the small stream he'd jumped over earlier. He weaved as he walked and fell a few times. By the time he found the stream, he was gasping and sucking air through his teeth. It wasn't much of a stream, but he lay down on its bank and buried his leg deep into the mud. It felt cool and dulled the intense pain. He looked at the stars as they skimmed across the sky and knew the poison in the bite was distorting his vision. He also knew the mud would draw out the poison and possibly stop the bleeding. It might even return some of his strength.

Holding the book in his mouth, he rested his head on the

riverbank. There were no tigers nearby. He heard something in the distance, but it was too far away to bother him. He breathed deeply and breathed slowly for the first time since the snake had bitten him.

When he opened his eyes, he could tell that time had passed—the light was different. It was not quite morning yet. He stretched his leg out slowly. The pain had lessened, but when he stood, it ripped through his hind leg and into his hip. He had lost some strength, he knew, and he was soaking wet and covered in mud, but the mud had washed the blood away. He sniffed the air. Still no rain, but it would start soon. He would get back hobbling on three legs.

Once more, Raif started his dangerous trip across the valley. He walked, stumbled, and kept watching. Then he heard them—the tigers. More than one, and they were somewhere nearby. Their roars rebounded through the valley.

Get to the mountains. Keep going. Their roars are terrifying. The tigers were killing something, but it was fighting back. I hope it isn't Beanstalk or one of his herd. He remembered when he was a cub, and his mother was hunting. Beanstalk had rescued him from a herd of ornithomimids.

The wolf moved more slowly now, concentrating to keep on a straight path. Fixing his eyes on Mascan's mountain, he limped through the valley. His tongue hung out of the side of his mouth as his teeth clamped down on the book. The noise from the tigers had stopped. He hoped they were too busy devouring whatever they'd killed, to hear him.

The beasts would be out now.

The wolf's pace got slower, and the land started to sway in front of him. He kept his eyes on everything, especially the ground. He wouldn't make that mistake again. He staggered and fell and picked himself up. His mouth felt stiff from carrying the book, and he was thirsty.

I wish I'd taken a long drink at the stream. I've not been thinking clearly, and now I will suffer the consequences.

He found his way around the boulders at the bottom of Mascan's mountain and crept along the hidden path. He stopped several times, dropping the book to catch his breath. When he finally saw the cave, he felt a relief he had never known before. Then everything fell into darkness.

He awoke to the sound of whispering voices and someone trying to take the book out of his mouth. He growled until he recognized the scent of the small one who wore glasses. He let him take it. Opening one eye, he saw the small one tuck it into his pants. *Good. Keep it safe.*

He listened to the loud one: "Look—two holes here; this is a snake bite."

As she gently touched the area around the bite. He didn't growl at her.

He watched the loud one out of half-closed eyes as she unscrewed the medicine ball. He smelled the potent odor and remembered Rex's injury. *Will the medicine ball heal me as well?* He could feel her fingers working the ointment into the snakebite. Before he fell into a deep sleep, he thought about Mascan. Was he still alive? Had INK done his job? Then he thought about his boy. *Was he still safe?*

25
THE SECOND POWER

Hank and Golden Eyes stayed on the side of the mountain until her tail stopped bleeding. She rested with her head leaning against the warm rock of the ledge, too tired and weak to go on.

"He took a chunk off the tip of your tail," Hank peered into her wound. "I didn't see it happen, but it's gone. There are two holes where his teeth ripped through."

"That might make flying more difficult," she hissed.

"The bleeding has stopped."

Golden Eyes remained silent, though Hank could tell she was trying not to shiver. She'd lost a lot of blood.

"If Ruby were here, she'd know what to do—and she'd have Mascan's ointment. Could one of the others go back to the cave and bring her here?"

Golden Eyes laughed in her odd hiccupping way. "Do

you think she'd climb on one of our backs and fly off a cliff as you did?"

He smiled weakly, trying to imagine it. He shook his head. "Then we wait for you to rest and get your strength back."

The flock crowded onto the ledge as the sun started to set. Moments later, Golden Eyes was asleep against the warming rock. Hank sat in the middle of the flock and leaning his head against the side of the mountain; he fell asleep listening to their raspy breathing and rustling feathers.

Hank awoke with a start and peered at Golden Eyes through the dark. She had stopped trembling, and her breathing was better. Looking up at the sky, he saw that Orion's Belt still held six bright stars. He thought about the others. Although he felt no pounding heartbeats, he could tell that one of his group was awake.

Probably Sam. He was the one who worried the most and the one who knew him best. Yes, Sam is awake and worrying about me. He's sitting on the grass outside the dark cave and looking at the same stars that I am. But something was different. He couldn't "see" Raif, and that bothered him.

Hank closed his eyes again and leaned his head against one of the pterodactyls. He was the second biggest in the flock and didn't seem to mind being used as a pillow. Far down in the valley, he heard something. *It sounds like rocks moving or grinding against each other. A rockslide, maybe? He* sensed something else. *Raif. Something is wrong. I can hear him fighting for breath. What had happened to my wolf? Is Ruby there to help him? Where is Mascan?*

Golden Eyes awoke as the first sliver of the sun peeked over the mountain.

"Everybody up! Time to go. We eat later."

The flock shifted into formation like jet fighters on an airfield. They moved easily around Hank, almost as if he were one of them.

Before they took off, he closed his eyes and tried once again to find Raif.

His wolf slept, but he was injured. He was too weak to stand, and his heartbeat was rapid and uneven. Hank kept concentrating, desperate for more information. *Raif wasn't alone. Ruby was with him. Good.*

Golden Eyes screeched her commands. Hank took three long steps, vaulted onto her back, and they were off.

They flew high over the valley. Hank watched three raptors run beside a narrow stream that trickled slowly through the middle of the valley. He wondered if it was the same group that had attacked them.

"We think that bit of water feeds into the fifth river, but no one knows for sure. It disappears underground just up ahead," Golden Eyes shouted over her shoulder. "Another one of our valley's mysteries."

"There. Can you see?" she was nodding her head at something below.

Golden Eyes had rested well on the mountainside. She now flew with great speed and was breathing normally. "That is the beginning of the fourth river, Ladon. It comes to the surface in front of that sheer cliff, but we don't know where the mouth is. No one has ever been able to find it."

Hank leaned over, peering closely at the river bubbling up from the ground. It seemed somewhat murky, almost cloudy, and the riverbed was invisible. "What do you know about Ladon?"

"Nothing, other than it's our smallest. A few humans have tried to find its source by going into the caves halfway up that cliff. They never returned."

"Do you think there are plesiosauruses in the caves?" He shuddered, remembering that terrible fight.

"Maybe. I've tried to get INK to go in, but even he refuses."

As they climbed higher, Hank got a better look at the valley's floor as it widened out ahead of them. Leaning over for a better look, he was surprised to see Rex's herd, some forty in all. There was no doubt that it was his herd—Rex was by far the largest. Hank could still see his eye injury. *Your eye looks better Rex. Ruby did an excellent job.*

"Can we get closer?" he asked.

Golden Eyes laughed in her odd way. "You think because you saved his life that his herd won't attack you? They could devour you in seconds."

"I don't think he would let them."

"Are you sure?"

"No."

"Good." She turned her head around, and for a moment her gold eyes pierced into him. "At least you have some common sense."

Hank remembered Golden Eyes had said her kind liked to fly over water. He wasn't surprised to see they were following the fourth river as it meandered north through the valley.

"How often do you go over the mountains to the other side?"

"Why?" she sounded irritated.

"Because I don't think we will be in this valley for much longer, and I want to know if I'll ever see you again. You've taught me lessons I'll never forget."

Golden Eyes was silent. "Perhaps you will see me again. Perhaps not. Only time will tell." Then she took her flock even higher, to a point where the air was slightly harder to breathe.

"There is the beginning of Colli Auf, the sixth river— Mascan calls it the river of gold. Humans used to blast and dig in it. They carried bags of gold stones out through a tunnel in the mountain to the other side. Many years ago, there was a tunnel collapse. We think people are buried inside those tunnels. But the man you call Floppy Hat returns. Although we have tried, we cannot find his secret passage in and out of our valley. But the gold returns. It paves the riverbed with small stones, and when the sun is bright, it's blinding."

She changed directions suddenly, and he shifted on her back to regain his balance.

"Pay attention, everyone! We are getting close to the fifth river, Alme Tulah. Watch for the animals. Fat white rabbits and foxes will be a tasty treat. But remember your training. Concentrate. A wolf or bear isn't afraid of our size. Don't fly too low. They can jump up and pull you down by your wings. I will fly closer than the rest of you."

His heart pounded. *What if she made a mistake and did get too close?*

He watched the ground get closer as Golden Eyes veered over the water. Then something strange happened. All at once, his vision changed. The shape and the colors of the water became brighter and clearer as if he'd refocused a lens. He could see perfectly through the water straight to the muddy bottom. And then he saw the eyes of a large ringed seal looking through the water, right at him.

"What are you doing?" Golden Eyes screeched. "Are you trying to kill me? I will drop you!" She changed direction and flew higher.

Hank looked down as the fat seal dove deeper and, in a few seconds, was almost out of sight.

Then, as suddenly as it started, the strange vision stopped. "I don't know what happened. I saw everything in the water as clearly as if I were a few feet away."

"I must talk with Mascan. This cannot happen. You took away my sight! I saw nothing as if I were flying in a thick fog. Even the air currents felt different. A few seconds longer, and I would have lost my bearings. Did you try to do this?"

"No! It just happened. Is that how much you can see?"

She turned her head quickly and looked him in the eye. "Remember when you were climbing the stone steps up to the plesiosaurus's cave? You felt I was nearby. I was two thousand feet above you, but I could see you perfectly. I could also hear you. You were talking to the girl who asks questions and telling her not to be afraid."

"What does this mean, Golden Eyes? I don't understand what happened!"

She remained quiet, taking the flock higher.

He tried to use his power and see what she might be thinking.

"Stop that!" she screeched.

He sat quietly on her back, waiting.

"It's your *second* power—and it's rare," she said, her voice softening. "I've heard about it but never seen it. The last time this happened was a hundred years ago. I was too young, and my mother kept me away from the fighting. But Mascan tells the story of a boy with great gifts. He didn't fly, but he took over the brain of a T-rex. There was a terrible war. It almost destroyed the valley."

As she climbed higher and higher, the landscape got smaller. Hank could see the rivers and forests and mountains of the whole valley.

"What kind of war?" he asked, his eyes sweeping over the valley below.

"It was between us—the creatures who have lived here for millions of years and humans who wanted to take the valley for themselves."

"What happened?"

"We won!" She flapped her wings and flew faster. "The boy helped us win."

"What happened to this boy? What was his name?"

"I don't remember. I don't want to remember. He left the valley. No one ever saw him again."

"What about the people you were fighting?"

"We killed most of them. A few got away. I would fly over your world looking for some who'd escaped. Then Mascan told me it was too dangerous. We had a big argument. Finally, I had to agree with him. It was too dangerous for me to leave the valley.

They continued to fly north for several minutes. Down below, Hank could see the meandering "river of gold" as it met with Ladon. The terrain was different here. The trees were smaller, more like shrubs. Snow covered most of the ground as ice formed and crusted around the riverbanks. Hank squinted down through the crystal-clear water; he could see many feet beneath the surface.

Why aren't I cold? he wondered. *It must be because I'm riding on Golden Eyes' warm back.* The steady rhythm of her wings and the constant flow of air relaxed him. He wondered how long they could fly like this and how far north they would go.

"Are you getting tired? Do you need to rest?" he asked as he leaned forward.

She hiccupped and flew faster. "We can fly until the sun begins to set. Watch now, young Hank. We are almost at the beginning of Alme Tulah, the fifth river. It holds much for us to eat, though there are no purple and green colors in the daylight. Soon we will fly lower again so that we can catch food. My flock is hungry. We will catch something for you as well. You will learn to love our food."

Her great wings shifted, turning back into a streamlined V that allowed her to dive. As they raced down toward Alme Tulah, Hank remembered the drawing in Mascan's cave. The small river spurted straight out from the cliff, halfway up the mountain where the tree line ended. There had been plenty of game: Arctic foxes and polar bears were part of the drawing. Were they going to attack a polar bear? His heart started to race, and he hugged Golden Eyes closely, crouching behind her massive crest.

They descended at an astonishing speed. The air rippled his cheeks, and his eyes watered. He felt the pressure on his face and scalp, and arms as the wind dug into his skin. He held on with his legs and arms as he watched the beginning of the attack.

Golden Eyes snapped her head around and screeched to the next pterodactyl in line.

"Take the fox. Now!"

Squinting hard, Hank could just make out a white fox running along the bank of the river. They were almost on top of it when Golden Eyes veered sharply to the right. The other pterodactyl reached down and grabbed the startled animal. The fox squirmed for a few seconds before the long claws snapped its neck. Hank stared at the animal: seconds before it had been alive and hunting for its *own* meal.

They continued hunting along the riverbank. Leaving the open water behind, they flew over solid ice and caught five more foxes and large white arctic rabbits. One of their flock flew closer to Hank and then, opening its beak, offered him a rabbit thigh. Hank shook his head.

Golden Eyes turned quickly. "Have you ever eaten fresh rabbit?

"NO."

"You never know. One day you might be starving, and you'd be happy for such a treat."

Moments later Golden Eyes shifted her direction. Peering around her head, Hank saw a polar bear diving for ringed seals. His heart pounded as he watched Golden Eyes prepare for her attack. She circled the bear, readying herself and her flock for an attack. He felt the tension in her wings as she flew lower.

The bear looked up, sniffed the air, and saw the flock of pterodactyls. It stood on its hind legs, apparently undisturbed by their imminent attack. Raising its front paws, it opened its mouth and growled.

"Hold on, young Hank! We will see how strong it is."

Golden Eyes repositioned her flock into two lines. They dove directly at the bear, aiming for its eyes. He was a massive male, and the scars on his face and markings on his coat told of many battles. He batted his paws with lightning speed each time a pterodactyl flew near. Hank held his breath. What would happen if Golden Eyes went in for the attack and he fell off?

Each time the pterodactyls tried to stab at the bear, he swatted them away. One of the youngest birds was swatted into the snow and remained still.

The bear stood his ground and released a raging growl. Then he stopped and walked away from the attack, paying no attention to the fallen bird.

Is he dead? Hank yelled at Golden Eyes.

She ignored him and screeched. "Another dive . . . now!"

This time, one of the birds drove her beak straight into the massive bear's snout. It howled, outraged, spun around, and started to run. The snow camouflaged its white fur, but Hank could still see every part of it. The bear ran straight toward the river's mouth, where it widened and flowed into the Arctic Ocean.

Seconds later, the bear reached the edge of the ice, pushed off with its powerful hind legs, and dove under the water. Golden Eyes glided overhead, watching the bear swim stroke after stroke under the surface. Hank leaned over slightly. He could see the bear perfectly as if he were wearing magnifying glasses. The bear's eyes were open, and its white fur waved in the water as it tugged at his coat. Each powerful stroke propelled the bear forward several yards. As the water pushed against its body, Hank could see the black skin underneath, as well as its small eyes, and the blood still streaming out of its large black snout.

Then the bear flipped over on its back, looked up from under the water, and found Hank's eyes. They stared at each other for a few moments before the bear flipped over again and continued swimming.

"Enough!" Golden Eyes screeched as the flock climbed to a safer height.

"So, you do have this extraordinary power, young Hank. You are just like the boy from so long ago."

"Is that why we followed the polar bear?" he asked. "So, you can tell if the first time was a fluke or if I do have this other power?"

"Indeed," she replied. "It was your first real test—your Fandian. We have been waiting for you. It has been a long time since one with your powers has been in the valley. Mascan will be pleased."

He sat perched quietly on her back. They changed direction and flew back toward the fallen bird. It was struggling to get up, and soon enough, it too was airborne.

It was an odd feeling, discovering a power you never knew you had and then not knowing why he had it.

He knew Golden Eyes was waiting for him to speak. But they continued to fly mile after mile, in silence.

I see nothing but a blurred jumble of colors and shapes. What could this mean? Why am I—Hank Rattler of 39 Ranger Road, with an almost forgotten father and an absent mother, the mysterious Mrs. Plunkett, and his protectors, Raif and Solvor— supposed to do for this secret valley of the dinosaurs? Did the boy who shared this power save the valley somehow. Am I to do the same? And what about the others? What were they doing here? How much did Mascan know?

"Is it true what Mascan said about my friends and me? Did our hearts really start beating at the exact same instant?" He broke the silence.

"You already know the answer, young Hank."

"Is it dangerous for others to know of this strange power of mine?"

"That's a question for Mascan, but I would think so."

"What is this power called?"

"We call it *jokotting*. It is rare and usually hidden from all but those few who need to know about it."

Jokotting. He turned the strange-sounding word over in his mind. He was sure he'd never heard it before. "Does Mrs. Plunkett know?"

Her hiccupping laugh was her only answer.

"Where are we going now?" he looked over her shoulder.

"You are becoming just like the girl who asks too many questions."

"Juliana asks excellent questions," he grinned thinking of her. "Do you think just because someone tells us something, especially when it's something extraordinary, we should believe it? Do you think we shouldn't ask questions?"

She remained silent.

The flock had turned, and there were flying south again. Hank was surprised to see them heading closer to the east.

"Why are we getting close to the cave with guns?" he asked nervously.

"Part of your Fandian. Can you see inside?"

"Twelve caves and many people. They have guns. Who are they?"

"They have all escaped from the mine. We cannot stop now. I am tired and the guns are too dangerous."

Golden Eyes veered away from the caves and climbed higher. "Your second power is extremely strong."

Sensing Hank's sudden fatigue, Golden Eyes flew smoothly and in a straight line. The others followed in perfect formation. He watched the valley spread out before him and saw the meandering rivers and their small tributaries. The sun was setting, and it painted the entire valley in a wash of vivid orange and yellow. Several minutes more brought them within sight of Mascan's mountain. He sighed and relaxed his grip.

"Keep concentrating until we've landed. Losing your concentration is a mistake that could kill you." For a split second, she turned and glared at him.

They landed on the side of the mountain just as the sun began to set. Sam was the first to run out of the cave. Hank, tired and hungry, almost fell into the waiting arms of his oldest friend.

Ruby shouted the first orders. "Bring him inside! He needs food and water. Hurry up! Don't drop him."

He smiled feebly, happy to see Raif limping along beside him.

As he sat on a bed surrounded by friends and cave dwellers, he found himself unable to speak. He couldn't find words to describe all that he had seen and done. Sam brought over hot soup and sat beside him, watching him eat.

Hank raised his eyebrow as he met Sam's stare.

"Mascan?" he asked between mouthfuls.

"There was a collapse in the tunnels that run between the caves," Sam said. "INK's been here several times. He found Mascan alive, but so far, not Drem. INK thinks Mascan will be able to walk out in the morning."

"You talked to INK?"

"Of course, we talked to INK. He's very brave to go into that tunnel to see Mascan."

Raif positioned himself quietly beside Hank, holding something in his mouth.

"My sketchbook!" Hank hugged his wolf. "How did you find it, boy?"

"He went into the valley last night and found it. But he was bitten by a rattlesnake and almost died. Even with Mascan's ointment, I thought I would lose him. He's still weak," Ruby said.

Raif growled softly and dropped the book into Hank's lap. His leg was swollen where the snake had bitten his wolf, then looked back at Ruby and smiled. *She is a great healer.*

He ran his fingertips over the teeth marks the tiger had

left on the book's cover. He slowly turned the pages. The fur from the tiger's tail had painted Golden Eyes blood across several pages. Hank closed the cover and buttoned the book securely in his pocket.

He looked at their waiting faces. "Today was part of my test—my Fandian. Some parts I hardly believe myself." He told them about the sabre-toothed tiger attack, hunting rabbits with Golden Eyes' flock, and the eye contact he'd made with the polar bear underwater. He also told them about the twelve caves filled with people with guns. They listened, wide-eyed, in silence.

No one was surprised when he fell asleep in the middle of a sentence.

That night, no one bothered to look at the stars, and so no one noticed that Orion's Belt had changed. There were only five bright stars in a perfect row; the sixth was barely visible.

26
THE SIXTH STAR

Hank's dream was strange, as dreams so often are. He was flying over the valley with Golden Eyes and her flock. The rhythm of her wings beat in his ears. Then it all became a jumble: Mrs. Plunkett; Sam's mother singing *Volare, oh oh, e contare, oh oh oh oh;* Solvor drilling his beak into the grizzly's eye; his Swiss army knife stabbing the plesiosaurus; Ruby's red hair in the plesiosaurus's mouth; Raif licking the blood from Rex's face; the sound of the raptors chasing them; 31 and 52 running away, Beanstalk's eyes looking at him as he pushed the six of them in the trees; his book fluttering below him and smacking into the sabre-toothed tiger; and Mascan behind the flower door.

Deeper into the dream, Hank was still flying with Golden Eyes, looking at the faces of the cave people. He saw a woman with part of her ear cut off, staring at him from deep inside the cave. He began to draw her face.

Then he woke up.

Everyone else was asleep.

Raif watched over them from his spot by the cave's entrance.

Suddenly Raif made a low sound in the back of his throat and left the cave. Hank followed, weaving his way around sleeping bodies. By the time he got outside, Raif was standing on a rock, looking up at Orion's Belt.

Hank looked at the stars, and his throat tightened.

"Oh, no," he muttered, looking at Orion's Belt. Five were bright and easy to find. The sixth star was barely there, twinkling weakly.

They needed to act quickly.

Then he heard Mrs. Plunkett's voice: *Think, boy. Use your brain. Panic can kill you.* He'd thought she was just a strange old woman who said things that made no sense. Now he would listen.

Mrs. Plunkett had told him that at this time of the year, during the twelfth crescent moon, the sun rose at 4:03 a.m. and set at 9:06 p.m. The position of the moon told him there would be about an hour until sunrise. He had wondered why she was sharing such useless information. Now he knew.

He checked his watch. It was one of the few times since he'd been in the valley that he'd bothered to check the time. He'd never needed to before. Now there was nothing more important than the ticking of his watch—3:03 a.m. The sun was already beginning to rise. They had eighteen hours and three minutes and a few seconds to get out of the valley.

He flipped open his book and looked at his drawing of the teeth from the first cave. He looked for any clues he might have drawn without realizing their significance, but he found nothing. Sliding the book back into his pocket, he looked up at Raif.

It's time to wake the others.

His heart began to pound. Inside, Sam, Ruby, Oz, Zebi, and Juliana opened their eyes at the same instant and sat up.

Hank signaled them all outside. They stood and searched the sky for Orion's Belt. Each one saw the fading sixth star.

"It won't be there much longer—maybe a few hours," Oz whispered.

"We have to get out before the sun sets today," Hank's voice was monotone.

"How long do we have?" Juliana asked, staring at the sky.

He checked his watch. "It's 3:06 a.m. We have eighteen hours, one minute."

"If we go back into the tunnel with Raif, do you think we'll be able to find Mascan? "Sam asked. "He'll be able to show us the way."

Oz shrugged. "It's dark in there. I walked in when you were gone and couldn't find my hand in front of my face. And I could still feel bats flying past me."

"I *know* he's still alive," Zebi said. "I can hear his heartbeat from the mouth of the tunnel. Isn't there any other way to get to him?"

Sam picked up Hank's wrist and rechecked the time. "We can return to the valley and try to get in through the pumpkin hole again. Maybe it didn't collapse with the rockslide."

"We need another plan," Hank said. "Sam, remember when we were building the pterodactyl for our science project, and your dad said we should start at the letter A and not at the letter M?"

Sam nodded.

"That's what we need to do here," Hank said, pacing back and forth, "start with Mascan and see where that leads us. If we try and go through the pumpkin hole to find him, we'll have to be very careful and use every power we have. Who knows what's in there?"

"Okay, that's a beginning," Zebi said. "I don't hear any movement in the valley right now. The beasts are not usually nocturnal, except for the tigers, but that's a chance we'll have to take. The cave people said it's rare to see them in the valley. We could go down the mountain now and try to find the pumpkin hole. But what do we do if this doesn't work?"

Hank rechecked Orion's Belt. "We figure out how to escape through one of the six rivers," he said.

"We can't use Ladon," Oz warned. "That's where the plesiosaurus was. We don't know for certain that we killed it or if there were any more in there."

"And Mascan said no one ever returns from Adamas, the third river," Juliana said. "So that leaves Calx, Ingemar, Alme Tulah, and Colli Auf, lost gold.

They heard Raif's low growl and watched as he started down the path that led to the bottom of the mountain and into the valley.

"Let's get our stuff and go," Hank said, moving toward the cave. "Raif must know something. It's time to stop talking and find Mascan. He's our best hope for getting out of here."

Sam hurried to keep up with Hank's longer strides. "There may be other ways to leave this valley besides the rivers. Maybe we could get out on foot."

"I think you're right. We only need one way to get us there safely."

The group followed Raif down the unpredictable twists and turns of the pathway. They were about to step onto the floor of the valley when Hank stopped. "Powers," he whispered.

"A sleeping herd of something big, about ten miles down," Oz said, his eyes darting in every direction. "A few small mammals, maybe rabbits? A polar bear and her two cubs are sleeping in a snowbank way up past the fifth river, Alme Tulah. Small brown birds perched in those trees across the valley, and a raven on a nest on the far cliffs. Nothing else."

Zebi thrust his head forward. "The wind is picking up over the mountains to the west. There's rain forming in the clouds, and the storm coming later this morning is from the northwest. Mascan sleeps inside the mountain, and INK is with him. He must have escaped from his other cave through his secret tunnel and made his way here. That large pine tree is dying, and it's full of grubs eating its insides. Something is swimming in the fourth river. Maybe another plesiosaurus, or maybe the same one."

"There's something putrid on the other side of those trees," Sam sniffed. He took a few deep breaths. "Maybe a fresh kill—uneaten? There's water seeping out of the bottom of Mascan's mountain." He breathed deeply again, closed his eyes, and exhaled. "I wonder if the waterfall hidden inside the tunnel has found its way into the cave after the rockslide. I can smell rain in the air. It's about a hundred miles away."

Hank turned to Juliana.

"Golden Eyes is circling overhead," she pointed straight up. "I can taste the blood and guts of freshly killed fish on her claws."

Ruby ran her hands down the wolf's back. "Raif's fur is standing up, and he's shaking," she stuttered. "He's never afraid. What's wrong with him?"

"He *is* afraid," Hank warned. "The last time he was in this valley, a Diamondback rattler almost killed him. He's also weak. The venom is still in his system. Ruby, rub more ointment over the bite marks. He needs more time to heal, but he doesn't have it." Once again, he looked at his watch in the moonlight.

"I sense no more rockslides or any beasts near us. It's time we find the pumpkin hole." Hank started down the path.

They tiptoed onto the floor of the valley and crept along, as quiet as assassins.

"Nothing yet," Oz whispered, squinting into the dark. "Pumpkin hole," he pointed up and to the left.

"Good eyes," Hank nodded. They headed up the small, rocky hill to the entrance. Once they'd all squeezed into the cave, they looked around. It was exactly the way they'd left it. Hank held his watch up to his face: 3:21 a.m.

It took them a while to find their way through the first two small caves. It seemed like years since they'd been there.

"I have one candle left and don't want to use it unless I have to," Hank said.

They found the lever in the wall and gently unlatched the door, leading them back into the cave of bats. They followed Raif, who quickly found the staircase.

"Hang on," Hank held up his hand. "Sam, do you smell anything bad? The last thing we want to do is trip over a dead man in the dark. Remember, we left him here when we were on the other side of the door."

"No, nothing gross like that," Sam said. "I only smell bat guano and . . . wait . . . bats are watching us."

They all stopped moving, their hearts pounding at the thought of the bats swooping down on them again.

"They know we mean no harm to Mascan," Hank said.

Following Raif, they crept up the staircase until they arrived at the landing in front of the flower door.

Ruby got to work, pushing and pulling the petals and stems in the same order as before. Hank stood on the stairs in amazement. He'd been ready to read out the notes he'd taken the last time she'd done this, but she didn't need them. She was going to open this secret door in complete darkness.

Zebi stood beside Ruby, cocking his head to one side, listening to the knocking, clicking, sliding, and twisting as each piece of the door gave up its secret.

Finally, the door opened with a creak. A faint light glowed from the back of the room.

"Incredible!" Juliana whispered to Ruby.

"He's over here," Zebi hissed, running over to Mascan's room.

The old man was asleep on a makeshift bed. INK watched them, hanging upside down from a rafter in the ceiling. Raif growled at the unblinking red eyes.

Ruby felt Mascan's pulse. "He's alive.

Within a few minutes, Mascan was sitting up and sipping water.

"Ah, you have found me, my brave young friends," he

exclaimed. "Ruby, you are very good at opening my flower door." He smiled at her, his old eyes narrowing to slits.

He sighed. "I've broken my leg. What a nuisance that will be in the winter. My bones are too old. Ruby, help me put it into a splint so that it will heal properly. Did you bring the amber egg?"

She whipped it out of her pocket.

Mascan unscrewed it and sniffed. "About two hundred years ago, I found a scroll in a forgotten library in Greece. There were notes the ancient Greek doctor Hippocrates had written about healing the human body."

He took a small amount of the ointment and, leaning forward, massaged it into his leg. He handed the globe back to Ruby. "Keep it safe and keep it secret."

He looked off into the distance. "I have some sad news," he said. "Golden Eyes' fledgling has been killed."

The six of them gasped.

"How? When?" Hank asked.

"She was a magnificent little creature and would have grown into a strong leader like her mother." His voice got weaker. "Mrs. Plunkett and Solvor had taken her far back into the woods. There's a big pond, almost a small lake, and Solvor showed her how to fly over water and hunt fish. A farmer shot her. She dropped straight into the pond. He had dogs with him, and they tried to retrieve her, but she sank like a stone."

"Why would a farmer shoot her?" Juliana whispered.

Mascan shrugged. "For sport, I suppose. Mrs. Plunkett is sad. She has always been so good at keeping things safe."

"How do you know all of this?" Zebi asked.

"Mrs. Plunkett and I communicate frequently. She is my sister—my twin sister."

Hank stared at Mascan. "Your sister? Why didn't you tell me before? Why does she live out there while you live here?"

"You know why she lives out of our valley . . . right next door to you."

"Is she my protector too? Like Raif and Solvor?"

Mascan nodded slowly, his cloudy eyes staring straight into Hank's.

"So, she's 403 years old too!" Sam gasped and looked at Hank.

Mascan nodded and smiled weakly. "We must continue our quest, Sam. You are troubled, Hank. Something else is wrong."

"Orion's Belt is changing," he replied.

Mascan took a deep breath. "How many stars now?"

"Three are still bright, two are weaker, and one has almost disappeared."

"You *must* leave by sunset tonight."

"Yes. We've come to you for directions."

"You understand what sunset means?" Mascan asked. "Not *one second* after the last sliver of light has disappeared.

If the sun dips behind the mountains and you are still in the valley, you will never be able to leave."

His words hung in the air like the blade of a guillotine.

Sam spoke first. "We need your help. We don't know how to get out."

Mascan suddenly looked older. He spoke as though he were in a dream state, and his voice was low. "This mountain has suffered an internal slide. Some of the tunnels remain blocked, but others are open. There is a tunnel that runs parallel to the one you arrived at from the other world. I have not tried to navigate its dark paths for a hundred years. If I could walk now, I would try, but I could barely walk to this cave with my broken leg. I can go no farther. And to send you on your own, with only my directions, is far too dangerous. There is no time for mistakes."

Mascan's blind eyes, one so brilliantly green and the other blue, looked toward the shelves holding his medicines and herbs.

"Ruby, can you bring me a few things from my bottles and wooden boxes?" He sighed. "Drem has still not returned, and I cannot find him in my visions. I fear the worst. Sam, stop huffing and looking at Hank's watch. It won't change the facts."

Hank wondered again if Mascan was almost blind.

"Two walking sticks are standing against that far door"— he pointed impatiently. "Bring them here."

"We're leaving you with three jugs of water and the food I found on your table," Ruby said. "Your ankle will feel better but not for several days. In the meantime, INK will stay with you. Don't do any walking for at least two weeks."

He rubbed his eyes. "How right I was, Ruby, to give you the power of touch. You have a gift. Guard it. What time does your watch say now, young Hank?"

"Exactly 4:46 a.m."

"Then it's quite accurate. Where did you get this watch?"

"It was my father's," he said softly.

Mascan reached out to feel the watch's face and run his fingers along the strap. A faint smile crossed his face.

"The dinosaurs will be starting to wake now. Be alert." He raised his hands and waved them away. "You will follow Golden Eyes to the Cave of Kings. Once inside the cave, you will find Colli Auf, the sixth river. Follow the river to where my two helpers take you. Do not fear them. They will not hurt you."

"The Bywyd stone will gather the strength of the light, and you will be set free."

Hank wasn't sure what Mascan meant, but he didn't get a chance to ask. The old man grasped Hank's wrist. "Remember Mrs. Plunkett, young Hank. Do that, and you will find the answer. Now listen carefully. This is what you must do when you get there."

27

THE ANCIENT COUNTDOWN

Several minutes later, on the ledge outside the pumpkin hole, Hank searched the early morning sky and remembered the first of the four phrases on the wall in Mascan's cave.

The purple will touch the crescent moon before the six entwine.

Hank looked at his watch. "It's 5:03 a.m.," Hank said. "Let's move."

Zebi took the lead, with the others scrambling to keep up.

"Why . . . do we need . . . to run . . . so fast?" Sam gasped.

"Because we don't want to be running out in the open for much longer," Zebi hissed over his shoulder. "The beasts are waking up, and we don't want to catch their attention."

Sam ran a little faster. *Remember your powers.*

A few minutes later, they stopped to catch their breath.

"There's a small amount of dust way down the valley," Oz pointed. "I'll keep watch."

The others were leaning forward, palms on their knees, chests heaving.

"We'll walk for a minute and then start up again," Hank said. "Watch for the Diamondbacks."

Juliana clenched her jaw as she stepped carefully across the valley floor. "Where are we going? No one knows where this Cave of the Kings is."

"Golden Eyes knows," said Hank. "Mascan said she would take us. She'll be here soon."

"We have to get out of the valley!" Oz said, his voice was tight. "Something's coming. I can't tell what it is yet. Which way to safety, Hank?"

"This way—toward the cliff. I remember flying over it. There are steps leading to ledges."

"Are you sure?" Zebi tilted his head and listened to the sounds coming toward them.

"It's our best option. What if it's the raptors again or some carnivore we've never seen before?" Hank's eyes swept around at all of them.

"We need to run," Zebi started running toward the cliff ahead of the rest.

Then ran like they'd run from the raptors. Hank cursed himself for not insisting they keep closer to the cliffs. They had strayed out too far toward the middle of the valley and left themselves unprotected.

"I can see the steps!" Oz was pointing to one side. "They're steeper than the ones to Mascan's cave."

Sam screamed. "I lost my glasses!" He slowed down, looking over his shoulder at the ground he'd just covered.

"Leave them!" Oz yelled, gaining speed, and grabbing him by the arm. "There's no time. They've seen us."

Ruby's face was beet red, but she kept running. "Where are they?"

Juliana lost a shoe but didn't look back.

They focused on the steep stone steps carved into the cliff. Zebi started to climb, calling out to the others behind him.

"Get up here! Now!"

Hank took one look at the steps and felt sick to his stomach. Unlike the other stone stairs, which climbed gradually to the caves from the valley floor, these went straight up. There was no way Raif would be able to climb them. He was too weak. And this time, they had no rope and no time to carry his wolf.

Ruby started climbing. When she was halfway up, Sam reached the bottom step. "I can't see!" he was feeling with his foot for the next step. He rubbed his eyes and glanced up at Zebi.

From up above, Zebi poked his head out over and spoke slowly. "You're fine, Sam. Reach for each step. One after the other, not too quickly."

Juliana was next. As she climbed, she turned to see what was coming into view behind her. A herd bellowed and kicked up dust as it burst through the underbrush. She reached up and grabbed the first step, and then the next and the next.

"I can't see what they are," Oz cried out as he skidded in front of the bottom step. He banged his head into the stone and opening the stitches in his eyebrow.

Hank was the last to begin the climb. He looked back at Raif and then over his shoulder at an advancing army. They hadn't seen these beasts before. There were hundreds of them—at least ten feet long each—and running faster than any of the dinosaurs they'd encountered.

He started to climb, quickly and carefully. Reaching the top, he rolled over onto the ledge and peered down, searching for Raif. He was easy to find with his bright white fur. Hank watched him run along the side of the mountain, searching for shelter. *Please let there be a gap in the rocks where he can hide.*

The six friends looked down the valley. The advancing dust made it impossible for anyone but Oz to see.

"What are they," Juliana asked. "Is it another herd of tyrannosauruses?"

"No, they're smaller," Oz's voice was even, calm. "It's a big herd. I think they're deinonychus. They're fast."

"How fast?" Hank asked.

"About twenty-five miles an hour. Maybe more."

"Herbivores or carnivores?"

Oz narrowed his eyes and stared ahead. "Carnivores."

"Anything else?"

"Yes," Oz said. "They're smart. They have big brains, and they use them."

"Is that it?"

"Forget the rest."

Hank snapped. "Tell me! What else?"

"Unlike the T-rex, they have long front limbs to grab hold of their prey. And on their hind legs, they have a deadly claw that looks like a sickle."

Hank went white. Reaching into his pocket, he felt his sketchbook. He dug his fingertips into Raif's teeth marks.

The ground shook as the herd got closer. The deinony-chus had long necks, with lightly built skulls, long forelimbs, and legs nearly fourteen feet long. Watching them emerge out of the dust, Hank took one look at their long legs and knew they would be fast, very fast.

The herd spotted Raif almost immediately. The largest one ran closer to the center of the herd, emitting a deep, horn-like signal. Then they charged after Raif.

At first, Raif outran the herd easily. He transformed into a white streak running across the valley, leading the herd away from Hank and his friends. But the gap between the wolf and the charging deinonychus began to narrow. Hank's heart sank. He could sense the herd's frenzied anticipation of the kill. Raif would be nothing more than a tiny morsel for a few of them, but it hardly mattered: they wanted him anyway. They were seventy-five feet behind him, then fifty, then forty. Hank fought the urge to close his eyes.

He blinked. The black shadow of Golden Eyes' enormous wings skimmed over the heads of the advancing herd. When the pack leader was a mere ten feet behind the struggling wolf, Golden Eyes made her move. Spreading her claws wide, she grabbed the shoulders of the startled Raif and yanked him up into the air. The leading deinonychus made one huge lunge as Raif was lifted just over their heads. The deinonychus angry roar bounced across the valley.

Hank watched as Golden Eyes struggled to find the proper grip to keep hold of Raif. She flapped her wings hard, pushing her body to fly higher and not let go of him.

They all held their breath, watching the dangling wolf in Golden Eyes' claws.

The herd slowed down and looked up, watching its stolen morsel carried away. Several continued the chase, snapping into the air. Raif swayed like a lion cub in its mother's mouth as Golden Eyes spread her wings and slowly carried him out of sight.

Hank took a deep breath and looked over to Oz.

"I can still see them!" Oz stared up the valley. "Golden Eyes is heading north. I wonder where she's taking him."

"He steered the herd away from us," Hank sighed. "He always protects me."

"He's a mighty wolf." Zebi said, squinting as he watched Golden Eyes and Raif become two dots in the sky.

"They're a few miles past us now. Do you think it's safe to keep going?" Oz asked.

"I think we should wait a little longer," Ruby watched the back of the deinonychus herd.

Sam shook his head. "No, we've got to keep going. We don't know where the other cave is, and we don't know what we're facing once we get there."

Hank looked at his watch. "Sam is right. It's 6:21. We've got fourteen hours and forty-five minutes left. Let's go."

28
MASCAN'S INSTRUCTIONS

They made good progress, keeping a fast pace while staying close to the side of the mountains.

"They're all heading north," Ruby said, looking over her shoulder at the back of the deinonychus herd.

Hank slowed down enough to pull out his sketchbook and find the drawings from Mascan's cave.

The purple will touch the crescent moon before the six entwine.

"Mascan said this valley is the place where the six rivers converge. He said the rivers could only join at the smallest point of the crescent moon. Then every living thing in this valley must drink from the convergence and have a chance to live for another year." He pointed to the sky. "Look: it's almost the crescent moon. They're traveling north to drink the water, where the six rivers join at the smallest point of the crescent moon."

"And the purple?" Ruby asked.

"The Northern Lights," Hank whispered, tucking his book back into his pocket. "The green and purple lights touch the rivers as they join. *That's* where they're going. And we have to find our way to the Cave of Kings in the middle of it."

Oz scanned the sky, searching for Golden Eyes. The wind had shifted; it was coming in from the southwest now as it carried bits of dust and leaves. The breeze picked up speed and began to howl. He got a glimpse of black clouds building on the other side of the mountains. They were in for a storm.

Zebi closed his eyes and turned his head slowly.

"Do you hear that?" Hank asked over the sound of the building wind.

"It's the same sound," Zebi said. "Children's voices. The same high-pitched screams. And a man is yelling. Rocks are falling, banging into each other."

"It's over at Floppy Hat's place, isn't it?" Hank asked.

Zebi nodded. "And someone's yelling out numbers—7 ... 12 ... 55 ... 31 ... 52 ..."

Hank looked at his watch. "We can't do anything. We have no time."

Zebi nodded as he looked back toward Floppy Hat's place. "Keep going."

Forty-five minutes later, the group stopped to drink from one of the small streams fed by the mountain run-off. As Sam took his turn standing guard, Hank leaned down to drink. The water was pure and clear, different from the well water he was used to at home. One after the other, they all drank their fill. Earlier, they had stuffed crusts of bread, and the fruit from Mascon into their pockets. They ate it now, not knowing when they might eat or drink again.

Hank glanced up at the western side of the valley and saw a curtain of rain and then a few lightning strikes coming across the mountains. Given the speed of the wind, he figured the storm would hit in less than an hour. As Hank leaned down to drink, he felt something shift under his shirt. He reached for it, remembering the few words he and Mascan had exchanged before they left on this final journey.

I have one more thing to give you, young Hank," Mascan said, pulling a leather cord over his head and handing him a small, worn pouch.

This is Bywyd—my ancient stone. I have used it many times during my long life. When you feel you are in physical danger, clutch the stone in your right hand and picture the image on the top of the amber egg, the one in which all the rivers join.

What does it do? Hank was turning the pouch over in his hand.

You will see. Keep it safe and keep it secret. It has lived with me for 403 years.

Will it save me?

"Only you are strong enough to control its power. And finally, remember Mrs. Plunkett, young Hank. Do that, and you will find your answer."

"Hank! Let's go." Sam's tone yanked Hank back to the present.

The mountain terrain was rockier in this part of the valley, making it harder to move quickly. Still, they stuck close to the mountains. Hank looked up at the clouds and caught a glimpse of Golden Eyes, threading her way in and out of view. The clouds were like thinly layered lace, and even from two miles below, he could see her eyes blazing down at him. He knew she couldn't fly that high with Raif and wondered where she'd left him.

"Zebi, what do you hear?" Hank raised his eyebrows. "Anything that sounds like Raif?"

"Nothing."

"Oz?"

"I'm looking, but nothing so far."

Golden Eyes glided in circles, catching the thermals, barely moving her wings as the air currents kept her airborne. He remembered how strong and confident she was, carefully altering her wings to move from current to current. But even she couldn't fly through a lightning storm like this.

Zebi stopped and raised his hand. "I hear Rex!"

"Where?" Hank scanned up the mountain.

"He's coming down the valley toward us. Why would he do that when the rest are going north?"

"We have to get someplace safe!" Hank shouted, searching the cliffs for a place to hide.

Ruby tilted her head and stared at him. "Do you *really* think he'd harm us after all we've done for him?"

"Maybe—maybe not Ruby. Rex is a carnivore. That means he eats meat. Any kind of meat."

"Over here!" Juliana yelled. She ran toward a large oak tree with branches low enough to climb.

"Don't you think Rex could knock that tree over if he wanted to?" Ruby shouted as she ran.

But Hank had already helped Juliana onto the lowest branch. "Climb! Now!" he yelled to the others.

Rex was getting closer. They watched him run over the valley floor, leaving footprints at least fifteen feet apart. Other dinosaurs, all making their way north, veered over to the sides of the valley, leaving a wide path for Rex and his herd. The ground started to shake, making the tree branches they were clinging to shudder like the back seat of a pick-up truck.

"Look at him go!" Ruby yelled. "He's not afraid of anything, is he? He really *is* the king of the dinosaurs. And look across the valley—watch the triceratops getting out of his way?"

Hank was surprised to see Ruby smiling. She didn't seem afraid at all.

"How does his eye look, Ozzie?" she asked.

"Better."

Rex's bass voice thundered out to them.

"There you are. I expected to see you heading up the valley." He came to a stop just below the tree and peered up at them on their separate branches. "Is it time for you to go? Are the stars disappearing?"

From his branch above Ruby, Hank answered. "Yes. We're trying to get out through the Cave of Kings. We have to leave by sunset."

Rex nodded his enormous head. "I've never seen the Cave of Kings, but I've heard much about it. It's quite famous here in the valley, especially among T-rexes. Golden Eyes says it's the most dangerous cave in the valley. You must follow Mascan's instructions exactly."

He looked up at Ruby and then at the others. A deep grumbling sounded in his throat.

Ruby climbed down to the same level as his head and peered around his eye.

"Well, Ruby Basher, have you done a good job?"

"Yup. It's holding together perfectly. Try not to get in any fights for a while. And Rex, you don't get to eat my friends or me no matter how hungry you are."

"If I were, I would have done so right after you stitched up my face. Remember Mr. Shaking Spear?"

She peered again at his healing wound, running her fingers over the injury. She felt the skin and sniffed at it.

"It looks pretty good. I don't see or smell any infection, but you've pulled all the stitches out!"

"The small birds peck at them while I sleep, and no matter how fast I snap at them, they always get away."

He looked up to the higher branches and found Hank.

"Where's your wolf?"

"I don't know. A deinonychus herd was chasing him. Golden Eyes pulled him into the air just before they got him."

Rex growled softly. "He's a smart wolf. You may still find him, but you don't have much time." He looked up and down the tree again. "It's about to rain. I do like the rain."

"Why?" Ruby asked, still prodding his wound as her nose almost touching his nose.

"Because it washes the blood away."

Oz spoke from the top of the tree. "What's wrong with blood? You're a meat-eater."

"It smells, and small rodents try to eat parts of me. I step on as many as I can, but they're too fast for me."

Rex turned his enormous head and brought his bright eyes close to Ruby's face.

"Goodbye, Ruby Basher."

Raising his head, Rex settled his gaze on Hank.

"Now go. You can't be late. Remember Mascan's warning." He swung his body around and plodded north.

The rain didn't arrive gently. It fell as if the sky had been torn open, and the sound cracked against the boulders. They were quickly soaked and were soon slipping on the boulders strewn along the bottom of the mountains.

The six of them looked for cover, but there was nothing. They sat with their backs against a large boulder and waited for the storm to pass.

Hank closed his eyes. At first, the water streaming down on his face bothered him, but after a while, he let his thoughts wander. *Don't get sick, and don't get hurt.* Mrs. Plunkett's words had never left him.

As the rain continued, Hank thought about their time in the valley. The plesiosaurus's attack had been serious, but Ruby healed well; her hair had even grown in fast, and her red curls now covered most of the injury. And her ability to open the flower door was remarkable. Perhaps he didn't need to worry much about her. Sam was a different story. Although he'd been impressed by his no-nonsense attitude after the plesiosaurus attack—a change from his usual timid approach to problems—Hank still worried about him losing his glasses. *I'd better keep Sam close.* Juliana had more confidence and still asked all her questions. Oz's power of sight grew stronger every day, and Zebi's power of hearing and his common sense, curiosity, and bravery were impressive. Finally, he thought about Raif.

Where have you taken my wolf Golden Eyes?

"How long do you think this will last?" Sam interrupted Hank's thoughts.

He peered up into the dark sky. "It's a big storm. The wind's picking up, and I think it's getting worse." Hank scanned the sky and listened to the approaching thunder.

"We need to find some cover," Sam said, squinting into the dark.

Hank nodded. "Stay here. I'll take Zebi and Oz with me and see what I can find."

"Bad idea," Ruby said. "You know the rule: We all stay together."

"You're right. Everybody up," Hank yelled through the wind. "We need to find someplace to wait out this storm."

Oz peered through the driving rain. "Up there," he pointed. "It's only going to get worse."

Golden Eyes had been waiting for this day for as long as she could remember. After all, she'd been trained for this since birth.

Find them, keep them safe, and then get them out of the valley when the time is right.

Those were Mascan's instructions, and she had tried to follow them. It hadn't been easy. She thought back to other children who'd been under her command over the years. There had been some near misses, but so far, she hadn't got anyone killed. She also remembered the many conversations she'd had with Mascan. He did not take his warnings lightly. He might be old and feeble, with broken bones, but his mind was still as sharp as ever.

The wind picked up and pulled her sideways, giving her a jab of pain. Her tail still ached. She thought about the sabre-toothed tiger that had almost killed them both. She wondered if Mascan knew. *Of course he does. He knows everything.*

She tried to ride out the storm in the air, but it was worse than even she had expected.

She had safely folded her flock into their favorite perch—a carved-out nook on a cliff several mountains to the north.

The wind picked up more speed, buffeting her from all sides. Down below, she noticed her little group was on the move, struggling to climb up the mountain. But she liked fighting the strong winds and knew there would be little time to play before the lightning strikes started.

"What are you doing?" she screeched into the sky, knowing they couldn't hear her. "Why go up that mountain? Stay where you are—a little water won't hurt you!"

In a matter of seconds, she dropped a thousand feet, trying to get a better look. The thunder boomed all around her, and the lightning moved closer.

I'll wait to see where they end up, and then I'll find shelter. The thunder is just loud—but lightning is dangerous and unpredictable. I may be the queen of the pterodactyls, but that doesn't matter in this kind of storm.

Once during a storm like this, one of her flock had dropped out of the sky. Golden Eyes had been flying right beside him one second, and the next, he lay dead on the ground.

Down below, Hank and the others had found a small cave.

"All right. Stay there for a bit and rest. At least you're away from the lightning".

She flew off in the wind to find shelter.

She knew something was wrong the moment she'd opened her eyes. It was much too late for her to be sleeping. Where was the rest of her flock? Her senses told her the storm had been and gone—maybe as much as a few hours ago. What had happened to her? *Maybe all the blood I lost has left me weak. Get going, Golden Eyes, or these kids won't make it out. And then what? Would they end up like the cave people? Half living, but confused and weak and sometimes dead.*

She took off like a fighter pilot on a bombing mission. She flew past the mountainside for signs of any fresh kills and was relieved to see none. *Where are they? Was it possible they were still asleep?*

Landing on the narrow ledge by the cave was awkward, but she managed. Peering inside, she screamed.

"Everybody up! Now! You've slept too long."

They jumped up at the horrible sound of her screeching. "Let's go!"

She sighed as she watched them clamor out of the cave and down the side of the mountain. *What was wrong with these young humans? The sun has already peaked and is starting its long, slow descent. They're running out of time, and the Cave of Kings and is still a distance away.*

"Faster," she screeched. "I can't pick you up one by one and fly you to the cave. You need to get there on your own two feet. I can only show you the way."

The company of six sped along, half tripping and falling as they looked fearfully up at Golden Eyes. She scanned the valley, searching between the herds of animals heading north for a flash of white fur. The wolf should have been here by now. Finally, off in the distance, she spotted him, streaking across the valley floor.

The wolf came bounding into view, barking out a sharp, throaty sound. She watched as Hank dove onto him and then engaged in what looked like a wrestling match.

How strange, she thought, *to do that to another species. Aren't humans odd?*

29
THE CAVE OF KINGS

Golden Eyes had not seen the Cave of Kings for decades. The sacred place was spoken of in whispered tones, even by Mascan. Those who knew of its existence believed they'd be struck by lightning if they ever divulged its location. Now, thanks to these six visitors, she would not only see it again but see it open for the first time in a century.

The wolf knew where it was. After Golden Eyes had rescued him from the deinonychus herd, she'd flown him over the entrance to the cave and pointed it out. Then she'd left him to rest and recover as she flew back to her human flock. Now she watched the wolf run ahead of the small group. He was fast and clever, heading straight for it as his pack of humans straggled behind. Every few feet, he would stop, look back, and growl at them.

An unremarkable outcropping of bushes camouflaged

the entrance to the cave. It looked utterly ordinary from the valley floor. No one would suspect anything this important to be so far up the side of the mountain.

Golden Eyes thought back to the only time she had seen the cave open, a century ago. She had so wanted to fly into it and explore the mysteries she'd only heard about in whispers and rumors. But Mascan had warned her: "Don't you dare go in, Golden Eyes. A cave can become your grave. And this is no ordinary cave. Poor air quality and falling rocks aren't its only dangers. In the Cave of Kings, you must be aware of the water."

She glided and then landed carefully on the top of the cave's opening and folded her wings. Mascan's warning rang again in her ears. *Okay, Mascan. I promise I won't go into the cave.*

As the group hurried up the side of the mountain, the wolf lifted his mighty head and howled. The sound filled the air with a note so pure and clear that anything living within miles would hear it.

She wondered if Mascan had heard it and then chuckled. *The old man hears everything. Of course, he has. Now he'll know we've made it to the entrance to the cave.*

Raif led the way as they pushed past the bush and then started down a darkened rock tunnel. Raif was leading, followed by Hank, Ruby, Sam, Julianna, Oz, and Zebi.

The tunnel was barely wide enough for them to walk through, perhaps six feet high. Cocking his head to one side, Zebi whispered from the back. "Raif's about twelve feet ahead of you, Hank. Judging from the echoing off the walls, I think this tunnel goes straight in for about thirty feet, and then it descends into something big—something *really big*."

Hank felt the rough rock as he crept slowly after Raif. "He's just a few feet ahead of me . . . now he's stopped."

Zebi spoke up from behind. "His heart isn't racing, so I don't think he feels any danger."

"What is it, boy?" Hank pushed up against his wolf, trying to sense what he was feeling. "We need to get into the cave, Raif. Can you help us?"

Raif growled a warning, deep and guttural. Hank knew his wolf and stopped. Instead, he closed his eyes and used all the intuition Mascan had given him. Hank sensed no plesiosauruses or Diamondback rattlers. He felt no life, no energy, and no movement from within the cave. Why was Raif waiting?

Finally, Raif crept forward again. Hank had seen him hunt and knew his wolf was listening for any noise, watching for the slightest movement or flicker of light. After a few minutes, Raif turned around in the tunnel and touched Hank's face lightly with the end of his snout. It was his signal. *Move forward with me.*

"Wait here," Hank whispered to the others as he crept behind Raif. As he inched along, he felt a sudden rush of air on his face. It smelled stale as if it had been sealed up for years. He reached his hands out to the sides and felt for the walls of the tunnel. It was widening now, and after a few more steps, the side walls were gone.

"I think I'm out of the tunnel," he whispered back. "Stay here. I won't go far."

He reached out and grabbed the fur on the back of Raif's neck. Taking a deep breath, he tried to assess his pitch-black surroundings. He sensed no danger, and beside him, Raif seemed calm. He turned around, stuck his head back into the tunnel. "Okay . . . slowly."

Moments later, the six of them stood on a ledge with their backs pressed against the wall. High up in the ceiling, six discs slid open, allowing sunlight to shoot straight down to the floor. Squinting against the light, Hank looked at his watch and blinked. It had stopped—the hands were still where they had been last time he'd checked. He held it up to his ear and shook it, which set off a ticking sound.

Sam looked at him and shook his head. "Forget about the watch, Hank. We have to figure this out and get out of here as fast as we can."

Hank nodded and looked down from the ledge at the cave below. Even with the sun shining through, the cave was dark, but round and enormous. The cave was bigger than the first secret cave, the second cave where they'd met Mascan, or the cave with the painting from the amber egg. The flower-door cave was roughly the size of one of their classrooms, and the plesiosaurus's cave was about as big as Mrs. Plunkett's living room. None of them were like this. The rock here was a sandy-gray color and the whole cave was carved, with arched entrances leading to what Hank assumed were more tunnels. A staircase carved into the rock went straight down to where they were standing.

Hank's eyes adjusted to the light. He started noticing more detail. There were five life-sized stone T-Rexes carvings on the floor with a carved platform for a sixth. The T-rex stood at intervals around the floor of the cave. The sculptor had not missed the smallest detail; even their huge teeth were precisely like what they'd seen in Rex's mouth.

"The Cave of Kings!" Hank whispered, and the words rolled around in his brain, and his eyes widened to take in every detail.

"Come on!" Hank said, running down the stairs. "Mascan said this cave was our way out—we have to figure out how." He glanced back and locked eyes with Sam. "We have to use our powers." Sam nodded.

The others followed Hank and stood together on the stone floor, looking up at the ceiling. They used the powers

Mascan had given them and looked for any hint to get them out of the valley. Moments later, the floor began to shake and turn slowly. They reached out and held onto each other for balance as the noise from the grinding stone grew louder and sounded like metal gears shifting into place.

"I think it's resting on a mechanism, and our weight activates it," said Sam, as the floor began to turn faster." He jumped back onto the lowest step, and the others followed. Then the floor stopped.

"It turned about four inches," Sam said, pointing to the first T-rex's foot and the corner of the last step.

Hank looked again at the cave's ceiling—his compass needle pointed to the east. On the east side of the ceiling, someone had cut six identical holes in the roof. They were lined up in a row, and each one looked about three feet in diameter. A matched set of holes also lined the west side of the ceiling. The sun poured in flooding the entire cave.

Hank closed his eyes and tried to remember the last bit of advice Mascan had given him.

"Just remember, young Hank, you are leaving during the twelfth crescent moon. When the sun reaches the last of the six holes, you will have six minutes to get out of the cave and into the other side. Three hundred and sixty seconds—not one more."

"This cave is designed like the amber egg, but instead of rivers, it has these five T-rexes on a circular floor," whispered

Ruby, taking the egg out of her pocket and holding it up to the light.

"Maybe it's more than the amber egg," Hank cautioned. "And put that away! Remember what Mascan said."

They stood quietly, but their hands and minds and powers joined.

This is our final test. Mascan said there was supposed to be a mineshaft here, but I can't see it. It's another puzzle, just like the flower door, thought Hank. Do you think it could lead to Colli Auf, the sixth river?

There's water somewhere, Juliana thought. *I can taste it in the air, and something big is swimming in it. I don't think it's a plesiosaurus, but it's not anything we've seen before. I think there are two of them.*

Sam took a deep breath. *That's all there is to smell. It's stuffy as if nothing has been here for years. I wonder why the bats don't come. Oh, wait! There is something in here, and it's coming toward us.*

Ruby scratched her head where the plesiosaurus had bitten her. *It's different than the other caves. Someone spent a long time carving this. Our job is to unlock its secrets in a few minutes.*

Zebi continued: *There's a mechanism moving under the floor. I can see it turning it like a giant plate. It might unlock a tunnel or staircase that leads to the river or outside the valley. I can hear the water that Juliana sensed. I can hear something coming toward us. I can hear it paddling through the water.*

There's rock everywhere, thought Oz, *but I can see gold through the layer of grime when I look at the statues.*

The sensation of their hearts and brains working together was strange and new.

Hank looked up again at the six holes on the east side. The sun was beginning to shine through the first one. *"Mascan told us the sixth river will take us out. We know there's water nearby with something large swimming, and some sort of mechanism is turning the floor. But why? This cave must mean something important to someone. Some of these statues are gold, not painted. I think when we find the water, we'll also find that the bottom of the river is gold."*

Ruby started to speak, but Oz held up his hand. "Leave him alone," he whispered. "He's figuring it out."

Seconds later, Hank pulled his compass out of his pocket. "Mrs. Plunkett gave this to me for a reason." The glass compass caught the light from the sixth hole, and the reflection lit up the palm of his outstretched hand.

"The sixth river is close. We can feel it and smell it. Oz, you might even be able to see it. The river has something to do with the moving floor. I think Zebi is right—if we make it move, we'll find the river."

One by one, they stepped off the staircase until all six of

them stood on the floor of the cave. It began to move slowly. Above, Golden Eyes stuck her head and most of her body through the first of the six holes.

"The secret is beginning to unfold!" she screeched as the sun's rays encircled her, making it appear as if her head was on fire.

The floor stopped turning. The T-rex closest to the bottom of the stairs began to shudder and rumble. Hank kept his eyes locked on the carving, afraid that it might break apart. The rumbling continued until, suddenly, the T-rex's eyes blazed, and two parallel rays of blue light shot out, stopping just above the center of the floor.

Raif padded to a spot near where the light stopped. His shining eyes held Hank's gaze. *Don't be afraid*, he seemed to be saying. *I am here.*

The floor began to turn again, moving them slowly toward the second T-rex. They felt and heard the same rumbling, and once again, the statue's eyes blazed, sending two more rays of blue light across the floor to join the first pair.

"The sun is moving to the second hole!" Golden Eyes screeched from above, her enormous gold eyes blazing down at them.

This time they were prepared as the floor turned. The third T-rex began to shudder and rumble. Two more bright blue rays soon joined the others.

"Have you noticed that each T-rex is different?" Oz stared at each one.

Ruby squinted at the face of the approaching fourth T-rex. "Why?"

"I don't know," Oz was looking from one statue's face to the next, "I don't think the sculptor was just carving statues of an old dinosaur. I think these are different, individual T-rexes.

"Do you think our Rex is here?" Juliana asked.

"Not yet," Ruby shook her head. "But one day, he will be."

"The sun is in the third hole!" came Golden Eyes' warning. "You must act quickly!"

The fifth statue was the loudest. Several seconds passed before the grinding noise stopped, and the two rays shot out of its eyes glowed more brightly than the others.

They all stood back, away from the ten rays of blue light, and waited. The place where the lights joined grew bigger. In an instant, it became a ball so bright; it was almost blinding.

"You know what you must do, young Hank," screamed Golden Eyes shaking her wings. "Now! Do it *now!*"

Hank stared up at the great bird. He had no idea what to do. Then beneath his feet, the floor began to quake.

"You are missing your chance!"

He stood gripped in a terrible vise. They would never get out of the valley, and it would be all his fault. They'd be trapped here forever because he didn't know what to do.

Over the roar created by the quaking ground, he could hear Mrs. Plunkett's calm voice—as if she were standing next to him: *Keep your head, boy. Panic can kill you.*

Hank took a deep breath. What had Mascan whispered to him when he clutched his hand?

The Bywyd stone will gather the strength of the light, and you will be set free.

Hank ran to the center of the floor. He pulled out the pouch and dropped the stone into his hand. It was a diamond as big as an egg. Everything around him slowly fell away. He held the stone, feeling alone in a small circle of space filled with light. The blue lights twitched and moved as if searching for something. Hank's hand shook, and he worried the stone would fall off. But it stayed, growing brighter and brighter as one ray, and then the next, and the next, were gathered into the stone.

It sounded like a thousand drums beating. Then it stopped suddenly as the lights vanished. The stone lay on the floor, and as he leaned down to pick it up and return it to his pouch, he heard Golden Eyes.

The water came without warning. It rushed out of the floor from every direction. In a few seconds, it had covered their feet; moments later it had reached their knees.

"The water is your escape," Golden Eyes screamed above

the sound of the rushing water. "If you do not take it, you will be locked in here forever!"

Ruby grabbed Oz's arm. "I can't swim," she cried.

The water was almost up to their waists now, and as it got deeper, it got quieter.

Golden Eyes spoke calmly from up above, but her words filled Hank with dread. "You have run out of time. The sun is rising in the sixth hole, and the water will only remain for another 180 seconds. When you get to the staircase, you will have another 180 seconds—a total of 360 seconds to get out of this mountain!"

Sam started to count. "One Mississippi, two Mississippi, three Mississippi . . ."

Hank heard a loud swishing behind them. He turned— and saw two enormous turtles swimming straight at them.

"They're called Archelon," Oz said calmly, wading to the front of the group. "We studied them in science."

"Are they meat-eaters?" Ruby's voice was barely a whisper as she hid behind Oz.

"Go with them," Golden Eyes yelled. "They will take you to the sixth river!"

The first turtle circled. Its horn-shaped beak was wide open, and its head moved from side to side as if it was searching for something to tear apart. Hank figured the turtles were about twelve feet long and seven feet wide. Their enormous shells had oddly shaped plates covered in leathery skin, and their forelimbs looked like powerful paddles.

Their big, black, shining eyes found each of them.

"They're our way out. I know it. I can feel it." Hank picked up Sam and placed him on the first turtle's back. "Three per turtle. Plus Raif. *Let's go.*"

Oz picked up Ruby and set her on the second turtle.

"You won't fall off Ruby." Sam tried to smile.

Oz put Juliana next to Sam before he and Zebi climbed onto the second turtle beside Ruby.

The water level in the cave began to go down as Hank shoved Raif onto the first turtle then climbed on. They sat right behind the turtle's massive head.

The turtles paddled toward an archway. Just before they passed underneath, Hank turned and looked back at Golden Eyes. She watched them with her piercing eyes as she leaned through the sixth hole—a sliver of light peeked over the top of her right wing.

Something caught Hank's eyes: on the wall just above the archway, he saw chiseled letters in the stone: DI BOUNAR-ROTI. Then the turtles rounded a series of corners into blackness.

The turtles moved almost silently through the water. The only sound was Sam's whispered counting . . . 32 Mississippi,

33 Mississippi, 34 Mississippi"—and the odd splash from a turtle's paddle.

It was getting darker. They all balanced themselves carefully. Hank stared into the darkness hoping to catch a glimpse of something, but there was nothing but Sam's clear voice . . .

". . . 110 Mississippi, 111 Mississippi, 112 Mississippi . . ."

The turtles stopped as Sam got to 113 Mississippi. Just in front of them, a pair of doors slid open. They shielded their eyes as they entered a large and brightly lit cave. Hank stared; mouth open in awe. Everything here was gold—even the bottom of the river where the turtles paddled. No one spoke as they floated past walls, elaborate carvings, and stacked chests, all made of gold and encrusted with diamonds.

Staring speechless at the cave, Hank remembered their first meeting with Golden Eyes when she tested Oz's power of sight.

Your powers can go farther, Oz. Beyond that northern river. Many miles farther than that polar bear and her cubs. What else can you see?

A dog sled with two men. They're carrying something big.

And what is it?

Crates of something. Machinery? Drills? And there are some small bags tied with rope on top of the crates.

What's in the bags, Oz?

Diamonds.

He looked at Oz, wondering if he too was remembering, but a moment later they were back in complete darkness. Then the turtles bumped hard against something and stopped.

Hank reached out and felt a wall and then stone steps. "It's a staircase! I think this is the mineshaft from the sixth river."

"Are we getting off here?" Ruby whispered as Raif jumped onto the stairs.

"Yes. Here—grab my hand." Hank helped her climb off the back of the turtle and onto the stairs. The rest clambered off, and a moment later, they heard the turtles paddling away.

Sam kept counting in the pitch dark: "181 Mississippi, 182 Mississippi, 183 Mississippi."

They started to climb, their feet carefully feeling for each step.

"Keep climbing," Hank urged them. "Put your hand on the wall to your left. Nobody trip. Nobody fall."

Below them, a splash sounded in the water. Ruby gasped.

"It's just the turtles, Ruby," Oz's voice was calm in the darkness. "I can see them now. I think there's light coming in around a doorway at the top of the stairs."

". . . 226 Mississippi, 227 Mississippi, 228 Mississippi . . ."

When they reached the top of the staircase, Hank felt around for the doorknob and pushed hard and fast with his shoulder. It didn't budge.

"Help me!" he yelled as ten hands joined his on the surface of the door. "One, two, three—*PUSH!*"

The door opened a crack.

"HARDER! ONE, TWO, THREE . . . *PUSH*"

They nearly fell over each other as the door gave way.

". . . 249 Mississippi, 250 Mississippi, 251 Mississippi . . ."

In front of them were three tunnels.

"Which one?" Oz yelled. "They all look the same!"

"But they're not—they can't be," Juliana screamed.

Hank watched and listened as Sam, Ruby, Oz, Zebi, and Juliana's voices faded away. He could hear Mrs. Plunkett's voice: *Keep your head, boy. Panic can kill you. You have the tools.*

Hank slowed his breathing and his mind returned to Mascan's last words to him.

Remember Mrs. Plunkett's gift, young Hank. Do that, and you will find the answer.

Hank dug deep into his pocket and pulled out Mrs. Plunkett's compass. The needle moved to the tunnel on the right.

"There!" he pointed and began to run. "This one."

". . . 319 Mississippi, 320 Mississippi, 321 Mississippi . . ."

They ran faster than they had from the deinonychus.

Sam was shouting. "334 Mississippi, 335 Mississippi, 336 Mississippi."

"We're almost out of time!" Ruby screamed.

Giant boulders fell from the ceiling and the walls. Hank watched in horror as the boulders were quickly filling up the tunnel behind them.

"Faster!" Zebi shouted over the roar of the rocks. He grabbed Juliana's arm and ran. "We're going to be buried alive!"

"Head for that light straight ahead!" Hank yelled as Raif ran beside him.

The ground shook like an earthquake beneath them. The noise was deafening, and dust filled the air as the ground shook beneath them.

They all looked at the bright sky up ahead and ran straight for it.

And then, suddenly, they were out.

They landed in a heap just as an enormous boulder crashed into place behind them, sealing the tunnel shut.

No one moved. Their hearts pounded, and their chests heaved as they gulped the fresh, clean air.

Hank counted Sam, Ruby, Oz, Zebi, and Juliana. Out of the corner of his eye, he saw Raif head off between some rocks. Somehow, miraculously, everyone was okay. Hank closed his eyes as the sounds from inside the tunnel faded away until everything was finally quiet.

"There you are!" The voice came from the bottom of the cliff.

Six heads peered over the ledge to see Counselor Frank climbing the rocks.

"We knew you had to get out of that storm somehow," he shouted. "Good for you for finding shelter. We've been looking for you all night!"

The counselor turned and waved at someone on the ground.

"They're up here—and they're fine!"

Hank looked over the ledge. Below, Mrs. Plunkett was standing with her arms crossed, staring straight up at him.

"Time to go home now, boy."

30

QUESTIONS ANSWERED

Hank turned and looked out the back window of Mrs. Plunkett's car. Sam, Ruby, Zebi, Oz and Juliana stood in a line, watching him leave. He raised his hand and wondered when he'd see them again.

"You'll see them soon enough." Mrs. Plunkett said, reading his thoughts as she pulled away from the camp.

"When?"

"You and Sam are trusted friends—best friends! And Ruby, too. You'll see them at school and in town. And perhaps they'll come to visit one day and look at some of my bones. Or the eggs! As far as the other three, you will meet again when it's time. I don't know yet when that will be." She gunned the motor as she navigated the dusty mountain road, her wrinkled hand on the gearshift.

"Is it true what Mascan said about the first beat of our

hearts?" He studied her profile as she concentrated on the road.

"Of course, it's true. Is that the only question you have for me? Your heartbeats?"

"The two boys we had to leave behind, from across the valley. Ruby thinks they work in a mine. They didn't have names. They just called themselves by numbers: 31 and 52."

"Ruby is clever. Yes, we think there is a mine there. But we can't get to it without being either shot or devoured. There must be a secret passage somewhere, but we've never been able to find it.

We know there are children in there. Also, grown men. We can hear their voices."

"When will Raif get back?"

"He's *your* wolf." She turned and looked at him sideways. "When do you think?"

"Soon."

She nodded.

"And Mascan—he's your brother?"

"My *twin* brother," she said with a smile. "How *is* he?"

"He was injured in a cave-in, but Ruby helped him, and INK is watching him."

She drove quietly along the zig-zagging roads.

"He's a tough old buzzard." She laughed quietly. "He's broken many a bone in his 403 years, and they weren't all his. INK will take good care of him."

"Did the grizzly bear die? Solvor drilled his beak right into his eye."

"That bear has guarded that mountain for many years. It was our mistake; we didn't let him know that the six of you were coming. He lost his eye, but Solvor didn't kill him."

"And the plesiosaurus? Did we kill it?"

"No." Her chin jutted out as she swerved to the left. "But he *almost* killed Ruby. Why?"

"Because we didn't use our powers." He stared at the dashboard.

"No, you didn't. Panic can kill you, but so can careless curiosity. Sam may be small and almost blind, but he remembers the rules and keeps his brain working, no matter what.

Hank watched as they left the mountainous roads and made their way into the foothills.

"And your sketchbook? You must have drawn some good pictures. We'll look at them over dinner tonight."

He slid his hand over the sketchbook still safely buttoned in his pocket. He was pleased to hear the excitement in her voice.

Leaning his head back against the seat, he stared out the window. The storm had blown through the night before and left a few clouds behind. He squinted up to the bright sunlight and then blinked. *What is that?* He rolled down the window and stuck his head out. *There she is. A tiny black speck in the sky. And she's flying so high.*

"Golden Eyes!" he whispered. He watched her soar high above the clouds. "She's making sure we're safe."

"She won't always be watching you," Mrs. Plunkett said, "but she's checking up on all of you now. Her eyesight and hearing are remarkable. She can see and hear everything we're saying in this car. It's almost as if she were perched right in that open window." Hank squinted up at Golden Eyes again and then turned back to Mrs. Plunkett.

"Golden Eyes told me to climb on her back and flew me to the top of the valley," he said, wondering for just a moment if he should continue. But he had to; if he was ever going to understand what had happened in the valley, he needed to be honest with Mrs. Plunkett. She was the only one who had the answers he and his friends needed.

He took a deep breath. "Something happened when we were flying in the north. We passed over a polar bear, swimming in the river below, and for a moment, it was as if I took away Golden Eyes' sight and it became mine. I was looking down at the bear through her eyes and seeing everything she would see. It was strange and incredible."

"Well, well." Mrs. Plunkett glanced at him, then looked back at the road. Hank noticed the strange look in her wrinkled old eyes—almost as if she were proud of him. "So, you *do* have it. You have the powers I always thought you would."

She took her hand off the gearshift and just for a moment, settled it on Hank's.

"Well, Hank, we're going to have some adventures together."

He blinked. *Hank. She called me Hank!*

A moment later she looked out of her rear-view mirror and frowned. She glanced at Hank and then far up in the clouds and found Golden Eyes.

Hank looked back and gasped. *There's a yellow car following us. It's the one from the night of the red snow.*

He looked over at Mrs. Plunkett. Her chin jutted out, then she nodded and pointed to Raif running in the hills beside them.

"Raif and Golden Eyes are your protectors, but you still must keep your wits about you and always remember your power."

"Will I ever see Mascan again?"

"What do you think?"

Author Bio

ARDYTH WEBSTER BROTT, CM
is a Canadian arts administrator,
author, and lawyer. She is
the co-founder and executive
director of the Brott Music
Festival, National Academy
Orchestra of Canada and
BrottOpera, based in Hamilton,
Ontario.

In December 2023, Ardyth was appointed a member of
the Order of Canada by Governor General Mary Simon "for
her contributions to the Canadian orchestral community, and
for her sustained support for youth involvement in music."

She has been inducted into the Hamilton Gallery of
Distinction, received the Negev Award, awarded the Hamilton YWCA Woman of Distinction Award, and Orchestras

Canada's Betty Webster Award. She has served on the Board of the National Gallery of Canada.

Ardyth has published several books for children, with *Hank Rattler and the Secret of the Cave of Kings* leading the way in her series created for middle-schoolers. She is also the author of *Jeremy's Decision* with illustrator Michael Martchenko (Oxford University Press, 1993). *Jeremy's Decision* was orchestrated by Canadian composer Paul McIntyre and performed by numerous orchestras throughout North America.

Ardyth co-founded the 36-year-old Brott Music Festival, National Academy Orchestra of Canada and BrottOpera with her late husband Boris Brott. Brott Music is Ontario's only and Canada's largest orchestral music festival. The NAO is the country's top professional training orchestra.

www.ingramcontent.com/pod-product-compliance
Lightning Source LLC
Chambersburg PA
CBHW030629020726
47493CB00006B/1627